AROUND ALIEN STARS

by
G. David Nordley

Brief Candle Press titles
by G. David Nordley
TO CLIMB A FLAT MOUNTAIN
THE BLACK HOLE PROJECT
(with C. Sanford Lowe)
AMONG THE STARS
AFTER THE VIKINGS
PRELUDE TO STARS
A WORLD BENEATH THE STARS

AROUND ALIEN STARS

Brief Candle
Press

DEDICATION
This book is dedicated to my late
Friend and connoiseur of non-human intelligence
Gerald Perkins

ACKNOWLEDGEMENTS

My thanks to all the writer's group people who have read and commented on these stories over the years, and to advice from Poul Anderson on winged sapients, Jack Cohen on walking whales, Bob Forward on antimatter, and Nancy Kress on extreme personality. Nancy, at least is still among us. Thanks also to Stan Schmidt and Trevor Quachri of Analog for buying these stories originally, to Lars Hedbor of Brief Candle Press, for taking them again, and last but never least, my wife Gayle Wiesner for her unending and insufficiently rewarded efforts to correct my spelling, grammar, and punctuation. As always, despite everyone's best efforts, perfection eludes me. Any errors are mine.

TABLE OF CONTENTS

Preface   i

Empress of Starlight   1

The Trimus Chronicles

   Poles Apart   42

   Network   83

   Final Review   128

PREFACE

While these stories take place in a more or less consistent future historical, scientific and technological background, *Around Alien Suns* was written by two different people who shared one body over time. "Poles Apart" and its successor novellas were written by a much younger man, still in early middle age, than the one who wrote "Empress of Starlight." "Empress" is a story by an author in his seventies, more experienced in writing, but often struggling to recall the right word for something--there must be a word for that--an embarrassing drag on the writing process but not a halt. Also, perhaps, the older me has become more weary of tales of conflict and violence.

But there were plenty of those on Trimus. There is a fourth Trimus novella, partly finished, which I've been promising to finish for years and may never get completed. Or maybe it will become a novel. In that, I hope to send my Trimus Monitor team properly off into the star-set, for it seems likely that being a policeman cannot last forever for any flesh and blood being; sadness is cumulative. It may be that I still need to get near enough to that final farewell myself to understand what it might mean to my characters.

While the Trimus stories have problems, plots, characters, beginnings and endings, one is also asked to think about the setting. I've introduced, by name, the concept of a "primitivist" as a way of getting readers to think not about "the future" of humanity, but the futures of humanity and other beings, separated by vast gulfs of intent as well as time and space. They are free to go their own way and only loosely connected to their common heritage. Some of them may drink deeply from the magic potions of technological advance, but others may sip but gingerly, using only what they absolutely need, and intentionally regressing on occasion. Even on this claustrophobic orb, we still have a few remote people living neolithic life styles, while others have sought to freeze lifestyles in the 19th century, or return (partly) to the more exciting times of the middle ages, or just go camping. The coming singularity does not necessarily mandate that everyone become cyber beings all the time; it gives people that option, but all the other options are still there.

"Empress of Starlight" is as much an exploration of an extreme character as an exploration story of extreme technology. It's a bit cautionary; while Dyson Sphere-like concepts have been kicking around for about a century, science fiction may have been slow to grasp just what the implications of that technology are. This is perhaps because we may think about such things without considering how other scientific and technological advances would mesh with the concept. To think of a Dyson sphere as just a source of energy for billions of space colonies seems a bit quaint. "Empress" asks us what checks, if any, may be put on such technology and its users.

Carl Sagan thought that the evolution of Intelligent beings may be the way the universe becomes conscious. In the future history of *Around Alien Stars*, the evolution of intelligence is rare, but not unique. Perhaps a few thousand other technological beings are about, including some whose birth worlds were among the first ordinary stars produced by the universe, and who achieved their singularity billions of years ago. The Kleth, Do'utians, and humans, are latecomers. The ancient don't get involved unless something really bad is about to happen, and on a scale of eons; normal galactic maintenance is left to younger and more enthusiastic local beings.

There is a kind of very loose galactic civilization with library nodes scattered around the galaxy, and a sense of letting others find their own way, similar to the "prime directive" of Star Trek, but more like a description of optimum behavior logically arrived at than an enforceable statute. I should add that there is no fantastical setting aside of Lorentz invariance in this universe. It is causal, actions have consequences, and it may take the local parts of a galaxy decades to centuries to react to anything happening elsewhere. This does allow for some uncertainty and problems that matter, at least locally. And, in a galaxy a couple hundred thousand light years across, 400 light years is local...

EMPRESS OF STARLIGHT

Somebody was stealing stars.

"A star eight times the mass of the Sun doesn't just suddenly disappear," Dr. Amber Cloud said, quietly, from her office at the rim of Shackleton Crater, Luna.

"It isn't completely gone. There's a coincident infrared source," Tony M'tonka replied three seconds later, bringing up a display of IC 2602, with the vanishing star's location marked. "And a pair of very faint polar jets. So something's still there."

"Uh-huh." Amber said. Even in the twenty-third century, graduate students should be kept guessing as to what their professors were thinking.

"Not only that," Tony continued. "But the Galactic Library files show this has happened before, at roughly 20 million year intervals. A new high mass star fades away just after it settles down to the main sequence. But it isn't gone. Ten million years later or so it shows up again, ready to expand into a subgiant, as if nothing had happened. Then, after another million years or so, it happens again."

"Uh-huh," Amber said.

"My best guess is that it's a Dyson swarm moving from star to star built by a Kardeshev class two civilization at work on something."

"Uh-huh." A teaching moment. "Tony, how do you define Kardeshev class two civilization?"

He frowned. "Okay, I'll bite. A classic Kardeshev class two

civilization used all the energy of a star; hence a Dyson sphere, almost by definition."

"Uh-huh. But, human beings, and every other star traveling civilization known, use a small part of the energy of many different stars. Where do we fit in Kardeshev's classification system?"

"Uh, well, we could build a Dyson sphere if we wanted to, so I guess we're type two."

"Do you think the Kardeshev classification system is useful?"

He hesitated before answering. "I guess I do because I used it, but I take the point. Maybe it's useful as a broad brush way of talking about scales of energy use. Maybe we're a one-point-nine or something like that."

Amber smiled. "Look up Nimmini'odd's treatment of galactic development thresholds."

"A Do'utian?"

"Yes. They've been at this much longer than we have. Anyway, a migrating Dyson sphere?"

"Do you have a better idea? It's not an eclipsing object; the Galactic Library files..."

"...have images from many different positions in the galaxy. An eclipse would only shade one position, and not for ten million years or so." She smiled and shook her head. "No, I don't have a better idea about what's causing this."

"Oh." Tony seemed finally at a loss for words. Time to let him off the hook.

"It is intriguing. Who else have you told about this?"

"Nobody, uh, except the Galactic Librarian."

Amber nodded. The Galactic AI at the Earthmind library mirror site would be discreet. It had started existence as a Troglian, from well rimward of Sol, and still took its native form for a few years when doing so amused it. Nothing much worries an immortal ten-meter-tall triped.

"Of course. Let me think on this a bit. I'll get back to you about this time tomorrow."

"Oh, thank you, Dr. Cloud, thank you!"

She nodded, touched the net to end the connection, and took several deep breaths. It was okay; nothing had gone wrong. Then she took the lift down to the crater floor and walked out into the unheated observation dome. Starlight provided the only illumination here, but her eyes adapted quickly. The cold and dry air bit into her—she was alone here and hadn't bothered with clothes; the digital coverall her AI had concocted for Tony had vanished with the connection—but she could tolerate that for a few minutes. Above, only about ten meters of nitrogen and oxygen gas and a few micrometers of graphene laminate separated her from the deep.

She located Theta Carinae quickly, to the right of the Southern Cross. A Pleiades-like jewel box of fifth magnitude stars surrounded the brilliant third magnitude Theta, about 465 light years away. With the benefits of little atmosphere extinction and genetic engineering to eliminate the various vision flaws her ancestors had to endure, she could easily see down to seventh magnitude. She located the place where the missing star should be; it was, indeed, missing. She touched the net to log the naked-eye observation with a smile. Tycho Brahe, take that!

She glanced toward the Moon's Southern Eye. The ancient 10-km spherical mirror had long been superseded by optical interferometers with astronomical baselines for serious work, so she pretty much had it to herself. There were no student projects underway now, so she touched the net to position the secondary reflector and get some digital data.

Amber now allowed herself to notice the cold and shivered. Time to go back inside.

She didn't meet anyone; she usually had Shackleton Rim all to herself. Astronomers had no reason to be physically close to their instruments, and hadn't for centuries; robots did all the technical work—and that was why she was here; not to do instrument maintenance, but because nobody else was *here*, and that lack of people lowered her stress level.

But that would end in a few decades. They were going to terraform the moon, fill its maria with real brine and grow pines on the lunar Appenines. Warm now, she shivered anyway. She could go to Mercury's south pole, but no great historic instrument graced the plains of Chao Meng Fu and the lightspeed delay would make teaching difficult. Besides, eventually, they would terraform Mercury. The Venus project was already well underway and Mars was a shirtsleeve environment. Biological immortality spurred lots of unexpected long-term projects.

She looked up at Theta Carinae again. Long term?

* ✳ *

"Alone?" Boris Malenkov asked.

Amber nodded to the transportation minister and shrugged. "That's in the application. Why not?"

"Ah, it's just surprising, that's all. I see you've addressed all relevant questions. The thing is that one would usually send either full crew or send purely automated mission. If there are human decisions to make, being alone creates a single point failure. And while I have no doubt you can upgrade your interplanetary license to be master of an interstellar ship, you'll obviously have no experience in interstellar flight."

"I don't know anyone I could ask to spend hundreds of years of their life for what may be no more significant than satisfying my curiosity."

"When you get back, as much time will have passed on Earth as has passed from Shakespeare's time to ours."

"Maybe I'll write a play. We all have indefinite biological lifetimes now."

He sighed. "Point taken. We are still getting used to the idea. You wouldn't get lonely?"

Amber smiled. Getting "lonely" was something she knew about other people in an academic sense, but not empathetically. "I don't get lonely."

"Contacting a Kardeshev type two civilization would be a lot more than satisfying curiosity. You'd be representing not just Earth, but the entire Galactic civilization."

"Such as it is."

"Such as it is. Slow, inattentive, hands-off, but that comes with astronomical distances. We are responsible members now."

"I am very responsible," Amber said, with a slight smile.

The minister smiled. "Realizing that everything is done by robots and we have a surplus in starships and propulsion capability after the 70 Ophiuchi affair, there are still trades involved and expenditure of IPA resources. If I were to find some other responsible adventurers, would you object?"

Amber's throat tightened. She was not a group person. But she could function like one, as long as she had plenty of downtime between meetings to recover from the stress. She had never married or cohabited—the thought of having to be constantly mindful of someone else's interests, discussing things, tolerating things...she shivered. But she wanted this mission. It was a once in a possibly eternal lifetime chance to do something unique and significant.

She smiled at him. "The only place I fit well in a group is at the head of it, and I don't like leadership. One always has to worry about underlings ganging up on you. I hate politics. As you say, everything is a trade, but all said, I would rather go alone."

Boris cocked his head to the side. "Well, I think there will be an expedition. The question is whether you will be on it."

People! Disappointment coursed through her. Her shoulders slumped. Briefly, she considered getting an interplanetary ship and doing the trip by fusion power. It would be like a ten-thousand-year round trip—Rip van Cloud getting back. Or maybe she wouldn't come back. She remembered the grade school bullies who hated her for being different. The high school cliques. Her lone date in high school had been going to the senior prom; the nerd who'd asked her was as awkward as she was, but they'd done it anyway—to the utter surprise of many of her classmates. It was her only date, however; he'd gone to

Cal Tech, she'd gone to MIT.

The minister seemed to notice. "Your personality profile isn't unique. I think we can find a compatible crew. Trust me. Your publication record, your student reviews, the detailed program you've put forth, all of this argues for your inclusion. From all indications, you do much better with people than you think you do."

That isn't the problem, she wanted to scream. She could deal with people; the problem was the price she had to pay inside to do it. She nodded and gave him a tight little smile to acknowledge the compliment.

"I'll get back to you," he said.

"Thank you," Amber said, as her mind stretched centuries back to the fate of women at the mercy of men's decisions, and centuries forward to the possibility of a triumphant return from a Dyson sphere—anytime but here and now.

After a month, Boris did get back to her. The expedition was on.

★ ※ ★

Four hundred and fifty-two Earth calendar years later, she gathered the crew of *SV Nicolas Louis de Lacaille* in Sphere One Park, the upper part of one of three spherical cabins, strung like three beads on the hundred-meter-diameter greater ring of the starship. Beneath its composite skin, this ring carried the superconducting cables that generated the magnetic field that had protected them from the lethal radiation of their passage, and the flares that coursed through this young stellar system. It was, she thought, like a wedding ring that bound her to the four other beings on this journey, and though her life depended on this loop of technology, divorce was never far from her mind.

Digital paint covered the dome overhead, and showed the sky ahead of the starship as if the dome were transparent and facing in that direction. Even at twenty astronomical units away, the huge object ahead covered nearly ten degrees of sky, almost twenty times the apparent diameter of the Moon in Earth's sky. It seemed utterly smooth at this distance and glowed a deep, deep red.

"So that's what a Dyson sphere looks like up close," Amber said, realizing they were her first words in a couple of hundred years or so of proper time. Relativistic time and cold sleep left her vocal cords intact, apparently.

"Close, not yet," Ga Tan said.

"Impressive, but close not yet," echoed his mate, Ko Tor. The Kleth female opened her velvety webbed wings and closed them, a gesture equivalent to a shrug of human shoulders. "Put a talon on the skin of *that* thing, I would."

Katella M'tonka laughed. "Careful. Seven-hundred kelvins down there."

Ko Tor chirped her amusement and added, "Suitably insulated, of course."

Kleth co-captains represented one of the ministry's inventive ways of dealing with Amber's social phobias, while leaving her to study the stars free of human politics.

"The interferometer pictures were more detailed, but couldn't capture this, this three-dimensionality," Tony M'tonka said. He was holding the hand of his wife, Katella, a physicist, who represented the ministry's other inventive solution. Did the ministry still exist? Amber wondered. It probably did; the pace of change lessened as lifespan lengthened. In fact, Boris was probably still running it.

Amber told the spacecraft AI, informally called "Niki," to increase the magnification. It looked as if the starship zoomed across the intervening twenty astronomical units in seconds.

"It's mottled at high magnification," Niki observed. "There appears to be texture as well. The surface looks like hexagonal parachutes, or jellyfish, joined together at the rim. There's a strong magnetic field and holes in the skin over the poles of the star for plasma to escape."

"I would put a talon on the skin of *that* thing," Ko Tor repeated.

"Interesting, yes," Ga Tan said with an impatient snap of his beak. "But first, let us see to our return system and our mining system for fuel for operations. Also, we K'Leth need a sphere big enough in to fly."

Amber nodded. The ship would soon take up orbit in a gap in the disk surrounding the tempestuous red dwarf binary, which, in turn, orbited the Dyson sphere at approximately Saturn's distance from the Sun. Their precursor robots were already fully employed with the habitat and the return system. There was little the crew could do to hurry the process.

"Yes," Ko Tor sighed, a low whistle in Kleth. "Proceed as planned, I'm sure we will."

That, Amber realized, was directed to her as the Expedition Leader. "Please do. Thank you for asking, but I only need to be consulted about exceptions." She smiled and nodded to her Kleth second. Then she turned to Tony.

"Tony?"

"Yes, Dr. Cloud?"

"I seem to have fallen into a surface examination. Could you check with Niki on the contemporary source survey?" The motions of stars in the chaos of a galaxy had only limited predictability, and their maps were half a millennium out of date.

"Got it."

"Ko Tor?" Katella asked, "Why don't we put together a feast for five beings who haven't eaten in seventy-five proper years?"

"Empty our gizzards are," she replied with a friendly chirp. "So off to the kitchen!"

Amber barely heard her. The surface scan had just reported 268.4 Kelvins on dome tops, just under the freezing point of water. The much larger areas between the domes were Venus-hot where they joined, but their surface was convex so they did not shine on the dome tops. As she watched, one of the domes emitted a long silvery projectile, which rapidly accelerated away from the Dyson sphere.

To where?

★ ❆ ★

Amber called the Dyson sphere the "Red Rubber Ball," and it stuck. Radiation pressure supported its surrounding "skin", so it was thin enough to be quite flexible. It also had negligible mass in astronomical terms, so Niki could work out the mass of the enclosed star by observing the velocity of a ring of orbital debris. It came out to be 8.245 times the mass of the Sun. A young star of that mass would normally have a luminosity of some 2000 Suns. Take away the sphere, and at their distance, their little scientific station would be hit by some 20 times Earth's insolation or more. With the sphere, the Red Rubber Ball was barely visible, though prominent in infrared.

The shell radiated far less energy than it received. Where did the rest of the energy go?

★ ❆ ★

Katella wanted her attention on the net. "Dr. Cloud?"

Amber wanted to say, "Not now, Katella, I have this nice juicy problem to think about," but she successfully suppressed that response. One had to get along with people, or they would become even more of a problem.

She kept her net voice cheery. "What can I do for you?"

"We've modeled the star's gravity field from how it affects the shape of the Dyson sphere, the frame drag, and gravitational lensing. We can then compare its shape with evolutionary models and..."

"Okay, okay. What's the result?" Amber didn't need an astronomy lecture from a physicist.

"Our best fit says it's turning off the main sequence, maybe thirty million years old, about 3000 times as bright as the Sun."

That was in line with the age of the cluster, but overluminous. "The sphere probably affects the star's effective temperature," she ventured. "Anything on the Red Rubber Ball itself?"

"It's apparently under tension, like a balloon filled with light. Small differences in the infrared intensity from place to place indicate that it adjusts its emissivity locally—probably to keep it centered on the star. It would need some kind of smart fabric to do that. We've got a neutrino telescope under construction but the best way would be to get a physical sample. We need to go there."

"We'll send a robot."

"You're no fun! Don't you want to be the first person to set foot on a Dyson sphere?"

"Yes, I am no fun and no I don't want..." Amber stopped herself. "Sorry, I didn't mean to be sharp. Katella, this isn't a relic; it's an ongoing operation of some sort, probably being run by an AI that hasn't chosen to communicate with us. We have protocols to observe. Also, remember that whatever is running this thing has about 12 times, ah, ten to the twenty-ninth watts to play with. Suppose the surface has a phased laser array?" Or *is* a phased laser array...

"You think it's a weapon?"

"I think it could be if it wanted to be. It's four times the Earth's orbit across." Amber touched the net and asked Niki for the resolving power of an array with a radius of two AU.

"Oh, my God!" Katella said.

She must have done the same thing.

$$\star \; \ast \; \star$$

As much as Amber hated meetings, she called one.

Tony was as grim as Amber ever remembered seeing him. "Earth is four hundred and fifty light years away. But if the surface of this thing includes a phased optical array, it could put about half the star's energy output on a spot as small as 100 meters on Earth."

"Only half of that within 100 m, darling," Katella said

Four heads looked at her as if she were crazy.

"Just being ironic. The intensity would be something like ten to the eighteenth Suns—an exasun if you like. Something like ten million trillion Suns per square meter."

"Or, defocused, a mere 13 trillion suns over the whole planet," Tony added, "at lousy efficiency. We knew this before we left, or we should have. I should have."

Ga Tan clicked his beak and spread his wings. "We too. Nobody thought about it."

Ko Tor waved her beak. "Cjo Dok egg, our name for a Dyson sphere is. A thought exercise, it was. About encountering one in reality no one deeply thought. For all that energy, no real need exists. So why build one?"

"If it helps, K'Leth is even closer to this than Earth." Ga Tan added, careful, as always to put the glottal stop in the name of his world, even when speaking astro-English.

Amber shuddered. Everyone looked at her. There was no calling back to Earth, or even Kleth, for marching orders to arrive 900 years later. She would have to decide, but maybe later. "That aside, does anyone have any idea of where those spacecraft leaving from the "cold hills" are going? The answer may lie there. Niki?"

The starship's AI displayed a graphic showing the convergence of the vectors of some 834 spacecraft that had been observed departing the Red Rubber Ball. "The vectors converge on a location about 2700 AU from here that's moving at 31.47 kilometers per second with respect to this system's center of mass, mainly tangentially, but with a significant radial component; the trajectory would be hyperbolic—not bound to this system. But I have not found an object there, yet. I will have more aperture available if I modify the return array."

Amber smiled to herself. The array of power stations and beam drivers their robots made to get them home would be a tiny sliver of a Dyson sphere itself and around a tiny star; many orders of magnitude smaller than the Red Rubber Ball. Call it the "Red Rubber Band," she thought.

"Let's hope whatever is running this show hasn't noticed us yet," she said.

"When we leave," Ko Tor added, "we must not toward K'Leth or Earth head, at least not to start."

Tony reached over to Katella and held her hand. An incredible exile had just become longer. But they had each other. Amber wondered what that was like, both the needing and the having.

"Perhaps," Amber said. "But we haven't tried to talk to it yet."

"Do we?" Tony asked.

"How else do we find out what this is all about?"

"Do we lie about from where we come?" Ko Tor asked.

"No, no," her mate responded. "We do not tell it, but we will tell it that we do not tell it. If intelligent, it will understand why. If not, it will not matter."

Amber considered that. In her mind, a spectrum of possibilities flowed between those two bookends. But she didn't want to discuss it now.

"If it is intelligent?" Katella asked. "But how could it not be and do this?"

"On K'Leth, we have little worms that build vast lacy colonies a hundred meters tall, with guard worms, worker worms, breeding worms, scout worms—but each worm is only a millimeter long and has a three-picogram brain with only about ten million cells."

Amber thought about bees, termites, and army ants.

"How do they...." Katella asked

"Little tiny tentacles their tiny mouths surround." Ko Tor put her four-fingered hands at each side of her beak and wiggled her fingers.

Laughter and beak clicking ensued, breaking the tension.

Eventually, it died down and Amber realized she would have to come to some sort of decision as to what to do next. As she realized she didn't know enough to make a decision, her choice became obvious.

"For now, I think, we gather data passively."

Katella shook her head. "But if it knows we're here, it will have that much more time to react to us. We should go to the Red Rubber Ball and find out what makes it tick."

"Do we use a shuttle or risk *Niki*?" Tony asked.

Ko Tor spread her wings and did a quick circuit of the dome.

Her mate clicked his beak. "*Niki* gives us at least some room to fly. The journey will take several weeks, at least."

Tony shook his head. "It's not designed to land, and the habitat modules aren't designed for microgravity."

"We can levitate magnetically and build a despin coupling device," Ga Tan said.

Ko Tor waved her beak. "Extra fuel will be needed for the thrusters."

"We have plenty of ice and boron in this disk," Tony said.

"We do," Amber said. "And it seems we'll be using it. But first we need to establish ourselves and get more data."

★ ❋ ★

The expedition established itself in the disk around "Double M," as they called a red dwarf binary that orbited the Red Rubber Ball. Their robots reproduced themselves and made a one-kilometer rotating spherical habitat with a ring lake around the inside of its equator and three houses spaced along its shore. A huge mirror gathered light from the rather distant and disk-obscured red dwarfs while other mirrors and lenses concentrated and relayed it to the inside of this habitat. The spin provided one Kleth-normal gravity, about forty percent of Earth's, at the maximum spin radius. They also finished the return beam system, getting it ready in case they needed to depart quickly. The Red Rubber Ball ignored them.

The inside of the habitat was a work in progress, which the crew took turns managing. On Amber's shift, to outward appearances, she stood on a terrace with her arms crossed near the "north" spin pole of the habitat, drinking in the view. In reality, she was hard at work, in contact with Niki, making decisions on where to put trees, streams, farms and roads on the ten-meter-thick shell of regolith gathered from the disks and painstakingly purged of radioactive isotopes by their mining and refining robots.

They'd brought a simplified boreal forest ecology with them, to be gradually introduced from Niki's stores of frozen embryos, spores, cysts, and files of genetic material. So far they had a minimally complex soil, grass, some saplings, and three cottages along the shore. Sheep would be next.

After a couple of years, their trees were higher than they were and Amber was knitting a sweater. There was nothing left to do but go to the Red Rubber Ball.

The voyage took three months. Short for interstellar travel, but, as Amber recalled someone saying about Pluto, a Chihuahua is still a dog. In terms of actual time they spent awake, it was three times as long as their voyage from the Solar System. Amber had not had to deal with people continuously for so long since her college days. Sometimes she screamed—but always behind closed doors.

The surface of the Red Rubber Ball proved an excellent conductor; the spinning starship could levitate over the mirror image of its magnetic field, almost a kilometer above its surface. Rather than build a despin device, they simply took a shuttle from the starship down to the surface. Each "mountain top" sat on about 50,000,000 square km of gossamer-thin reflective material—billions and billions of concave light-sails joined rim to rim to make the Red Rubber Ball a photon balloon. The more-or-less flat top was still ten km in radius. Ko Tor attached the shuttle to the surface less than fifty meters from the last Red Rubber Ball spacecraft exit tower.

Even in spacesuits with a month's worth of supplies, Amber weighed almost nothing. Gravity is the weakest force in the universe and at two times Earth's distance from the center of the eight-solar-mass enclosed star, it fell to an eightieth of Earth's gravity.

"Potential entrance one," Ko Tor said. With a spacesuit covering his wings, he looked like a hunched-back demon out of a late medieval artist's nightmare.

Their high resolution imagery showed a number of circular somethings near the spacecraft exit; the first one looked like a smooth hemispherical bulge about two meters in diameter. Up close, it was still a smooth hemispherical bulge about two meters in diameter.

"Radome?" Ga Tan speculated.

Amber looked at the dome closely. Its surface was barely pitted; clearly, it was regularly maintained.

"Not a way in, I'd venture," Katella said. "Let's jet over to number two on the list."

They finally hit paydirt at number sixteen. It looked like an ordinary circular plate, but they happened to watch a bristly robot emerge from it. The thing had a body about a quarter meter in diameter with a fuzz of arms projecting at more or less equal intervals around it. It seemed oblivious of them.

"Play back the recording of the exit," Amber told Niki.

That told her where the hinge was—a simple, universal solution to a simple, universal problem. Their nanobots made quick work of the mechanism, and the door opened.

Inside glowed in a diffuse way like a huge room, the windows or light fixtures of which were out of view. The lack of reds struck her; objects were white to gray with occasional hints of blue, green, or rarely orange. A sparse latticework surrounding a giant tube vanished into the haze of the depths below them.

"Who does not want to be among the first into a Dyson sphere?" asked Katella.

In for a dime, in for a dollar, Amber thought. "Okay. The open hatch might be noted, and a closed hatch would block our data stream. Let's go quickly."

Along with a half-dozen head-sized, spider-armed exploration robots, they dropped in one at a time, checking their fall with brief thruster bursts when their velocity built up to a meter per second.

After an hour or so, their scenery changed. The haze ahead of them began to resolve into some kind of industrial-mechanical landscape.

Amber signaled for a stop. They braked and clung to the scaffolding like sparrows on the Eiffel tower. "Now we'll send a robot first."

The robot video resolved into a forest of spacecraft identical to the one they'd just seen exit. They sent their robotic eye closer to the tube; there was no reaction.

"To our right," Ga Tan said. He used his own eyes, much better than human ones.

Amber turned up the magnification. A large cylinder glided toward a spacecraft near the launch tube, which opened a hatch along its side and took in the cylinder. The bottom part of the launch tube then rotated, revealing an opening.

"A breechloader," Tony commented.

The spacecraft lifted slightly on its tail and glided sideways into the tube opening. Another rotation of the tube bottom closed the opening. A slight vibration ensued.

Data poured in from the robot. The cylinder massed 5.34 tonnes, the spacecraft 42.68 tonnes. The neutron activation spectrum...

"Gammas? Pions..." Katella asked.

"Annihilation products," Ga Tan said. "P-bar, neutron annihilation to be precise. There's antihydrogen in the cylinder. Very cold, from the narrowness of the spectra."

"Fuel," Katella said. "The spacecraft are antimatter fueled."

Ga Tan's spacesuit didn't allow his beak movements to be seen, but Amber imagined it waving negatively.

"It doesn't make sense for the trip to the target area. This launch tube is an accelerator, an electromagnetic gun. It easily provides enough velocity and does it for a tiny fraction of the energy needed for an antimatter engine's fuel cycle."

"If the antimatter isn't the fuel," Amber said, "It must be the cargo."

Her suit alarm beeped. "We've got company. Ascend. *Now!*"

They hit their jets and zoomed up parallel to the launch tube. Whatever was following them moved much faster, however. Amber recalled their exploration robot; it would come up from behind their pursuer a minute or so before it reached them.

"We can send the other robots to the side as it gets near us," Ko Tor suggested. "We can englobe it."

So quickly do the hunted become the hunters, Amber thought. Her feelings had changed as well, from a touch of fear to the anticipation of a predator about to pounce. That, she realized, was dangerous.

"Stay vigilant," she said. "This is likely a convenient first responder, a scout of opportunity. There could be billions of these things here in a matter of hours.

"Yeah, the first of the Dyson sphere's version of a flash mob," Tony added.

"But if we catch it, we might have a way of talking to this thing," Katella said.

Amber thought she heard a hint of the tiger in Katella's voice. The younger woman was right, of course. Assuming they could capture the pursuing robot non-destructively, they should have a channel to whatever passed for the controlling mind of this operation. Capture? With a mental effort, she shifted her thoughts from offense back to defense.

"What might this thing do when it reaches us?" she asked. "Simply observe and report? Or will it recognize us as foreign and attempt to... remove us?"

That got clicks from Ko Tor. "We should go to the side, too. Let it chase a robot." The Kleth female opened her belly pack. "I will use a space blanket to make one look bigger.

They jetted away from Ko Tor's decoy and found pieces of scaffolding to cling to. The decoy adjusted its speed so that the pursuing robot closed on it where the humans and their robots were waiting.

When the pursuer got within a few dozen meters of the decoy, it blasted it with a laser, putting a quarter meter hole right in the middle of Ko Tor's space blanket. That was not where the robot was, however, Ko Tor having set the decoy up asymmetrically. The decoy played dead, however, and when the alien robot closed in to what it had shot, the rest of their own robots pounced on it.

It got off three shots, disabling three of its attackers, but that was all; the remaining two stuck to it like burrs. There was a bit of a whirling mechanical stalemate for a few seconds, but then their original reconnaissance robot caught up to them and the three overwhelmed the alien and disconnected its laser and maneuvering jets; snip, snip, snip.

With the alien robot disabled, the crew approached. Ko Tor slapped some space tape over what appeared to be its cameras.

Amber wrapped a space blanket around it; it would have to power down whatever it was using as a power supply or overheat, she thought. Besides, the space blanket had a conductive layer; it made a good Faraday cage.

"That was way too easy," she said. "We need to get out of here before its buddies show up. They all glommed onto their captive and hit their jets, trusting their interlinked computers to get them to the hatch with zero delta-v left.

About fifty meters from the surface, Tony sent, "Here comes the posse. I'd say a couple hundred of them. We should get to the hatch on time, but not with a moment to spare."

"Send one of the robots ahead to open the hatch," Katella sent. "When it's open, have the *Niki* get its lasers ready."

What was on the other side of that hatch, now? Amber thought. How much did whatever was controlling the sphere know? The response should still be local, she reasoned; it had only been about eight minutes since they'd captured the robot; even at light speed, news of it could have only gotten about the distance from the Earth to the Sun where they were. About one AU. The circumference of the Red Rubber Ball was over six times that. No, half that distance, round trip. How smart was a half-AU patch of this thing? Was there a central brain? Was it near here? Events were happening too fast. She needed to think. She needed more information.

"We're not going to the hatch," she sent. "Off to the side, two kilometers longitude, with the hatch as the zero meridian and the star's equatorial plane as zero latitude."

"What are you doing?" Katella said, "We'll get caught inside."

"No, I understand," Ko Tor said. "Caught *outside* we could be!"

"We should stick an antenna through," Ga Tan said, "and contact our spacecraft to see what the situation is."

"Dr. Cloud, we should head for the hatch. It isn't that smart. No response to our queries..."

"It doesn't have to be smart, Tony," Amber sent, "just experienced. Think white blood cells. And no more queries."

"Oh. Okay."

"Tony!" Katella shouted.

"Not my call," he replied. "Radio silence."

Amber, the two remaining robots and the Kleth changed their thrust vectors, as did Tony a couple of seconds late. Katella, apparently realizing she couldn't out-tug the five of them, did likewise.

Perhaps a kilometer away from the hatch, the humans and their captive reached and clung to the underside, a millimeter or two of alien composite away from the surface. Any wrong decision could get them all killed, she thought. Not doing anything would almost certainly get them killed.

"Do we risk contacting the ship now?" Tony asked Amber, helmet to helmet.

"Yes. We need to put a tiny hole through, enough for an antenna, but maybe not enough to trigger maintenance concerns."

Amber wished she had a needle. In a sewing kit? In the emergency medical supplies! She pulled it off the upper arm of her suit, irrationally worried that the zipping sound of the geckro would alert some alien menace. That didn't happen and when she opened it, there was indeed a needle inside.

Ko Tor and Tony set it up. A robot claw held one end of the needle. They got ready to flee if something bad happened when the needle poked through; but nothing did. They found a frequency the ship used that was quiet around the Red Rubber Ball and got their link.

Niki sent a disturbing video of a cluster of menacing, laser-equipped maintenance robots over the hatch, but which ignored, so far, the immobile shuttle just a few meters away.

"They would notice the rocket exhaust if it moved," Ga Tan said.

"How else can we move it?" Katella said, clearly impatient.

Amber imagined the shuttle gliding over to their location without rockets, somehow.

"Too bad it doesn't have legs," Tony said.

"It does!" Ga Tan exclaimed. "It has robot legs—the legs of the robots inside it. They can carry it in this gravity. If they do it slowly and don't harm anything, maybe the movement won't be noticed."

Amber nodded. "We'll move it very slowly and unthreateningly. First we sacrifice another robot, however. We'll move it toward the group at the hatch, slowly first then more rapidly until they do something. Then we'll know the threshold."

She told Niki what to do. It printed and deployed a sacrificial robot, which was vaporized when its speed reached half a meter per second.

Using a hatch on the other side of the shuttle from the mob of mechanical menaces, a trio of robots slowly emerged and gently worked their way beneath the aerospacecraft, one under each delta wing, and one under the nose. There was no reaction from the Red Rubber Ball's robots.

Niki's bots slowly lifted the shuttle. Then, with infinite patience they began carrying the shuttle toward the explorer's location at a slow walk.

The Red Rubber Ball's robots stayed guarding the port.

"They must be like frogs," Tony said. "If something stays roughly in the same place they ignore it. I bet the maintenance bots would react differently. This is like an ant colony, or a beehive. No intelligent central direction, but every worker and drone knows what to do."

"Maybe." Amber didn't know how much she trusted that model,

but it seemed to be working so far.

"We'll have to break something to get out," Tony said. "It may not like that. We should close it up quickly after we go out. But how?"

Amber nodded. They could laser a hole and get into the shuttle in probably less than a minute. But then what would happen? If the shuttle were recognized as hostile, it would likely be vaporized. There would be no getting away; "out of range" did not apply to Dyson spheres.

Amber looked at the suture kit. Was there enough thread to sew it up after they cut through? Would they have time? What else did they have?

"The vacuum tent doors are big enough, and self sealing," Ga Tan offered, obviously thinking along the same lines. "If we can relocate them."

"Space glue we have," his mate added. "One door to the inside surface of the sphere we glue. Into the tent we go, that door seal, through the shell cut, through the cut go, and let the door close up after us like an air lock. A maintenance problem it would be, but not an ongoing one it would seem. Worker bots rather than soldier bots would respond."

"That's a good theory," Amber said. She didn't have to say they would probably be dead if it was wrong.

After an extended discussion, however, nobody came up with a better idea. Go slow and don't upset the natives seemed to work.

It took them less than an hour to rig their ersatz exit lock. It took perhaps another hour of talk to plan and replan their "escape" from the Red Rubber Ball; once in the shuttle, they would slow-walk away from the cold hill and float well away with cold-gas jets, then ascend at minimum acceleration and rendezvous with the *Niki*. Then the starship would ascend magnetically as far as it could before using its engines. They could only hope that the starship's fusion engines, ignited at a distance, wouldn't elicit a response. There had been no response coming in.

That left eight hours, approximately, before the shuttle had walked to their position.

"I think we can take a rest now," Amber said. "The shuttle won't be here for a few hours. I want to be alone for a while." Then she put her com on auto, clambered a couple dozen meters away from the group, clipped herself to a strut and hung there. She exhaled in a great gasp and then began shaking involuntarily. She tried chanting *nam yoho renge kyo*, and let the stress of dealing with people and situations ebb away. Gradually, her shaking subsided and her breathing became more regular. How much of that her crew saw, she wasn't sure. *Nam yoho renge kyo*. The universe gives us the power to choose our destiny, though I walk through the valley of the shadow of death, word-fame is the one thing that lasts forever...

❋

She woke to a gentle touch on her shoulder.

"Dr. Cloud?"

It was Tony. She groaned and shook herself awake.

"I'm here."

"The shuttle is almost here, and there's been a development."

She followed him over to their soon-to-be exit, where the data rate was better. Soon, she looked down on their cold hill through the *Nicholas Lacaille*'s eyes.

It had taken the better part of a day for the shuttle to glide its way over to them. As it did, a collection of "warrior robots" had formed over every potential exit on their cold hill. Only by good luck, they were nowhere near one. There were thousands of them. Were they being produced locally? If the Red Rubber Ball didn't have a laser array now, it could develop one rather quickly, she realized.

"We can depressurize the cabin and use the nose-wheel maintenance entrance," Ga Tan said. "We place the nose wheel just ahead of the slit and the doors will impede views from the side. We can lower the back of the shuttle to impede the view from that direction."

They'd done some additional planning to counter the increased number of warrior robots. Amber nodded her approval. "Let's get in the lock."

They crowded in and sealed the door behind them.

"I've got a boarding order," Katella announced. "Ga Tan should go first as he's the pilot. Then Dr. Cloud, myself, Tony, and Ko Tor with the robots, in case there's some rear guard action."

There was silence. Amber couldn't read Kleth body language in space suits, but she didn't have to.

"One doesn't separate a Kleth pair in these circumstances, Katella," Amber said.

"Don't lecture me," Katella snapped. Tony put a hand on her arm, but she shrugged it off. "What?"

"Kleth mate for life," he said. "Literally. If one dies, the other dies as well."

"Huh? If we don't all get in, we all die."

"Ko Tor will follow Ga Tan," Amber said. "I will stay with the robots until you are all aboard."

"We greatly appreciate that," Ko Tor said.

"It's not optimum," Katella protested, "and everyone's lives are at stake. We should at least discuss it longer, Dr. Cloud. You shouldn't just be making arbitrary decisions."

Nobody answered her, but Tony put his helmet against Katella's so they could speak in private with the radios off. She pushed him away.

They did not have time for this, Amber thought; they had to get aboard the shuttle. The Kleth, at least, should not have to pay for this human comedy with their lives. Katella had followed the last time. She would again, by force if necessary.

There was a surgical knife in the medical kit—hardly bigger than a penknife, but enough to cut through the alien fabric. Before uncertainty could grip her, she plunged the knife into the skin of the Red Rubber Ball behind the gap and pulled the blade steadily down along it. The fabric pulled aside quickly, and, under a surprising amount of tension, formed a nearly circular hole.

"Ga Tan, Ko Tor, now!"

The Kleth complied without a word.

"Bastard!" Katella said.

"Tony," Amber said.

"Who are you married to, her or me?" Katella shrieked, the shriek muted by the comm software.

"We have to go, Katella. Now." Tony said calmly and quietly. Then he turned and followed Ko Tor through the opening.

Amber queried their robots about any sign of reaction from the Red Rubber Ball. Maintenance robots were on the move but no sign of warrior robots yet. Amber motioned for Katella to move through the opening. The other woman just hung onto a strap near the tent entrance and did nothing.

"He's yours if you go to him," Amber said. "I don't mate. But you must go to him or perish here."

After taking another few precious seconds, Katella let go and pushed herself over to the opening and up through it.

Amber motioned the robotic crew up and in with their captive first. They were essential and she didn't want to enter the shuttle in close proximity to Katella. Then she went through and commanded the tent door to seal behind her. It couldn't; it appeared to be trying at the ends but the tension must be too great.

Amber pushed herself down to the gap and grabbed the two sides close to an end of the slit and pulled them together. With the stress relieved, the seal worked its way up toward her hands, almost like a zipper being pulled by an invisible hand. With as much strength as she could muster, Amber slid her suit-gloved hands up the gap without releasing the fabric and pulled it together again. The seal followed. She could see the far side of the tent bulge; maintenance robots or worse were there. She pulled the fabric together again, and the seal advanced to half way.

A metallic arm rent the far door and protruded through, thrashing around.

Amber pulled one more time, and the sealing mechanism took

over, now overpowering the tension of the now smaller gap. It closed with a snap she could feel through her suit.

Some loose Red Rubber Ball skin was left on either side of the tent seal. Remembering what got them there in the first place, Amber took the surgical knife, still in her leg pouch, and sliced off a ragged square. Then she pushed herself away from the Red Rubber ball and up into the shuttle's wheel well.

She saw the surface glide away beneath her as the carrying robots began moving the shuttle, perhaps a little faster than when they took it here. That rate had some margin built into it, and now was the time to use that margin.

In a few minutes, maintenance robots converged to where the opening had been, but ignored the creeping spacecraft.

Amber entered the maintenance hatch and watched the nose wheel rise, very slowly, behind her. When the doors finished shutting slowly over it, she slammed the hatch door shut, sat down with her back against it and shook like a leaf while the shuttle repressurized. *Nam yoho renge kyo.*

Then, without saying anything to anyone, and not being asked anything by anyone, she went toward the rear of the shuttle, wriggled one of the tiny shuttle bunks and accordioned the side down behind her. *Nam yoho renge kyo.*

Through a trembling haze, she monitored the shuttle's slow, hour-long walk to where the slope of the cold mountain began to get warm. Then the robots let go and clambered back aboard through the air lock as the shuttle took flight, hidden by the bulge of the dome, and began its slow climb up and away on its attitude control thrusters.

Enough self indulgence, she told herself. She was still the leader of this expedition, however flawed. She had duties. She replicated a half pint of beer in the bunk alcove's tiny printer, chugged it, took another deep breath, raised the bunk side, and made her way to the front compartment. Katella had plunked herself down in the command seat, but that would mean nothing to Niki, so Amber chose to ignore it.

Amber supervised the rendezvous with the *Niki* from the shuttle pilot station. She filled her mind with the details of the operation to keep it off the people problems that she would have to deal with after they settled back into shipboard routine. The shuttle glided through the main ring nose first along the rotation axis of the starship, then matched its spin with its bottom aligned with the number three hull from which it had come. The hull's shuttle bay doors opened and the shuttle cradle rose up on telescoping supports and locked onto it. The starship compensated for the change in the hull's mass and angular momentum by pumping fluids back to the other two hulls as the shuttle descended in the complex mechanical ballet that kept the spin center fixed.

The human crew exited the shuttle in silence and headed for their compartments. The Kleth headed for the sphere on dome to stretch their wings.

At dinnertime on the second deck of sphere 3, Katella pointedly ignored Amber. Fortunately, Amber had a peace offering.

"Katella..."

"I don't want to talk about it."

Maybe I should go through her husband, Amber thought. No, that relationship seemed to be a problem for her. The Kleth? She had presumed on them too much already. It was hard to tell, but she thought she could detect the beginnings of an attitude of condescension beginning to work its way into their dealings with the humans. No, she would have to do this. Deep breath.

"It's not about that," she said, lying as pleasantly as she could. She reached into her flight suit pocket and pulled out transparent envelope with a scrap of cloth in it. "I cut this out at the last instant. It was why we went there in the first place, as I recall."

She held out the sample of the Red Rubber Ball's skin to Katella. "It's as light and strong as you might imagine; about five grams per square meter."

Katella took the sample, eyes wide with interest. "Probably full of circuitry. It could tell us a lot, along with the robot..."

"I hope so."

"Okay...thanks." Katella turned and slid down the center pole to the lab area below.

Had she achieved a truce? Who knew? Amber sighed and ordered herself a beer. When it came, she ascended to the dome above and drank it alone, losing herself in the stars.

★ ❋ ★

When they got back to the Double M habitat, they had woods, fields, and a small flock of sheep. Relationships got back to normal. In another couple of months, Amber had the sheep shorn and knitted sweaters for everyone; for the Kleth, that meant a kind of vest-like poncho arrangement with fasteners at the bottom. They expressed diplomatic appreciation.

In spare moments she tracked the progress of the antimatter-cargo spacecraft they'd seen depart from the Red Rubber Ball. On its present ballistic course, it would reach the convergence point in about four months. Should they follow it? If so, when?

They continued watches, with someone "on duty" for data collection operations and habitat minutiae. Since the *Niki* came from the Solar System, its day, and thus the colony day, followed a human convention of 24 hours, but whereas human beings divided this into two 12-hour segments, the octal-raised Kleth more naturally divided it into three 8-hour segments. That, it turned out, was best for people as well. So Amber was on 9 hours, including an hour overlap with her predecessor. This evening, that was Ga Tan. While their shift could be done anywhere, they'd established precedent of a face-to-face handover; in this case, Ga Tan flew over to her house.

"Anything new on the Red Rubber Ball?" she asked as he alighted.

"It continues to ignore us," he replied after a second or two.

They did have a sense of humor, she recalled.

"Thank chaos for small favors. How's Ko Tor doing on the "warrior robot?"

By itself, it was little more than a telop; it responded with a limited suite of behaviors to a higher level external direction. But it had a database.

"She's found the map of the 'cold hill' segment we entered. She thinks each segment is largely self-sufficient and interacts with the other segments only as much as needed to keep the Red Rubber Ball centered, if that. The segments can modulate the net photon pressure by changing their emittance."

"That sounds more like a sponge or a jellyfish than a colony of bees or ants."

"*Oh ga so da*, on our world. They are quite successful, but not self-aware. If that is the case here, we won't be able to ask it why it does what it does. It wouldn't know."

She nodded. What did a sponge know about why it pumped water through its various holes?

"Yes. It may not know. Or maybe we don't have the key. What intelligence does it need to run the place and maintain it?"

"About that of a colony of oh-ga-so-da, I think. Consider all of the complex biological material in a living cell; systems to fight parasites, recognize the other, reproduce, and so on. The Red Rubber Ball is less complex, actually. It doesn't need to be self-aware, or intelligent as we understand intelligence. Perhaps just as well."

Yes, just as well. They'd gotten away with an invasion an intelligence might not have tolerated. On the other hand, an intelligence might have responded to their questions.

"The Red Rubber Ball sends ships, or at least one ship, with an antihydrogen cargo off to an object a few thousand astronomical units away. It does not know what it is doing or why. Perhaps something there knows."

Amber had seen the data collected since they'd been away. A series of occultations of very faint objects had revealed a very cold circular shape, presumably a sphere, about twice the size of the Sun where the cargo ship trajectories converged.

"Any thoughts on the black disk?" she asked

It took him a few seconds to respond—consulting with Ko Tor, probably.

"It is probably a sphere, and from the way it bends light, about a twelfth the mass of your sun, a tenth the mass of ours."

"And so cold?"

"That is a mystery. We are in its equatorial plane, so the poles are not visible to us and it may dump heat in that direction. There is evidence for a strong magnetic field."

"Do we go there?"

There was a pause, a shift of the crest and a slight flap of his wings. She'd gotten good enough at Kleth body language to guess that he'd found something ironic or humorous in the question.

"We should go carefully, with robots going first. After we have a better picture."

Amber nodded. The better picture would come from the large synthetic aperture telescope they were building. With hundred-meter mirrors a quarter of an astronomical unit apart, they would be able to see whatever there was to see on the surface, with starlight.

"You've got the con." Ga Tan took flight, rising high toward the spin axis until he was a lonely small silhouette against the green of the far side of the habitat.

I should print myself some wings, Amber thought.

✱ ❀ ✱

Tony and Katella invited everyone over for dinner and a mysterious announcement the day after the SAT went operational.

"The 'Black Rubber Ball' has a satellite," Tony announced. "It's a torus."

Amber looked up from her coffee. A torus implied artificial gravity, which implied biology. "Spinning?"

Tony nodded. "Slowly, enough to give maybe half a meter per second acceleration—a twentieth of Earth gravity—but that may just be an outer shell. It's about forty km in radius. No effluvia that we can detect."

"No question of what the antimatter is for now," Katella said. "In a thousand years of spaceflight, human beings have encountered only four other biological intelligent species."

"If that's a biosphere, it must need gigawatts," Amber said. "It should be bright in the infrared. It's not."

"Maybe they've come up with a heat sink that we don't know about," Tony said. "Yet, anyway; we're a bit behind the galactic times."

Ga Tan clicked. "Both of our cultures are near the top of most technological S-curves; progress comes slowly. If I assume the shell is to attenuate cosmic radiation, it's primitive. Superconducting loops form a much more efficient shield."

"A stone age space donut. What is it guarding against? Debris? Meteoroids?" Tony speculated.

"Weaponry," Ko Tor said.

They were all a bit quiet.

"They'd have a lot of antimatter by now," Amber said. "How are you doing with the captured robot's communications?"

More clicks from Ga Tan. "We can command it around as if it were one of ours. We should be able to communicate with whatever it can communicate with. But there are no assurances of a higher level mind to talk to."

"Can we replicate it? With some improvements?" Amber asked.

"It should be printable. I'll need specifications for the improvements."

"There's one more oddity," Katella said. "The elements of the Stone Donut's surface are depleted in radioactive isotopes."

"Well, so are our habitat and ships," Tony replied. "There's nasty stuff in these young systems, bad for electronics as well as life. The front end of our replicators sorts that out."

"Yes. But I mean *really* depleted. As if over ten billion years old."

"You think it wasn't built here?" Amber asked. The Dyson sphere surrounded a star only a million years old or so.

"That's one hypothesis. Or the isotope composition may have been specified a long time ago."

"By who?" Ga Tan asked, as he lightly fluttered his wings. He was dissatisfied with his state of knowledge.

As they all were. They exchanged glances, as if looking for answers in each other. Who, indeed?

★ ※ ★

Amber found that another year of Black-Rubber-Ball data and analysis improved their picture only marginally. Their most-likely model had the Black Rubber Ball as a shell around a sphere of pure hydrogen ices about seventy times the mass of Jupiter, though compressed down to a Jupiter-like radius. If the hydrogen model stood up, it was on the edge of becoming a star—depending on its composition; the amount of helium and deuterium were critical in this calculation and could not be determined remotely.

There was nothing more to do but to get samples in situ, and it would be better, they agreed, to be close enough to that operation to supervise it. The Black Rubber Ball was nearer to the solar system than the Red Rubber Ball by a few light days; if they screwed up bad enough, they could at least provide a bit of warning.

There was no chance of that, she told herself—no intelligence to anger, no awareness to threaten Earth—only an opportunity to solve a great mystery.

They made plans; there could be no mass beam station at the Black Rubber Ball, so the *Niki* would have to decelerate and reaccelerate on fusion engines, which required it to carry many times its mass of hydrogen and lithium; even then, their velocity would be limited to about 0.15 c and the journey would take several years. In the context of the centuries of offset they were accumulating with respect to the Solar System, she thought wryly, it mattered little. But they did use cold sleep.

★ ❋ ★

"By the authority granted us by the First Fledgling Aviary of Dar-Kleth," intoned Ga Tan, spreading his wings wide above his shoulders, "we award the rank of *Master of Mindflight* to Anthony."

They were all on Kleth, or as close to it as the dome of Sphere 3 could reproduce. Cool zephyrs of mint and orange scented simulated wind chilled them as Kleth's constellations brightened in the sky above them. The huge crescent of Bar As Do, ragged with mountains and craters, sat horns up on the horizon while the Bo Go leaves clattered in the wind like the hooves of tiny antelope on pavement.

By tradition, the Kleth awarded their equivalent of a Ph.D. after sundown the day after first new moon following the fulfilling of the requirements. Niki had reproduced the sky of Og Go Kan, the aviary of the educational institution awarding the degree by Ko Tor's proxy. Niki's Kleth side was no more than 434 years behind the times on such matters.

Amber caught the brief frown on Katella's face as she gave Tony the traditional brief congratulatory hug, as did Ko Tor and Ga Tan. Otherwise, it was all celebratory. Tony had started his Kleth degree long before their ship left and managed to set a record for, as far as they knew, the amount of sidereal time as an undergraduate of the aviary school.

★ ❋ ★

They passed two of the Red Rubber Ball's freighters on the way. This colony of machines moved at a far more patient pace than biological intelligence. As the second freighter receded, Katella called a meeting in the Sphere 1 Park about the rubber ball skin. She didn't ask Amber for the meeting; she just called it herself. Amber made no protest. It was a minor thing and probably just an oversight on Katella's part.

"As I thought," Katella started, "it's smart fabric. But it isn't very smart and can't do very much. It can contract or relax, report contact with other objects by mass and pressure, and pass along other messages, amplifying those beneath a certain threshold. The dots on the outside are photon emitters—millimeter wave to red light. It also has a lot more energy storage than it needs for that. In fact, the whole shell of this Dyson sphere seems to be a kind of battery."

"If the whole shell can store as much as the sample, how much?" Ga Tan asked.

"An order of magnitude or two more than the star puts out in a second," Katella said.

"Is that legal?" Tony asked.

He may have been kidding.

Or maybe not. The elder races were still around, however unobtrusively, and that was too much power, Amber thought, way too much. Unbidden, the thought of wielding that power came to her head, and she suppressed it. She shot a glance at Tony; he didn't look like he was kidding. She glanced at Katella. Katella was looking at Tony as if he'd just put his foot in his mouth.

Could I talk to you, tonight? Tony sent.

Amber thought for a bit and decided. *Sphere 2 park, 1900.* It wasn't a question. She was the Expedition leader, and marriage counseling was part of the job description.

"If it's illegal, Dear, where are the cops?" Katella said, her voice dripping with derision.

Amber touched the net. *Niki, we are the cops, aren't we?*

It depends on the nature of the contemplated action and the proximity of other potential actors. Generally, lack of consultation is not an ethical reason for not taking timely action. Ethical duties of a mature civilization, Best-Hugger Silversmith, Galactic Library Legacy Document 149344939546089, filed about eight billion years ago.

She knew it. Every space struck boy or girl had read it; the literal translation of the author's name was unforgettable. It was in the standard emergent civilizations section (according to the Galactic Library node at Proteus). It was nothing one really expected to come into play.

I have no Library records of Dyson spheres being held as contrary to ethical traditions per se. Partial Dyson spheres have been used to power intergalactic travel for billions of years.

"It does seem to have been around a long time without attracting galactic notice," Amber agreed. "But so have a lot of things. We have a responsibility to our planet, and this part of the galaxy, to find out as much as we can without hitting any trip wires."

"Nuts," Katella said. "We should grab control of it."

"Maybe," Amber said. "But carefully."

★ ✹ ★

That evening, Amber arrived about an hour early. A dip alone in the Sphere 2 park pond seemed like just the thing to release the tension of dealing with people for another day. It was roughly oval, about seven meters across, and about a meter deep over most of it. Its area happened to cover all of the central core of the sphere—it was tertiary radiation protection in addition to part of their limited ecology and recreation systems. Nothing in a starship went to waste and almost everything served more than one purpose. She laid her clothes on a bench by the shore; there would be plenty of time to dry and dress before Tony arrived.

He showed up fifteen minutes later, stripped and dove in, apparently without noticing that she was there; as she was swimming in the other direction; the first indication that she wasn't alone was the splash. Then his body brushed by her before she could even react.

She froze. This was totally wrong by so many standards; naked with a subordinate, married, man in a conspired rendezvous that *she* had selected. She imagined her trying to explain it to the extrasolar affairs bureau. But the extrasolar affairs bureau was 450 light years away, however heavily it weighed on her mind and not available for consultation.

Get a grip, she told herself. She was the authority here; she had to decide what to do and that would be that as the Kleth went along. They wouldn't intervene in human sexual affairs. Or would they? She'd intervened in a Kleth sexual issue—a welcome intervention, to be sure—but an intervention nonetheless that had put their biology ahead of what at least one member of the crew thought was overall safety. The same crew member who would go ballistic if she knew about this. Of course, not taking the swim would not have risked this. Was there something inside her that wanted to take this risk? The conscious mind was such a small part of overall motivation, she knew.

Niki, am I in trouble?

Not yet. Your instincts may be better than my analysis in this matter.

"Dr. Cloud?"

"Sorry. I was a bit caught by surprise. This is awkward."

"It's not anything new, really, we've done laps together in the basement pool."

Bright lights, chlorine, tired muscles, marked lanes, so completely unsexy as to hardly be worth a thought. Not this intimate splash under a simulated dark starry sky. She decided to ignore the intimacy, for now.

"Okay, Tony, you called this meeting."

"I need to talk to another human being about a human being. That leaves you."

Oh, God. Of course, it did. "You know, you should get out of this pool, get your clothes on and get out of here as fast as you can." Or I should.

"Do you want me to?"

Yes! No. He was a crewmember. She had a responsibility no matter how awkward the circumstances. "What I want..." She was kneeling in the muck at the bottom of the pond now, very controlled, innocuous muck, but muck never the less that she didn't want higher up on her body. But kneeling made her breasts visible. Was that an unfortunate circumstance, or an excuse? Was something primal running her behavior and getting rationalized? He was staring at her breasts, of course. He wouldn't be normal, otherwise.

The humor of the situation saved her. She actually let herself smile. "What I want seems to be under internal dispute. Okay, let's talk. But let's move out where the water is a bit deeper, and sandier"

She floated, and sculled forward in a breaststroke, washing the muck off her legs and putting her chest underwater. So she got a few moments of respite.

In the center, sitting on clean sand, she said the obvious. "Katella is being a little more assertive than you care for." More than any of the crew cared for, recently, actually.

"Yeah."

"Have you talked to Niki about this? He has a ton of psych data, and is totally secure as far as sexual matters are concerned." Too late, she thought of an exception, but that didn't apply to this. *Sorry, Niki.*

My ton of psyche data is telling me it isn't important. You're doing okay.

Not fabulous, not outstanding, not the right thing: just "okay." Goddamn AIs that were that smart.

"I'm on edge all the time," Tony said. "She...it's like she wants to run me like I didn't have a mind of my own. Nothing I do is good enough."

The man was actually in tears. Instinctively, she wanted to hug him. No. Not naked. She settled for touching his arm.

"Well, this may pass. See what Niki says."

"How long do I have to wait? I've been waiting some time now and it's getting worse."

"I'm going to talk to Niki."

Niki?

I don't monitor private conversations. The public area data seem to support what he says. Katella sees herself being treated as the number five in this crew, less listened to and appreciated than either of you or the Kleth, and she thinks she is better than all of you. In matters of internal knowledge, she may be right. In dealing with complex circumstances, what may be called judgment, she doesn't do well, however. Emotional issues may be clouding this judgment more than usual for your species.

Are you being smug, AI?

Ha. I see where you might think so. Not intentionally. In any event, she is not your immediate problem. Tony may be borderline suicidal.

What!!??

He was very much in love, and that is falling apart, leaving him with little to fall back on emotionally.

Except me. Or drugs. Or cold sleep.

There are downsides to all those possibilities. You may be the least damaging.

She shivered. *Yeah. Got it.*

She looked Tony in the eyes and saw a lot of pain. When had this started? Was she, herself, responsible in some way?

"How long has this been going on?"

Tony looked down at the water.

Amber touched him again. "Were there problems before the mission?"

He nodded.

"And neither of you said anything?"

"We both wanted to go very much. It was our chance to be part of history. It was the opportunity of a lifetime. And I wanted to be with you."

Amber took a deep breath. "I was your professor. Now, I'm your expedition commander."

He nodded. "You're beautiful. You're brilliant. You listen to me carefully and never get angry or harsh. You are a safe place to come to when Kate gets troublesome. I need you."

She had been entirely too good at pretending to be someone she wasn't.

While she was thinking, he embraced her. He was a child, she thought, half her age and totally besotted with her. A lethal combination of maternal instincts and reproductive imperatives clawed for control of her mind. Out of pity, as much as anything, she found she could give him what he needed, and not without wanting it and caring for him. In fact, she cared for him far too much, in her position. She should get fired for this. The people who could fire her were 450 light years away. She gave in with a sigh, returned his kisses, returned his hugs, and welcomed him into her. When he was done, she kissed him again, briefly, to let him know she was okay with it.

They didn't say another word as they dried and dressed. She

touched him briefly, to indicate that he should stay a while, and then she left the park, went down to her room, took a pill, then had a hot needle shower for half an hour. There had been no "right" decision, she told herself; what she had done had seemed the least wrong and the least stressful at the time.

She needed to be away from people and away from such decisions. If she could only stay here by herself, 450 light years away from them and everything.

★ ✳ ★

After the six-month trip and a gentle deceleration on its fusion thrusters, Amber stationed the *Niki* at the forward Lagrange point of the Stone Donut's fifty-eight-hour orbit around the Black Rubber Ball.

That put their ship a good 2.2 million kilometers away from the center of either object, at the expense of a fifteen-second lightspeed control loop lag with the robots. Their avatars would have to move slowly, and decide a lot of things on their own. The human operators would "feel" what the robots felt, but be along for the ride otherwise.

Ga Tan set up the virtual reality command deck on deck 2 of sphere 3, just under the active galley. He'd learned Amber's coffee habit. They would send three of their "Trojan" warrior robots in, with the humans linked to each and the Kleth watching over the operation. The warrior robots were non-flyers, except for occasional rocket jumps, and Ga Tan thought human instincts would work better.

Amber settled into a chair and put her hood on and found herself transported, at least visually, to the open airlock of Shuttle Number 3. She practiced moving the robot by telling it what to do, not trying to move individual arms or legs. The VR system moved her limbs fifteen seconds later and let her feel what they felt. The weird part was the feeling of resistance she got as the robot's limb pushed something; that the hood and its software managed to find and stimulate just the right part of her brain to do that was always a wonder to her.

"Okay, I'm in. Tony, Katella?"

"Good to go," Tony said

"The time lag's a nuisance," Katella said. "We should bring the ship closer."

Amber sighed. They'd discussed that, and she'd made the decision. That was probably Katella's main problem with it; not the time delay but the fact that Amber made the decision on where to put the ship and Tony cheerfully complied. Should she try to think of something polite to say? Or just ignore Katella's challenge?

"You'll get used to it, dear," Tony said, taking Amber off the hook.

Niki, in its shuttle persona, reported that they'd engaged the traffic control system of the Stone Donut, mimicking one of the Red Rubber

Ball spacecraft. With their captured robot's operating system and the radio traffic of several spacecraft arrivals in hand, Niki had made short work of the alien berthing protocol.

The shuttle hovered in the microgravity above the spin axis of the Stone Donut and matched its spin rate. The surface looked smooth, but radar, looking several meters into the shell, told a different story. It had been repeatedly cratered, repaired and smoothed over.

There were five hatches, at what seemed to be random angular spacing, on the inner part of the donut. They would have been invisible to the eye, but clear on the subsurface radar and thus on Amber's computer generated view. Spacecraft going to the Stone Donut went to the center of the donut's rotation, in its metaphorical donut hole, then matched rotation and coasted down to the surface in a radial direction to its inner surface, picking up angular velocity as they went. Their shuttle was about to try the same thing.

"We're being hit by an electron beam," Tony said. "It's part of the berthing system. We get a static charge, which the Stone Donut uses to manipulate the incoming spacecraft."

Would this really work? Amber wondered. They had not succeeded in contacting a "higher mind" of the Stone Donut, nor found any digital evidence of any such thing. What they were doing now was the cybernetic equivalent of turning a doorknob—on someone else's house, without invitation.

"It's formed an array of positive locations around the hatch area, mostly spinward. We're being pulled forward," Tony said. "Very gently."

A small hole formed below them and grew to the size and approximate shape of their spacecraft. Programmable matter, Amber thought as the spacecraft coasted into a huge, featureless hanger. It's used here, but not at the Red Rubber Ball. Why?

A platform rose up out of the hatch and their shuttle was placed on it. Then it was drawn in. The hatch closed over it and all contact was lost. Their avatars were on their own.

Contact was restored an hour later. The avatars had succeeded in linking with its computers and they now had full access all of its systems.

"It's like trying to communicate with a swarm of bees," Tony said as the shuttle ascended from The Stone Donut. "It does what it does, but it isn't conscious in the sense we are."

Ga Tan lifted his wings slightly, a sign of uneasiness. "It may not be conscious of itself, but it is now conscious of us. If our activities match that of some threat it has encountered in the past, it can annihilate us."

"We could take control of it," Katella said. "In self defense."

"Such an attempt may trigger defenses," Ko Tor said. "While it may not be conscious in the sense that we are, it has survived for billions of years."

"We should find out more," Amber said.

"Yes, like what is inside the Black Rubber Ball?" Tony asked, rhetorically, for he answered his own question to the extent he could. "Something as massive as a very small star, but very, very, cold. Absolute zero, to the degree we can measure from out here. The shell is held in place by magnetism generated by superconducting loops. We can tell from the Stone Donut's orbit that the mass is almost entirely concentrated in the center."

It was maddening, Amber thought. They now knew what it was doing, delivering antimatter to the Black Rubber Ball, and how they did it. What they didn't know was what they were delivering it to, nor why.

Ga Tan seemed to read her mind. "If you are thinking of following something into the Black Rubber Ball, that may also trigger defense," he said.

"There's nothing else to do," Amber said. "We may be able to suppress the defense. Niki is working on it."

For once, everyone seemed to agree with her.

"We can't hover above the surface; the gravity is nearly eight meters per second squared—almost Earth normal."

"For us, way too much," Ko Tor said.

"We'd have to land a shuttle. An uncrewed shuttle."

"Chicken," Katella said. "We're in control now. Let's see for ourselves."

"Amber," Tony pleaded, "It's a singular opportunity. We've beaten the risk down to nothing."

"We don't know what's in there!" Amber said.

"Caution is best," Ga Tan said.

"Best caution is." Echoed Ko Tor.

Suddenly, Amber's crew threatened to split on species lines—her worst nightmare. Time for a compromise.

"We send the robots in first," she said. "If it looks safe, we'll go in to view the cargo delivery. There, I hope I've made everyone equally unhappy."

Ko Tor clicked her beak. Tony shrugged. Ga Tan was immobile and Katella looked like she was looking to bite Amber's head off. But no mutiny happened.

★ ❄ ★

The Sphere One Park sky served as their remote viewing area. They did not view from a particular robot; rather, Niki absorbed all the robot video and reconstructed their display as if seen from an imaginary flying disk inside the Black Rubber Ball.

"Here it is," Niki said.

Utter blackness greeted them. "I can see no light inside the Black Rubber Ball at any wavelength," Niki said.

"Have the robots form a centimeter wavelength synthetic aperture," Amber said. "Illuminate the center."

"Way ahead of you," Niki replied, to chuckles and clicking beaks. "Here we are in centimeter waves."

A featureless ball appeared about twenty degrees above their artificial horizon toward park "north," ninety degrees from where the main ring pierced Sphere One.

"The ball is seventy-five thousand kilometers in radius at its equator, about seventy one thousand through its poles; we're looking down from the north pole. It's rotating every 13 hours and has a huge, axisymmetric magnetic field. But in a perfect vacuum, no radiation belt. I brought the robots in through the North Polar lock; it does not seem to be much more than a lock, though there are extreme contamination reduction measures. To honor that, I have the robots using the magnetic environment for propulsion. We haven't had to use thrusters except for a couple of times."

"What happened then?" Amber asked.

"The gas was ionized by lasers and attracted to the shell's inner surface, where it was absorbed," Niki replied. "I can find no ambient gas inside the ball; only occasional transients."

"The getting must be absolute," Katella remarked.

"Getting?" Ko Tor asked

"High vacuum terminology for removal of any stray molecules," Katella said.

"English language human jargon," Amber said, getting a frown from Katella. "Continue, Niki."

"The central mass is mostly degenerate cryogenic metallic hydrogen with a very pure H_2 molecular surface layer. We do see a rather diffuse background of annihilation gammas; that's consistent with antimatter being used for something on the surface of the Black Rubber Ball shell. *What* it's being used for is not obvious and probably occurs in nanoscale operations. There are also gamma events on the surface, consistent with antimatter leaking down there; these events probably keep the surface a degree or so above absolute zero.

"The shell is very thin smart fabric, as with the Red Rubber Ball, with embedded superconducting solenoid loops circling the entire shell like lines of latitude at milliradian intervals. A combination of loop stress and repulsion keeps the sphere taut and magnetic alignment keeps it centered on the Iceball."

"Profoundly isolated, that sphere is," Ko Tor said. "Some kind of experiment? Part of a gravity telescope? A probe of the galactic magnetic field?"

"We need a forensic technological archeologist for that," Tony said. "Me just physics dude. Uga uga."

Katella started laughing uncontrollably, as did Ko Tor, in her way, after Niki provided the colloquial explanation. When she regained some composure, Katella kissed Tony lightly on the cheek.

Amber had never seen any display of affection between the two before, and it sent daggers of fear and guilt through her. What had she done? Things were clearly different than she thought. How could she get out of this situation?

✳ ✳ ✳

Two days later, while Amber was doing laps in the Sphere 2 basement pool, Katella came in, stripped and dove in after her. *You've got to be kidding me*, Amber thought. *When one of that couple wants something, they catch me naked. How much does Tony tell her?*

"You screwed my husband," Katella said when she caught Amber.

Amber stopped and stood; this pool was a meter-and-a-half deep circle; at least. She was frozen into silence. How was she supposed to handle something that wasn't supposed to happen? Abject apologies? Try to explain? Get tough?

"In grad school, all those late nights, you screwed him. That's why we're here, isn't it?"

Saved by not saying anything at all out of fear, Amber shivered in the release of tension. "No. I was his professor."

"I don't believe that."

"Why?"

"Because he loves you, wants to be with you, drools over you. You had to be screwing him." Katella's voice was cold, steely.

"Unrequited obsession can be the strongest of attractions, Katella. And imagination can be much more powerful than reality. Perhaps I should screw him now and get it out of his system?"

"Damn you!" Katella's expression changed then, into more of wonder than anger. "You meant that, didn't you? Like it was some kind of astronomical problem to be solved. You don't feel. You don't understand at all."

Niki?

The chances are very good that she is just venting and it will blow over. Just wait until she's done, and leaves.

"Listening is part of my job, Katella. If there is something you feel I don't understand, perhaps you can explain it to me?"

"Chaos! Ask Niki. He's more human than you are." With that, Katella splashed out of the pool, grabbed her clothes and caught the lift pole for the next deck up. Why not, Amber thought. The Kleth wouldn't care and Tony had seen it all before.

Not for the first time, Amber wondered if Katella were right, in a way. *Am I some kind of mutant? Do I lack normal human intuitive responses? Is that why I want to be alone so much?*

★ ✳ ★

Progress? Amber asked Niki.

I've gradually infused myself into the Stone Donut's systems. They aren't designed for conscious AI, assuming I count as conscious, of course.

You fool me.

I'm programmed to fool you.

We'll leave that there. Anyway, does the Stone Donut have a brain?

It does now—a printed copy of my starship brain. What I'm working on is an overlay of broader band interconnections. The original setup was very distributed, simple by our standards but still containing eons of experience and patterns. There was some very stringent configuration control, so that every module had the same behavioral set. My work is an overlay; you said to keep the original intact so it could be studied. But to add the overlay as well, there needs to be an increase in capacity of trillions of modules and metamodules. It will take weeks.

Can the Stone Donut be made habitable?

Yes. It seems to have been originally built for a construction crew of living beings, somewhat larger than human, from the architecture, but there are no pictures, history, nothing to say who except some recognition codes.

Military security, maybe. Whoever did this didn't want to be traced.

Maybe, somewhere in the Galaxy, there is a record.

How long ago?

Radioisotope dating of the basic parts of the station indicates that it is made of material about 9.7 billion years old.

But nothing saying when that material was used?

Not yet.

Are the builders still around, somewhere?

Almost certainly not.

Almost?

Ten to the minus thirteenth, based on many reasonable assumptions.

★ ✳ ★

"Time to strap in; at its current speed, the cargo carrier is five minutes out," Katella said.

Amber checked the video from the *Niki*. The carrier had matched velocity with the Black Rubber Ball a week ago. Now it deployed a solenoid loop field generator, and fell toward the north pole, using the solenoid field to brake against the Black Rubber Ball's field. It was a propulsion system that made a great deal of sense, given its destination's magnetic field, but it took forever.

"It's carrying a lot of antimatter," Tony said. "Roughly five tonnes. Mix it with an equivalent amount of matter, and the energy released would be almost a zettajoule, roughly a tenth the energy needed to get the *Niki* up to speed."

"Which would be used over tens of days," Katella said. "If it were released in a second, we'll be dealing with a zettawatt! I've always wanted to use that word in a sentence. It's exciting!"

"It also gives us some insight into why this is a fully automated operation and the skin of the Stone Doughnut is five meters thick," Amber said. "Think of an asteroid a kilometer across hitting a planet at thirty klicks."

Tony and Katella had landed about a hundred kilometers from the pole. They were strapped into their acceleration seats, ready to head south at five gravities on a moment's notice if something went sideways.

But nothing did. The carrier slowed drastically, floated on its magnets into the lock, which cycled, and came out the other side. Inside the Black Rubber Ball, it continued down toward the Iceball, accelerating rapidly to a few kilometers per second in its balance between magnetism and gravity.

"Well," said Tony, "that answers one question. The antimatter isn't being used at the surface."

"But there's nothing like a processing facility on or near the Iceball's north pole."

"Not yet, anyway."

"We should bring the shuttle in," Katella said. "We can establish a polar orbit that dips over the pole at just the right time."

"Too much contamination, I think," Amber said. "The interior is very clean for a reason and we don't know what that reason is." Once again, she was in opposition to Katella, but the younger woman simply hadn't thought things through. And she was putting Tony in a bad position again. Maybe this time she'd thought quickly enough, however.

"Niki, run the numbers on shuttle effluvia and see what Ga Tan and Ko Tor think."

Amber could almost see the relief on Tony's face.

Katella frowned, but she really had no reasonable objection.

The answer was a bit of a surprise. Ga Tan spoke for the group on the *Niki*. "We're going to print a magnetic shuttle with a set of cameras, super clean, with a sealable clean observation room if someone wants to ride it. It will be ready in a couple of days."

"I'm going," Katella said.

It was a good solution, Amber thought. But the fact that it had been adopted without her own input was a symptom of how far things had gone.

"Very well," Amber said. "I'm curious as to what goes on in the Stone Donut and now that we have access to its data, I want that with as little time delay as I can get while this operation is in progress, so I will be there. Tony, it's your choice as to where you want to be."

She touched the net for Niki. *Pack and send all my personal effects over to the Stone Donut. I will be there for some time, assuming it survives. I'm going to need one of the shuttles as well. Connect me with Ga Tan.*

Ga Tan?

Yes, Amber Cloud?

In the event that I do not return with the exploration group, you will need to lead the group back home.

I sincerely hope that it does not come to that, but I recognize and accept the responsibility. Will I have Tony's support?

A good question, she thought. That Ga Tan asked it was a good sign.

Almost certainly, but if there is any question, appeal to his sense of responsibility. I sense that Katella has erred too many times to have his unquestioning loyalty or perhaps even his affection; the bonds between our pairs are not as strong as among the Kleth.

Understand. In such circumstances, we will do our best. We want to get home, too, of course. With you if possible.

Understand. Thank you. But the universe may have its own plans.

Amber had not yet crossed her Rubicon. If she were to leave, and live here permanently, it would a betrayal, a violation of promises, explicit and implicit.

Tony would suffer the most; she was his safety valve, and he had given her, however unsought, a glimpse of being loved despite her aloneness. But she did not want, and could not tolerate, the continued permanent companionship and responsibility for someone else, even someone who loved her. Neither could she fight Katella for him; even success in that would tear her up inside to the point of suicide.

The people who had sent her out here in good faith, at her insistence, to whom she had pledged to do this, would be perplexed and disappointed at first, then perhaps angry at how she had desecrated this artifact for her own ends, and finally fearful once they realized the literal power she could command. The relationship could become testy, but it would be much dampened by the 450 light years between them.

Her Rubicon was waiting, uncrossed as yet, Niki willing. But she had set foot on the bridge across it.

* ❋ *

Three days later the Red Rubber Ball's antimatter carrier approached the Black Rubber Ball's north pole. *Shuttle One* sat on the surface of the Black Rubber Ball. Tony and Katella, in the magnetic shuttle a hundred thousand kilometers over the north pole of the Black Rubber Ball, watched the radar picture with their eyes on the deck window in case something visible happened. Ga Tan and Ko Tor monitored from the *Niki*. Amber, in *Shuttle Three*, watched from less than a light millisecond from the Stone Donut, connected to its data feed in near real time.

Her excuse of monitoring events from there wasn't entirely a deception. After nine billion years, she had to think of this alien system as an evolved being, however different it was from beings like Amber or Ga Tan. To survive this long, it must have left the design, if not the purpose, of its makers far behind. Her version of Niki modeled every input and output, every algorithm as they functioned. Activity was clearly increasing. It was also responding to her data taps. On some level, it knew they were here.

What is this thing? It could be a scientific experiment, but it could also be a weapon of unimaginable power. But, it had no apparent defenses.

Hours passed; the universe had no respect for human time sense, Amber thought. Things took forever...or they happened in milliseconds. Amber tried hard to clear her head of feelings, of pleasing people, of Katella, of Tony. Focus, focus.

What if it were a weapon, or part of a war effort in some way? If you build a weapon and you don't want it to fall into the wrong hands....

A self-destruct mechanism?

Niki, get Katella and Tony out of there, now! If the antimatter hits the Iceball surface, what should happen, in detail?

If the cylinder hits the surface as solid ice, its surface layers will annihilate as it penetrates the Iceball's outer molecular layers. That will create gigawatts of half-GeV gamma rays and a cloud of antihydrogen around the entrance point. The cylinder will bore down through the surface like a hot knife in soft butter, perhaps as much as ten kilometers. Then the pressure of reactions at its front end will slow it to a stop. It will vaporize and mix with the hydrogen under high pressure; this will take only a few tenths of seconds; it will be essentially an explosion. The radiation will be largely absorbed by the surface layers, heating them to stellar interior temperatures. Except

*for a narrow cone directly over the entry point, observers would see
only neutrinos at first. The blast wave will take seconds to make its
way to the surface.*

*Okay, Niki, so we'll have a horrendous flash on the surface from
the antimatter ignition and fusion reactions, and a compression wave
to the core. The Iceball becomes a star?*

*Yes, if the core ignites. The new star would expand into something
resembling a T-Tauri star before settling back to a very late red dwarf
or a brown dwarf, in a time frame of about ten million years or so,
with a horrendous stellar wind to start with. But it would take hours
for the core ignition wave to reach the surface.*

Will the Stone Donut be safe?

Easily, it seems designed for even worse eventualities.

What might those be? she wondered.

Tony, Katella, she sent, *I think the mechanism intends to ignite
the Iceball and make a star out of it. It might be a self-destruct
contingency that we triggered. Get out of there, now, at maximum
acceleration. I'll be safe in the Stone Donut.*

Once they were on the *Niki*, the starship itself could surf away on
the plasma wind, not entirely unlike the intentional fury that pushed it
to the stars in the first place. They and the Kleth would be okay inside
its magnetic field.

*Niki, put an image of the magnetic shuttle on the right and the
surface on the left.*

She saw the magnetic shuttle stayed put for a few precious seconds.
Katella! If she threw orders at the woman, she would only resist more.
Amber could only watch and hope that Niki, the Kleth and Tony could
move her. Or maybe not.

Niki, can you stop or slow down this process?

*No. It's completely autonomous, as far as I have been able to
determine. The system is not evolved for centralized control.*

Amber would have work to do. For now, she was helpless.

The container with its load of antimatter descended inexorably,
now only a few kilometers above the Iceball's surface.

Finally, the magnetic shuttle rose rapidly toward the surface of the
Black Rubber Ball. Not soon enough, she thought. Not soon enough.

The container slowed and stopped its descent a few minutes later.
Its extremely cold cargo, rendered jet black in the radar visualization,
began to slide out from it, picking up speed as whatever fields had
contained it began to lose their grip on five tons of antimatter in a
hundred and seventy gravities.

The magnetic shuttle reached the polar lock.

As soon as the antimatter cargo cleared the container, the latter
accelerated upward against gravity at an impressive three gravities,
given it was using magnetic repulsion alone.

The black cylinder fell in the high gravity, but less fast than it should. *Its own magnetic field?*

Diamagnetic, Niki sent. *The field lines are converging, so there's a repulsive force.*

The magnetic shuttle emerged from the surface and flew into *Shuttle One*'s hold.

Niki. Amber crossed her Rubicon. Perhaps some would think of it as a sacrifice instead of a desertion. *Pick them up and evacuate, now. Ga Tan is in command. I am staying here. Go home, I will relay any data until the end. But if there is no end, I am content. There is so much to learn, so much to discover.*

Amber, Tony sent, privately. *Please...I love you.*

I know. That, in part, is why I must stay. I cannot return that kind of love. But do this for me; support Ga Tan. It will be difficult, but I think you understand why. When you return, give Katella a chance. People learn and change. But if not, there will be other loves.

We need to get into the Stone Donut, Niki reminded her.

Deja vu hit her along with the acceleration. Her prom date, those many years ago, had hoped for more after the dance. She had disappointed him with similar words and spent waking moments in the wee small hours of the morning ever since wondering about "the road less traveled."

"We're away," Tony reported on audio minutes later, his voice professional and controlled, "accelerating south at five gravities."

They will reach escape velocity in ten minutes, Niki said.

It might be enough, Amber thought as she entered the Stone Donut's axial lock.

The antimatter cylinder hit the ice surface, sending a target pattern of waves moving rapidly away from the impact point. It left a momentary crater that collapsed as fast as it formed. That was all.

What the hell? Katella sent. *That was five tons of solid antimatter!*

It was up to Ko Tor to voice what was both obvious and impossible. *The Iceball, or at least its outer layer...must ...of liquid, or perhaps superfluid, antihydrogen be.*

I recommend you do not stop accelerating, Amber sent. *If the shock of this impact was enough to trigger star birth, the T-Tauri winds will be made of antimatter!*

Then she decided to burn the bridge over the Rubicon.

Niki, I think we need to throw some rocks. Big rocks.

★ ✳ ★

The *SV Nicolas Louis de Lacaille* did not stop at the base at "Double M" and reached a third of the speed of light by the time the antiproton plasma wave reached the beam projector complex with its very attenuated, but still lethal, radiation. Forewarned, the robotic facility coped with it.

Its job was done in any event. The tail end of the acceleration beam had already been completely generated and projected. That spent the next month furiously overtaking the starship to deliver its load of momentum.

★ ✳ ★

Katella, Tony, Ko Tor and Ga Tan stayed in cold sleep for the three-gravity acceleration. They revived for their first scheduled waking period ten ship years later.

When they woke, Niki had a message for them. But first he sent them to an observation station in the main ring, a place with real windows where they could see the blue-shifted stars in their direction of travel wheel around with their own eyes.

"Ahead of us, about ten degrees from the sun, is a rogue kuiperoid, maybe the mass of Phobos or so. It's about three o'clock from Sirius, if you can spot that. I've sent you a marking circle."

"I have it," Tony said. "But surely we can't see anything that small by starlight."

"That is about to change."

As Niki said that, an impossibly brilliant star appeared in the designated place, then faded with twinkling embers.

"Good morning," Amber's voice said. "As you see, I survived the birth of the Antistar. I am now in control of the Red Rubber Ball, and I am repurposing it as an astronomical instrument. One of the things I can do is to vaporize things at an absurd distance to do spectroscopy on their content. I may actually file papers on this, assuming the institutions that publish them still exist. I may also send other messages to you, and I have taken special care to see that nothing unwelcome lies on your path home.

"The Stone Doughnut and the Black Rubber Ball had been floating through the spiral arm, using star after star for antimatter production for over nine billion years. The builders left no trace of its purpose that I can find, but the Black Rubber ball had reached the limit of its storage capacity. Still, the last antimatter delivery didn't quite push it over the edge. That took several thousands of tons of normal matter. I have no regrets; it would have happened in a few years, or a few million years, anyway.

"As a star, rather than an Iceball, that antimatter is now safely out of reach of anyone with designs on it. Trillions of years from now, it will become a ball of cold antihelium ash, its surface radiating half-GeV gammas and more from infall. But I'll leave that problem for future generations.

"With the Red Rubber Ball, I now control more power than any individual being should control. I am not sure I am entirely sane by human standards, and perhaps that combination will provoke an interesting response from the ancients of the Galaxy a few millennia hence. But, for now, I feel content and more relaxed than at any time in my existence. I am an Empress of Starlight, with extraordinary powers for hundreds of lightyears around me, and only the speed of light and my own values as a constraint. So, Katella, don't be an asshole."

"Seriously, I ask only this of all of you. Treat each other kindly, and at least make sure everyone understands that I am alone by choice, and I want to stay that way. Bon voyage."

THE TRIMUS CHRONICLES: POLES APART

...to establish a single planetary society in which all three spacefaring races take equal part; to find and develop common standards of civilized behavior, which may serve as a model for galactic civilizations to come.

- Compact and Charter of the Planet Trimus, Preamble

The human ship, almost four Charter units long with a huge square cloth sail, was new to Lieutenant Drinnil'ib. What, he wondered, were primitivists doing this far north? He hailed the ship, but instead of a verbal response, his voice brought a scurrying of the small two-legged beings around its deck. Before he could repeat the hail, a sharp, explosive, report split the air and something with a singing line attached went 'thwunk' into the sea beside him.

What in the name of the Compact? he thought. The line brushed over his nose and he stuck his tongue out to grab and examine it. The line came under tension, and he let it slide through his manipulators until the end came along.

Pollution! The thing was sharp. It nicked the muscular fingers on one fork of his tongue before he clamped down on the line with the other, forcing the humans to try to reel him in with it. That should slow things down a bit, he thought.   He raised a front claw and wrapped the line around it to ease the strain on his tongue. Then he held the object in front of his eyes. It was solid metal of some sort, and barbed:

something that could have killed him if it had hit him the wrong spot.

The thought and his reaction were almost simultaneous; he snapped his tail and bent his body downward. Not an eighth of a heartbeat later a tinny pop reached him through the water and another of the things zapped by. They *were* trying to kill him!

He let go, pulled a knife from his pouch, and slashed the line between the barbed missile and his foot. Then he swam first toward and then away from the ship, holding the line with his foot, and felt a satisfying give in the line after it jerked taut. He had some momentary misgivings - humans were fragile and he might have hurt one. But perhaps not: the tension on the line resumed quickly. Another slash of the knife took care of that. Drinnil'ib shook the remains of the rope from his claw, dove beneath the ship, and kept pace just below its hull.

Reaching back to his pouch, he replaced the knife with his gun and contemplated the plank belly of the offending vessel. Two, he thought, could play perforation. It took ten explosive rounds to put a fair sized hole in the hull; the layers of polluting timbers were a twelfth of a Charter unit thick. But when he was finished, the ship was leaking so badly it would have to head for port too quickly to bother any other Do'utian.

Satisfied, he breached the surface immediately behind the ship, fired a shot in the air and roared a challenge: "I am planetary monitor Lieutenant Drinnil'ib and you have just assaulted me. What in the name of eternal repudiation do you think you are doing?"

Shouts sounded and sails rose. He grabbed the rudder of the ship with his front foot and wiggled it vigorously. Finally a face surrounded by reddish hair appeared over the railing on the rear of the boat.

"What in hell are you doing here, Monitor," it shouted at him. "This is primitive territory - you damn techs are supposed to leave us alone."

"Not when people start getting killed," Drinnil'ib replied in a more conversational tone. "You can play your games but you have to observe the limits."

"Don't screw around in what you techs can't understand," it yelled. "Just leave us alone!"

Drinnil'ib rocked the ship again. "You're going to sink right here if you don't acknowledge that you can't sail around shooting people, wherever you are. It's against the Compact."

"All right, all right, I hear you. Shooting at you was a big mistake. But next time, stay out of human whaling waters, Fish-man."

The polluting idiot didn't seem to show a trace of remorse, however Drinnil'ib thought he might be misinterpreting their body language. Just to be sure they didn't misinterpret *his*, Drinnil'ib gave the harpoonist something very easy to understand: he emptied his lungs of moisture filled air right at them, soaking the speaker and sails. Then he

kicked the ship away in disgust and sounded. Ten Charter units deep,
Drin put the barb in an evidence wrap, and exchanged his gun for his
communicator and filed his report. He'd just gotten an object lesson
on how some of the killings might have happened, but he would need
human help to get to the bottom of it. A good excuse to look up an old
colleague. With measured beats of his muscular tail, he headed for the
northern reaches of the western continent.

✶ ✳ ✶

*As the tide-locked satellite of a superjovian infrared primary,
Trimus has three symmetry axes: north-south, east-west, and inner-
outer. This gives it three sets of geographic poles and three distinct
climatic regions that allow for all three species to live in comfort. The
arctic and antarctic match similar regions on Do'utia. The cool region
surrounding the far pole matches the climate of the most populated
areas of Kleth. The Earthlike near hemisphere is warmed both by
Aurum and Ember and ranges from temperate near the east and west
poles to tropical directly beneath Ember. Trimus' close orbit about
Ember gives it an effective day which is about twice the day of the Kleth
homeworld, one and a half times that of Earth, and three times that of
Do'utia. For the last, however, what counts is the four hundred and
seven day polar season cycle produced by the half-radian inclination
of Trimus' orbit to the local ecliptic, and this is almost the same as on
Do'utia.*
- Planetary Monitor's Handbook, Introduction.

The morning sun was a tiny red ball in the mists next to the great
ruddy crescent of Ember as Drinnil'ib propelled himself upstream
toward the human city with powerful tail strokes. The murders, he
thought, struck at the purpose of Trimunian civilization by pitting one
species against another.

Trimus was supposed to be the galactic laboratory for peaceful
interspecies cooperation. But Ember had circled Aurum eight-cubed
times since its settlement, and only the collective memory of the Kleth
and the mechanical memories of the Humans went back that far.
Some, he knew, felt this purpose had faded along with the need for
experiment; preempted by distances of time and space so great that the
residents of Trimus no longer represented the cultures that sent them.
If they ever had, he thought wryly. Beings who would leave their home
worlds forever to take part in an idealistic interstellar experiment may
have had more in common with each other than with their various
contemporaries.

But as far as Drin was concerned, the millennial-old civilization
of Trimus had become its own reason for existence. Forget the rest
of the galaxy and their occasional starships: to survive in peace with

each other and their planet, its residents had to put the discipline of reason ahead of the natural inclination to group things by shape. To be a monitor was a calling, and he had no greater loyalty than to his world and its ideals, except, perhaps, to reason itself.

Headquarters said that Mary Pierce would be waiting for him at the marina landing past the watchtower at the base of the main channel bar, wherever that was... There! He caught the echo and eased himself to the right and into the deep cool channel. The harbor bottom was a backwater fairyland of human bubbles and Earth-life reefs, and the channel led through that like a wide black road. At its end, the cigar shapes of human submarines lay in a neat row, safe on the bottom from the winter ice. He put his legs down, released a bubble to settle himself firmly on the concrete and with even measured strides hoisted his body into the warm air of the eastern continent.

A tiny tailless being, much smaller than the arrogant, hairy faced barbarian that had cursed him earlier, waited for him at the end of the ramp, covered with a form-hugging cloth that Drinnil'ib knew was an even better insulator than his doci of blubber.

"Afternoon. Drin?" it called, the high pitch indicating it was a human female.

"Greetings," he rumbled and reached forward with one of the branches of his tongue to shake her hand. The familiar taste of the air around her put him at ease. "Mary? I'm sorry but it must be eight years since we last met. It's really good to see you again."

Now that he knew it was her, it was easy to pick out the subtle individual characteristics of her almost-naked simian face and match them to his memory; the slight bend in the cartilaginous growth that housed her nostrils, the upturned angle of the hair on the upper ridge of her eye sockets, and its yellow-white color framing her face. It was a clean face, unmarred by any unnatural growth or scar, and he knew other humans considered her beautiful. He would agree, judging from the esthetics of functionality and also from the esthetics of the curve.

"You look pretty magnificent yourself, chum," she responded, but then shook her head. "I only wish the occasion were a happier one."

He bobbed his massive head in the planetary convention of assent. "Five more dead, four Do'utian and one human."

"Butchered?"

"Neatly, intelligently, as last time, except the human. The sea left too little of him to tell. But this," he held up the barbed projectile, "may be at the bottom of it."

"Primitivist hunters?"

Drinnil'ib hooted. "Not primitive enough, it seems. This was propelled by chemical explosives."

There were always some from every species, from every generation, romantics who wanted to live in the reserved areas by their instincts without having to learn the science and culture that got their ancestors to Trimus. A disease of the character, he thought, which could not be eliminated without eliminating character itself.

"I am sorry, Drin," Mary said, "for what our children have done. They form communities, the communities evolve, get recruits, and no one seems to care. Some of those places haven't been visited in a century."

Drin gave a sigh of toleration. "It is in your nature to hunt and in ours to endure the hazards of the sea. But without a trained intellect to guide, any race..."

She shook her tiny head in negation. "Some things are *wrong*, and always have been. Everywhere for everyone. Killing is one. They know the Compact, that's a minimum for letting them go out there. So it's up to us to find which 'they' are responsible and take corrective action." She shrugged her shoulders and spread her arms. "A policeman's lot is not a happy one."

A quote he didn't recognize, but one that fit. Lieutenant Drin bobbed his head again.

"Oh, the duty can be interesting."

"Ha! Well, my sub's ready to go; we can leave any time," she said. "But I thought you might like to try Cragen's sushi before we head out." She bared the exquisite miniature ivory chisels of her teeth to him in a human gesture of good feeling. Was there, he wondered, some art in this reminder that both of them were occasional carnivores? He would have to ask her on the journey. Meanwhile, the sushi sounded most pleasant. He hoped they could find a cubic doci of their rice wine to go with it.

About one of their traditional 'gallons,' if he recalled: "And a, um, gallon of two of, um, sake? To go with it?"

She laughed "Just what I was thinking, Drin. Let's go."

Glensville, on the northing Graham River, was easily cool enough in winter to be a congenial tropical vacation spot. He just had to remember to move slowly to avoid building up too much body heat. Great banks of melting snow lined the road, and ice covered the dozen park lakes scattered among the stone and wood human hives. Cheerful humans sliding on long flat boards attached to their feet waved to him as he ambled down the main road with Mary.

Cragen's was one of the few above-water taverns on the eastern continent that was set up to serve Do'utians. There were two there when he arrived with Mary: the poet Shari'inadel and a large Do'utian man with fresh white scars on his flukes and a deep, raw crescent behind his blowhole. Those were unusual wounds for this area - the sort of wound that one got in a beak fight with another Do'utian. So, Drin thought, this Do'utian must be primitivist of sorts - the kind that got his jollies on the southern beaches and came back every now and then to partake of the benefits of civilization.

The other turned its head, saw him, and hissed. Most impolite, and for what reason? Drin's lack of scars? His civilized bearing? His human companion? But this was a human town!

"I do not know you," Drin stated formally. "I am Monitor Lieutenant Drinnil'ib and I ask respect."

"Gota'lannshk. The sea has been generous with you, pretty monitor. But don't press your luck, beachmeat." The voice was a slurring, low pitched, rumble.

Drunk. Spoiling for a fight. Drin gave the other a sharp warning hiss, then turned away to ignore the reaction and cool his own rising irritation. He heard no response.

"You don't like him, do you," Mary whispered.

"I've never met the man," Drin replied, beak shut, letting the words escape softly through the fleshy corner of his mouth. "But what he is does not swim well in my thoughts. His companion is a poet, named Shari. I know the family - she's their first egg in two centuries, and quite indulged. She could be just the sort of dissatisfied romantic that runs off for glandular adventures in the south, and then lives to regret it. I think she is being 'offered' a place in that ogre's harem."

"Her choice, isn't it?" Mary asked.

"Choice implies an intellectual process, but he's playing on her instincts. Look at that one, and do not judge human rustics so harshly. He appears to have engaged in mortal combat for the fun of it."

Mary coughed. "Drin, Cragen's has some giant squid fresh from the farm. I'll split it with you, nine hundred ninety nine parts to you, one to me."

"Can you eat that much?" Drin rumbled. After his journey, a meal ashore would be a welcome.

"Try me!"

"You're on." Drin made the order. "Someday I'd like to try this squid in its native ocean, though." A fantasy of his; when would he ever find time in his life for a round trip of ninety years?

"That's where you'd have to eat it. You're too fat to walk around on Earth." She had a point. Twice the gravity of Trimus would have disadvantages, and he had been gaining a bit lately. Well, he'd swim that off on this trip.

"Maybe you underestimate me," he rumbled. Cragen's did not, however. The squid arrived - more than enough for even his appetite.

They talked strategy. The nearest concentration of humans who might know something lived on the islands near the warm inner pole. Whether or not these folk pinpointed the murderers, Drin made clear that he would need to talk to the Do'utian exiles near the south pole; to placate, to gather evidence, or both. Then would come the older human communities on the southern edge of the undeveloped West

Continent.

"Cites of stone, ships of wood. Reports of warfare and slavery."
Mary shook her head. "At the very least, they need to be reminded of
the Compact."

"That was certainly my experience," Drin agreed.

★ ❋ ★

*A common civilization requires a common language, common
measurements, and places where all three species can meet
comfortably. Human English shall be the common language because
it is the only language all three races can pronounce acceptably.
Numbers and measurements shall be in the Kleth octal system, which
is easiest to learn, is compatible with cybernetic binary systems, and
is more widespread than human base ten or Do'utian base twelve.
Common architecture will follow Do'utian proportions, so that
Do'utians will not be excluded from the social interaction needed for a
common civilization.*

- The Compact and Charter of Planet Trimus, Article 6

*The "charter unit" is identical to the Kleth "glide," precisely
eight to the eighth times the strongest line of neutral sodium, (also
approximately the peak wavelength of Aurum's spectrum). This is
about a traditional Do'utian "tail," once related to the length of the
average Do'utian, or almost ten human "meters," once defined as
1/23420 (1/10000, base 10) the distance from the equator of Earth
to its north pole. The common "doci" (from duo-octi) is 1/82 of this,
about the size of the adult hand of any of the three races.*

- Planet Monitor's Handbook, Appendix C.

★ ❋ ★

The journey to the inner pole archipelago left Drin fit and trim,
and he enjoyed the taste of the exotic tropical fish. But to reach the
island, they left cold south-flowing bottom current and he felt like he
was gliding through a hot bath. He looked forward to the south polar
waters, and sent an almost joyful greeting to Mary when caught the
wake-sound of her submarine returning from her inquiries.

Nominally, the archipelago would have been reserved for Kleth
primitivists, but they were very few and needed little land, so warm-
loving human refugees from technological civilization had gradually
spread among the islands. Here, near the inner pole, the infrared
radiation from Ember came in almost directly overhead, almost
doubling the distant orange sun's modest daily contribution. The
more or less permanent high pressure system kept skies clear unless
the night fog rolled in. But it was clear tonight, and the gibbous, pink-

belted almost-star dominated the zenith.

"Were there any witnesses?" Drin asked as Mary came alongside. She was lounging on the deck behind the submarine's pilot house, and last rays of setting Aurum painted her a rich gold. She had no need for her insulating garment, and he watched muscles play under her thin epidermis as she got up to greet him. A strange shape, yet one that fit its owner as well as any in nature.

"No witnesses - not really that many people around. I found one man who heard about some whalers and got him to tell me he's seen them even in tropical waters. Says they're operating out of a city on a half-flooded volcanic island off the southern edge of the West Continent reserve. I checked the recon and there is some sort of primitive city there. Hasn't been visited by monitors for years."

"Were the people forthcoming."

She shook her head. "There aren't many people here, and those who are here act frightened. I had to offer, well, an incentive to the only person who admitted knowing anything."

"I'm surprised the area isn't more heavily populated. This must be close to the original human climate, you don't seem to need artificial insulation here."

"No, we don't. And it does feel good!" She shook herself and her flesh rippled in a way that reminded him of a jellyfish, but much faster. "But it's enervating. Most people's minds need more stimulation from their environment. The people who live here don't even ask to replace the occasional death - children are too much work. They just live for pleasure."

Ages ago, Drin remembered, humans had arranged their genes to be infertile without deliberate medical intervention as a population control measure to go along with anti-aging measures. The idea of being constantly driven to act out the reproduce process horrified him, but humans apparently enjoyed it. Of course it wasn't as messy with them.

Mary shook herself again. "Cooling off now, though. Time to kiss lotus land good-bye."

She waved and vanished down the submarine's hatch. They sounded together and slanted west toward the cold current and their joint adventure.

Half a day later his dorsal ganglia were running things while he was deep in thought about just how primitive things could get. He understood much of the attraction of the undeveloped areas. All spacefaring people were descendants of those for whom the unbuilt beach and the untrod planet exerted an irresistible call. But his last trip had been eye opening in other ways.

He had little basis for comparing what he'd seen to the depth of cultural degeneration Mary said she had experienced on her hothouse island, but all the same, he shuddered to think of how she would find on the shores of the south polar continent. At least humans without machines could still construct buildings. Ancient Do'utian women had mated and calved on the open beach. Without shelter, their retrgressing descendents would have no choice but to do the same. Despite himself, a shudder of prurient interest ran from his chest through his tail at the thought of beaches nubile young mothers, blatantly receptive in the free air.

"Lieutenant Drin?"   Daydreaming! How long had Mary been calling him?

With the flick of the tail, he glided over to the submarine and brought his right eye up to the center of the diamond hull. Its electric drive fields made him tingle as they pushed seawater toward its tail.

"Lost in thought, I'm afraid. What do you have?"

Mary was back in her artificial skin and all business. "Here's the recon on that primitive city." A relief map appeared on the holoscreen next to her. The flooded caldera surrounded a lagoon on three sides, and the forth appeared to be filled in by a simple stone dike. Large and small masonry buildings lined the shore of the lagoon.

"Mary, I think the cold current must flow by there, see the trench to the south?"

"Yes. Good eating?"

"It should be, and if so, we should find some Do'utian primitives nearby. I suggest we stay with the plan, head south first and gain what intelligence we can from the victim population before confronting this set of potential perpetrators. ... Mary?"

"Yes Drin?"

"In our early days, there were tests for reproductive rights. Death swims and beach fights. Bloodlust beyond reason. These occasional hunting deaths seem, in a way, like some of those old tests. I fear I will not be proud of how some of the Do'utian back-to-nature crowd might be living."

"Do you fear more than embarrassment?"

Yes, he needed to say. Yes I fear my own primitive instincts. So why did he hesitate to tell her? Mary was a friend and colleague, and any infirmity on his part could affect the mission.

"Mary ... we have never needed to revise our mating instincts. In our cities, with the privacy of our rooms, there is no need. In fact, we must make an effort to replace those of our colony who are lost by accident - an embarrassing and very private effort for both beings concerned. But with everything out in the open... I'm not sure how I will..."

Peals of musical laughter twinkled like bells from the hull of her ship, for so long that Drin became concerned for her health. Finally, she pressed herself to the transparent hull.

"Drin, my friend ... look, don't tell what I'm going to tell you to any other human, especially the other Monitors, okay?"

"My word on it," Drin said, curiosity clawing at him.

"Well," she laughed, "in order to be accepted and get what information I kind of went native. I allowed; hell, Drin, I enticed, my source to perform our mating act with me. I mean I was all there, and he was all there, and it just felt like the natural thing to do. In the line of duty, I told myself."

Drin swam in silence for a while thinking that to say the wrong thing would be harmful to his friend. But he soon realized that to say nothing at all could seem even worse. He reviewed what he knew of human mating. "Was this person physically suitable?"

This occasioned more laughter. "He was. Oh, yes. Exceedingly so."

"And you left this pleasure to return to your duty with me? I find this very admirable and hope, to the extent that we can compare our temptations, that I shall be able to exhibit similar moral strength."

"Moral strength? Drin, you are a forked-tongued devil."

After a moment, he realized this was a compliment. He gently pressed a shoulder to the window so that only the eighth of a doci or so of diamond hull separated their bodies. He easily felt the warmth of her flesh through this transparent, uninsulated, section. This communication of friendship had no intellectual hazards.

But his mind returned to duty. "Perhaps," he rumbled after a while, "we should ask the Kleth Monitors for backup in case we find we need eyes overhead when we visit this city. I know a certain Officer Do Tor who has a sense of humor and does not dump everything into their racial memory."

"Perhaps," Mary laughed again. "I think I met him when the last starship visited, six years ago. Gold wings, silver crest? Flighty little yellow thing under his claw?"

"The very one."

"Why not? The more the merrier."

★ ❋ ★

Following planetary engineering, only the north, east, and outer poles will be intensively settled. The remainder of the planet will be reserved for biological study and kept free of large settlements or significant technological effluents. The primary objective will be to observe how the three merged ecosystems evolve from their original design point. Low intensity visitation, consistent with these objectives, may be tolerated by those who wish to experience life in the wild.

- The Compact and Charter of Planet Trimus, Article 12

★ ❋ ★

"I have never seen such a cold, desolate wasteland of rocks in my life," Mary remarked as they approached an outrageously voluptuous antarctic beach. *A fish for every taste*, Drin thought.

She had parked the submarine and rode on his neck toward the shoreline, her warm thighs smooth against his sandy outer skin. The idea that she often had eggs, of a sort, waiting in a part of her body so near to him gave him ridiculous and perverted thoughts - thoughts that unwontedly stimulated certain secretory organs below the tips of his manipulators. Some, he had heard, had experimented with interspecies stimulation and considered it a form of art. Thank providence, he thought, that such thoughts on his part could remain private. But if Mary ever said that she wanted . . . No, no. Consign that idea to the abyss. Too much chance of giving offense.

It didn't help at all, as they neared the beach, that he could see at least four unabashedly pregnant young Do'utian women lolling thick-necked on the smooth pebbles in the sun. The beachmaster was nowhere to be seen, a circumstance that ran his biological thermometer well past its set point. He wondered if Mary understood how hard this would be for him?

"That beach is an indolent paradise for us, I'm afraid. I'd much rather talk to the head man than that naked harem, but he's left them unprotected. This isn't good. Uh, Mary, if they become aggressive with me, it might be best if I just let nature..."

She patted the top of his head, firmly enough for him to notice.

"I'll never say a thing. Promise." She put her arms around his neck, as far as they would go, and pressed the soft parts of her body against the back of his head, laughing. It was not at all unpleasant. Then, suddenly, she stopped.

"Drin," she spoke quickly, "to your left. What is that in th - DRIN!"

Instantly, he rolled his eyes around and slipped his tongue into his pouch, triggering his sonar with one manipulator and grabbing his weapon with the other. Then he saw, and knew instantly that it was too late to do anything.

A tall pole, perhaps half a Charter unit high, supported a white pennant at its end, snapping in the offshore breeze. The other end was firmly buried in the side of the corpse of a Do'utian man, bloated, floating in the swell. He shuddered as the wind shifted and brought the scent of death to him.

"Are you okay?" asked Mary.

"Yes. But I would prefer to approach this upwind. How are you?"

She was a trained monitor, and, he hoped, not as affected due to the difference in species. Fortunately for him, the wind shifted again.

"I'm fine. Look, why don't I check out the victim and the murder weapon while you interview?"

It made sense, but he was hoping for her presence to bolster his resolve not to be swept away by instinct on the beach. He belched in self disgust; was he not master of himself?

"Very well, Mary. I'll take you over to it, I need to get closer anyway. I suspect the victim was the beachmaster here, and if so, these women have been widowed. I should be able to tell from his scent - he will have marked them. Widowing can be a very painful death sentence in primitive circumstances - an unbirthed egg turns poisonous in a month or so.

"So my human primitives kill five Do'utians with one harpoon?"

"Mary, they are not *your* primitives," he rumbled. "Don't take so much on yourself. It's not very professional." He extended his tongue behind him and placed manipulators on both her shoulders. "Besides, there are no reports of harems dying because of the other murders." The thought struck him: why not? "We don't know the whole story," he finished. No, indeed.

He felt her five thin bony fingers cover his three thick muscular ones. She grasped tightly, and he could feel some warmth, though not taste her skin, through her water suit. He could not fathom what feelings ran through that alien mind nor what awful images from her past this fresh corpse might conjure. But he could recognize sadness in her, and try to give sympathy.

His own feelings were proving harder to manage. There was a primal urge in his species to avoid their dead, and thus, the evolutionists believed, avoid whatever circumstances might have lead to death. Then there was what waited for him on the beach. He shuddered.

"I can tell you'd rather not go any closer, Drin," A splash surprised him, and Mary swam in front of his left eye. Humans, in general, were clumsy in the water. But they were fearless and some like Mary were competent, if slow. "I'll take it from here. Looks like about as far to the corpse as to the beach. No problem; I'll just swim in when I'm done, or I'll buzz for you if I need back-up. Okay?"

He rumbled an assent, she bared her teeth to him, flipped and started pulling herself through the water toward the victim climbing through the waves with steady pulls of her front limbs. The wonder, he reflected, was not that his simian friends were slow in the water, but that they could swim at all, and even appear graceful, in their own way, while doing so.

"I'll be expecting you. Take care," he called after her. Then, with mixed feelings, he sent himself toward the beach.

The approach was not the simple landing of a human boat ramp. Jagged rocks were all over. The beachmaster had chosen well: an adult Do'utian needed care to reach the shore. Drin exhaled and settled firmly on the bottom to ignore the random swells. Legs extended, he picked his way carefully along, a Charter unit below the surface, while holding his sonar transceiver high over his head, hearing the image it received through his earphones. There! The a sandy path opened through the rocks. He followed it. It zigzagged to an open gravelly area under the breakers that seemed safe enough, but he chose to pick his way through the smooth stones along its side just in case. Carefully, he emerged onto the beach.

The women cowered together as soon as they saw him. Very well, he'd take it slowly.

First though, he traced his route with a sharp tongue tip on his comset's screen and sent the resulting image to Mary. While she could float over larger outlaying rocks that would disembowel him, there seemed to be only one place where the breakers might not dash her to pieces. He also sent a brief report to Monitor Central and inquired about the status of his request for Kleth support. Scheduled, they told him.

Chores done, he returned his attention to the widowed harem. Widowed because they had been very clearly scented by the dead beachmaster, and the deceased's neobarbarism seemed to have extended to marking them physically as well as with his scent - some of the scars were still unhealed.

A medical team would be needed. While, contrary to his initial assessment, only two of them were gravid, with the beachmaster gone they would both be needing egg relief soon. Also, all four were clearly undernourished.

He filed a quick report for Do Tor on his comm unit, then walked forward to them slowly, mouth politely open, tongue and manipulators spread to signal peaceful intent. Still, they cowered. They were young, very young, despite scars and abrasions on their hides that most of his people wouldn't acquire in eight times eight times eight years - and would probably remove if they did.

"I'm Lieutenant Drinnil'ib from the Monitors. I don't mean any harm," he said. "I'd just like you to answer some questions."

It must be the smell of the beachmaster's death that frightened them into silence. He had come close enough to carry some of it, and they probably thought he was responsible.

They keened and backed away as he approached. But a cliff surrounded the beach, and soon they could back up no further.

If they could smell the death, then there was no reason to try to keep it secret. He was hoping to avoid the legendary consequences. Nonsense, he told himself. These must be at least semi-educated people, living in primitive conditions by choice.

"I'm sorry to have to bring you this news. I've come from the North Pole colony investigating the reported deaths of several people in this back-to-nature area. I'm afraid I have one more to investigate. By what I smell, the latest victim was your husband. I'm sorry. I assure you I had nothing to do with his death before the fact." Lieutenant Drinnil'ib reached into his pouch and produced his badge, a holoprint two docis on edge - big enough for them to see easily. It gave off his scent as well.

The smallest of the Harem, with deep black scars on her forelimbs finally walked forward, then lower herself to her belly in supplication. "No," he protested. "I don't want you to do that. Stand up! Speak to me, please."

She keened again, then opened her mouth wide. It took him a few heartbeats to register what he saw, and then a few more for the horror of it to sink in. Where the two branches of her tongue should have been, with their manipulators that signified their species' rise from the beach should have curled, was nothing but a blackened stump, so short it would be useless for feeding or speaking.

He quickly pulled in his own tongue and lowered his belly to the gravel, to be on her level. Then he gently touched his beak to hers in sympathy. She shut her eyes and lowered her beak in sadness, and he did the same. When he looked up again, the other three had joined them. The gravid ones were looking at him expectantly. Oh-oh.

"Look," he explained, "I'm not part of your culture. I'm a Monitor. This is strictly a professional visit." Their eyes showed no comprehension, and their bodies began to sway back and forth on their legs. They came closer, swaying and keening. The first female kept nuzzling him. He tried to back away, but froze.

From then on, he noted his body's response with what was almost detachment. Body temperature up. A tightness at the base of his tail. He wanted to keep his mouth shut to avoid tasting whatever chemicals they were putting out, but a groan worked its way out from deep inside him, his beak yawned open involuntarily as reason left his brain. The women were beside him, keening, holding him between their bodies, their beaks locked wide open, pressing his most private areas. The need to give overwhelmed him. He let his tongue caress his their tails, almost as if it were someone else's.

He never saw the eggs emerge from their throats, but rather felt the smooth bumps against his underside, an emptying feeling in the base of his tail, and a slight coolness in that area as his consciousness slowly faded back in.

Afterward, of course, he remembered everything with the humiliating clarity of a terapixel hologram. Especially when he looked back at two white eggs covered with sticky yellow goo. And especially when he looked up and saw little Mary Pierce standing about eight Charter units away, mouth open in what must have been a look of horror.

Setting aside his embarrassment and disgust, he tried to remember what needed to be done. Back home, in a hospital, the eggs would be sprayed clean and anointed with all sorts of healthy fluids, wrapped in germicidal barriers, and placed in an incubator. The nearest thing to an incubator they had here was a Do'utian pouch. His was full of other things, but the women had pouches, too.

It was then that he realized that since none of the women had tongues, he would have to place the eggs in their pouches himself. He shut his eyes, moaned, and buried his beak in the sand again. He couldn't do this.

"It's okay," he heard Mary say. "I'm afraid I don't remember what the handbook says about Do'utian midwifery, but if there's anything I can do, just tell me."

He lifted his head up. "The hand book doesn't say anything. It's supposed to be too private. But ... but the eggs need to be cleaned off and placed in the women's pouches. They can't do it themselves because their former husband disabled them. I'm ... I'm afraid I'm not up to it."

"No problem, buddy. I think they accept me. Must be your scent all over me. Is it okay if I wash the eggs in the sea?"

"Yes, I think so."

She did this quickly and efficiently, taking each egg in turn, cradling and talking to it as if it was a fresh born human. Drin refrained from telling her that there would be nothing inside the eggs to hear her for eight-squared days. Done with the washing, Mary took the smaller egg and approached one of the formerly gravid women, who looked accusingly at Drin and backed away. Then a strange thing happened. The smaller Do'utian women quickly moved in front of Mary and offered her own pouch.

When that member of the harem had accepted both eggs, she came over to Drin and slowly scratched the sand with her beak. It soon became clear that she was writing. When she backed away, Drin could read, fairly clearly, "I GRI'IL"

"You can understand me?" Drin asked, wonderingly. Obviously, she could not speak.

She nodded.

"Your name is Gri'il?"

She nodded again.

"Do you want to leave?"

Gri'il did nothing, then nodded slowly, followed by a vigorous head shake. Something wrong.

"Will you follow me back to the North Pole? To civilization?"

She was still a very long time. Then she began painfully scratching the gravel again. What she wrote was "DANGR HUNTRS."

Mary saw this, went up to Gri'il, wrapped herself around the Do'utian woman's foreleg, and began her own type of keening. Soon, they had all joined in.

"I'm going to get some fish for everyone," Drin said to no one in particular, and trotted back to the shore. The mutilated Do'utian's were ill nourished and couldn't feed themselves. Besides, he needed something to do alone. Away from all women of whatever species.

★ ❈ ★

Individuals who wish to visit or reside in the wild regions, alone or in small groups, may do so without interference so long as they respect the rights of others and do not significantly disturb the environment. Introduction of chemical industry is specifically prohibited. Alternative societies are permitted so long as the individuals who join such societies are free to leave such when they wish. Do not interfere with suicide or risk taking that amounts to such. However, murder will be treated no differently than in the civilized areas.
    - Planet Monitor's Handbook, Law In Reserved Areas

★ ❈ ★

"Gri, Ohghli, Donota, Notri, do I have it right?" Mary asked. Human memories, Drin thought, were amazingly poor considering their technological prowess - on the other hand, perhaps necessity had made them superlative inventors.

Drin rocked her submarine by putting a little extra into his next propulsive tail-stroke. "Your memory is either much worse than I think or you find a certain humor in my situation. I think I would rather not have my thoughts in that current so often."

"My apologies." The comset relayed the drop of pitch in her voice that Drin associated with increasing concern. "But they're your wives now, aren't they?"

"No! I have made no commitment. There is no registration. Except for Gri'il, none of them seems to have any intellectual understanding of their lives, or that of the broader race. None of them is a suitable mate."

"I'd guess it will be hard for them to understand that," Mary suggested, more right than she could know.

"Very hard. I approached them under circumstances that make biological bonding almost inevitable in nature. And Gri had the eggs..."

"She seems the responsible type, and educated somehow."

"She will have a tale to tell. I suspect she is a truant who dove into the back-to-nature business just a little deeper than her inherent depth. The others, I think, must have been born here. They seem virtually feral."

"What will happen to them?"

"I think Gri'il will return to civilization, sadder but wiser. The feral women ... I don't know. The experts will have to decide - they may be happier as they are."

"Mutilated?"

"No, we'll fix that. But, they may be unable to adapt to civilization now. I cannot know their minds, or even if they have developed what you and I would recognize as a mind."

"That's heartless," Mary accused. "They love you."

"You don't understand the biology. I think our conversation should find different currents now."

But it didn't. Mary's attempt at match making left him in no mood for conversation at all. There was silence instead, a silence that should have been filled with plans as they approached the primitivist human settlement.

It was shockingly big, even by his standards. Primitivism in humans, Drin realized at the sight, didn't really mean living without technology. It meant living with a technology so primitive that it could be sustained without any meaningful education at the expense of ceaseless, boring labor; a technology of hand-hewn planks, poles, and rough-cut stones in huge piles, piles made all the larger by beings genetically designed for twice the local gravity.

The entrance to their harbor had been choked down to a canal by massive stone walls and guarded by massive wooden grates. The stream that issued from this was putrid. Drin turned away.

"Pollution! Mary, I think I would prefer to walk in."

"Understood. There must be two thousand people in this place, and that's the only outlet. The air isn't a whole lot better - lots of smoke. It's a couple of degrees over freezing; cool enough for you?"

"A nice balmy day."

"Why don't you try riding on top of the sub? You'll have to keep your tail off the rear electrodes."

Drin released a bubble of humor; the idea of him riding on a human submarine was indeed bizarre. But the water stunk like rotting carrion. "If you can steer without your forward fins, I could hang onto those with my forelegs. Then my tail wouldn't reach the electrodes."

"The sub says that's no problem. Climb aboard."

He swam into position, curled his front toes around the rounded edge of the flexidiamond fins and released some buoyancy gas to hold himself down. The submarine rose under him and broke the surface. The air stank as advertised, but only when he opened his mouth.

Soon Mary climbed out of the nose hatch to join him. She'd put her monitor uniform jumpsuit on over her insulated tights and looked academy sharp. Remembering that humans relied almost exclusively on visual identification, he pulled his monitor badges out of his pouch and stuck them on his front shoulders.

In front of them across the harbor entrance lay the top of the harbor wall with an opening just a little wider than the submarine, the massive wooden gate was solid above water and dwarfed even Drin. It was guarded by heavyset humans in thick-belted robes around which were buckled long, heavy, cutting tools; called swords, if he remembered correctly.

"Open the gate," Mary yelled. The men did nothing. Drin tapped her on the shoulder with his tongue to warn her, and she covered her ears. He took a large breath.

"PLANET MONITORS. OPEN THE GATE," Drin yelled, two octaves lower than Mary, pouring air from his bladder as well as his lungs. The human guardhouse resonated nicely with his undertones and a satisfying crash emerged from its open door. Various stones and pieces of rotten mortar came clattering down the sides of the wall. One of the men extended his hands, palms out as if to plead for patience, while the other dipped into the now-steady guardhouse and emerged with a pair of colored flags. He faced the harbor and started waving them in various incomprehensible patterns.

Soon, they heard a screeching and groaning of hidden wheels and levers as the left gate swung ponderously open. From aerial holos, Drin knew the breakwater was eight squared Charter units thick, but even so, the narrow canyon revealed by the opening gate made him shudder a bit. He slipped a branch of his tongue out the corner of his mouth into his pouch and wrapped its fingers around his weapon. When the noises stopped, the submarine nosed through the half-opened gate. It had only a few doci's of clearance on either side, but it maintained this clearance with mathematical precision as it moved smartly into the channel.

About halfway through, a red-robed human man jumped onto the hull from a ladder just inside the gate, landing without stumbling despite the vessel's speed. He looked at Drin, then at Mary, apparently unsure of whom was in charge; the male Do'utian or the female human.

"Who are you?" Drin rumbled. The man shook and looked around, as if for somewhere to jump, and finding nowhere, finally faced Drin.

"Yohin Bretz a Landend. I'm ... I'm your harbor pilot. We've got to go to city gate - Lord Thet will talk to you there."

"Yohin Bretz a Landend," Mary said, "I'm Mary Pierce from the monitor bureau. This is Lieutenant Drinnil'ib, my colleague. This is my boat; Lieutenant Drin doesn't need one. We are here to investigate the deaths of several Do'utian primitivists in this region."

"Huh? Whalers playing games with the fish-people, I'd guess." Bretz looked down at the submarine. "What do you draw?"

"Draw?" Mary clearly didn't recognize the term. Drin did, from his readings in human nautical literature, but kept silent so not to embarrass his partner.

"Yeah, *draw*. How far down is the bottom of this thing?"

"About a third of a Charter unit," she answered.

"What's that in meters?" A human chauvinist, Drin thought.

"It's a little over three of the old meters."

"Uh huh.   So the keel's a about twice your height below the waterline?"

"Yes."

The pilot shook his head. "You'd displace thirty ton less without the fish-man on board, I'd guess, and ride a meter higher. Well, no problem, the channel's deep enough, but you'll have to stay in it. You've got to go hard aport as soon as you're out of the dike canal and steer for the big stone mill you'll see on the shore. Bear a bit to the port of it to lead the current, if I were you."

Drin rumbled a bit, and Mary smiled, recognizing his laugh. The submarine could follow the channel on sonar or with blue light without any help from the pilot.

"We'll do just fine," Mary said, "thank you. Now you can call me Mary, what can I call you?"

"Yohin, or Mr. Bretz to be polite."

They emerged into the harbor, a roughly circular body of fetid water. The air was thick with the smell of fish and dark with wood smoke. Now and then a flake of white ash would fall on them. Rough wooden human buildings lined the shore except for the far end. There, across the middling stream that struggled to flush the place, was a large stone wall, more vertical and smoothly finished than the dike across the harbor entrance.

Against this dock were tied wooden ships including several small round vessels not much longer than Drin himself, set with triangular sails, and a massive square-sailed ship - perhaps ten Charter units long. The last also had a strange, forward-projecting bow and two rows of oars with which it could presumably maneuver without wind.

"Hey, we're in the harbor," Yohin shouted. "Don't you have to do something to turn this boat? How the...?" His eyes went wide as the submarine turned to the channel without Mary doing anything. Drin rumbled again.

"Tell me, Mr. Bretz," Mary laughed, "Are you happy here?"

"It puts bread on the table. Feeds me and my wife, gets me some respect. Even got a couple of slaves. I've been doing it a hundred fifty years. Yeah, I'm happy. Don't need any fancy stuff."

"Slaves?" Mary asked. "You have slaves?"

"Sure," Yohin said. "Someone's got to do the work while I'm out piloting. Be a shame if my wife had to, and I'm too tired after a day of this."

"Are the slaves happy?"

"I feed 'em well. They don't know anything else, so why shouldn't they be?"

Drin hissed. This manifestation of disgust, he realized, was wasted on this human pilot. "Do your slaves want to be slaves?" he asked. Yohin turned to him in surprise.

"They were captured fair and square. They know the game. What business is it of yours, Mister, excuse me, *Lieutenant* fish-man?"

"The primitive lifestyle is supposed to be voluntary. No one should be compelled to live like this."

"Look, I didn't set this up. But if you come after my slaves, you got an argument with me. Maybe from them too. What would you do with them? Send them to some machine school so they can contemplate their navels for the rest of eternity? They're better off working for me."

"Now, lady," the pilot waved his hand at the other side of the harbor, "you've got to turn this tub sharp starboard and make dead on for the flagpole on the end of the fort ... however you do it."

The submarine turned as if to the pilot's command, and he nodded judiciously.

"Never knew a woman could run a boat. But you do okay."

"I've got a lot of help," Mary said. "Yohin, I can imagine you doing this in one of those sailing ships with the wind blowing, using only your judgment and what you can see from the surface. I respect the skill you need to do that."

The pilot nodded his head again and bared his teeth again. Mary, Drin realized, was gaining trust.

This human, Drin thought, had found whatever Gri'il had been seeking when she left civilization for the beach. The question was whether the failures should be allowed with the successes, particularly if the failures were involuntary.

"You said something about the whalers playing games with the Do'utians. What kind of games?"

"I heard there's a deal where the fishmen try to outfox the whalers. Them that lose are meat, but word is that's how they want it."

Drin rumbled his skepticism.

"Who sets up these games?" Mary asked.

"How the hell should I know? Maybe Lord Thet does. You can ask him, we're almost there."

The submarine's hull was well below the level of the dock, due in part to Drin's massive presence. From sea level, he couldn't see the rest of the top of the dock. The angle got worse as they fetched up next to the stones.

Carefully, using the wall as an additional point of balance, he swung his tail over the side of the submarine, reared up on his hind legs, and hooked the rippled pads of his front toes over the edge of the stone wall, bringing his head above dock level.

The man waiting for them on the dock by the city gate was probably

Lord Thet. He was a head taller than Mary, gray-robed, and had thick black hair all over his face so that only the eyes and the nostril wattle showed when his mouth was shut. His robe covered either armor or what would, for a human, be an exceptionally large body. Others of his kind, holding metal tipped spears, stood beside him. Perhaps fifty humans carrying some sort of primitive wood and cord weapons stood well back of the primitivist leader.

Mary was able to scramble up his back and jump from his shoulder to the stone platform. Undignified, but it got the job done. There was a fair amount of wind and harbor noise, but Mary left her comset on her belt, where it could see and record everything. Drin listened through his earphone.

"Hello, I'm Mary Pierce, Planetary Monitor."

"You are not wanted here," Lord Thet stated - with aggressive impoliteness, Drin thought.

"Your name?" Mary asked.

The man remained silent, but the comset camera got a good look at him and the Monitor net quietly relayed the information through their earphones. He'd left civilization early in life and, despite his commanding presence, was largely ignorant of things beyond what he controlled.

"You are Jacob Lebbretzsky, otherwise known as 'Lord Thet' according to your voice and features. I'll be gone fairly quickly if you answer my questions," she told him.

"Don't overestimate your authority, Monitor. Your superiors are not that interested in us and your charter is open to interpretation." Wishful thinking on his part, Drin felt - while the Monitors would bend over backward not to be overbearing, there was no question about the final outcome.

But only he and Mary were here right now, things were nowhere near final, and if this egomaniac idiot had talked himself into believing he could get away with minor violence... or if someone else had talked him into believing...

Drin spoke quickly with his beak shut so that only Mary could hear him, on her earphone. "Mary, this fool could be dangerous. He's gotten so big he's forgotten what's backing us up."

She raised a hand to acknowledge him, but continued to face Lord Thet. "Someone's killed at least four Do'utian primitivists," she told him.

"Have the fish-men accused us?"

"We found the bodies."

"Death happens. Only the untested live forever."

An ancient Do'utian philosophy, Drin thought. Why was he hearing it from an ignorant human primitivist? Do'utians did not die of old age, but reproduced slowly enough that in the natural state, mating battles, disease, and accidents of the hostile sea were enough to maintain a population balance. But humans had eliminated aging and limited fertility with genetic engineering in historic times.

"You hunted them, don't you," Mary pressed. "Your people hunt them in ships, as if they were animals."

Lebbretzsky was silent for a heartbeat or so, then said, "The contest is more even than that. There is no opportunity for heroism on either side without the opportunity for death. And the deaths let us raise new children uncontaminated by your machine culture."

This made Drin hiss as he thought the stinking harbor, the human slaves, and the feral Do'utian women in his 'harem.' The sound got the momentary attention of the human, who probably had no idea of what it signified.

"Mr. Lebbretzsky," Mary responded, "I take your statement to mean that you know what I'm talking about. It has to stop, and the persons responsible must be reeducated. If you attempt to conceal them, then you will be a candidate for reeducation yourself."

Drin saw the man raise his arm as if to strike Mary, then put it down. Lebbretzsky, Drin realized, might be so ignorant and so deeply into these murders that he felt he had nothing to lose in an attack on a Monitor. Drin slipped a manipulator into his pouch holster for the second time. The movement of his tongue seemed to go unnoticed, or at least uncomprehended.

"Woman. Tell your superiors that your presence is an insult. Tell them that their interference with our culture is an interference of our rights to live and die the way we want. Tell them that we have not murdered anyone, and that the next time they want questions answered, not to send women and fish to ask them."

"Pollution!" Drin sent. "The victims were stabbed and butchered! But be careful, Mary."

The man continued: "There are no murders, woman Monitor. Now get out of here, or we will do what we can to eject you. You may have better weapons, but we are not afraid to die."

"Drin, better call that Kleth back-up." Mary said aloud. Drin almost rejoined that he had done that hours ago - then realized that Mary was saying that for Lebbretzsky's benefit,

"Lebbretzsky," she continued, "I don't care what you think it is, attacking and killing Do'utians with harpoons is murder just as much as if you did it to me. The cultural group can deal with the why's later, but my job is to stop it, now. Who has been doing it? Where are they?"

Drin tensed. Mary, in her fearless eagerness to erase what she saw as a blot on her race, was pushing a bull on its own beach. Wrong species, but in this case, Drin feared some convergent evolution. As if to confirm his thoughts, the big human drew a long knife. Mary backed quickly away from him and got her gun out. Drin put a manipulator in his pouch and keyed his comset by feel. He dumped everything they had so far into the Monitor net - just in case he and Mary didn't survive her abuse of Lord Thet's hospitality.

"All right," Mary yelled. "Lebbretzsky, drop the weapon and lie down. You are in custody. You can arrange representation after you've been secured."

"Mary..." Drin sent. Too late. Lebbretzsky's hand seemed to flick and the knife flew at Mary. Her gun got it on doppler, flashed, and a smart bullet locked on the thing and knocked it out of the air. The two humans stared at each other in silence for a few seconds as if in a momentary stalemate. But here and now Lebbretzsky had overwhelming numbers. He made some kind of a signal and a hundred darts flew at Mary, some at Drin. He and Mary both fired as fast as their weapons could, but Mary was hit.

"Got my leg," she said with professional calmness. "Drin, let's get out of here."

Drin roared and with the occasional supreme effort his race could summon, pulled himself over the edge of the dock and scrambled toward Mary. The human archers paused in surprise and he flung his tongue out to his injured partner. He was just able to grab her leg with one manipulator and was pulling her to him when the primitivists started shooting again. He reeled Mary in with one manipulator while the other sent smart bullets at the legs of the crossbow archers.

Mary, a small moving target wasn't hit again, but despite both their guns knocking dozens of darts off their trajectories, he was hit himself. They irritated like the spines of the giant dagger snail, but none seemed to reach below his layer of fat, and none had hit his eyes. Some of the men with swords charged at him. He waited until they were too close, then quickly turned and swept the polluting snail-brains over the side of the dock with his tail. Then, with Mary firmly in his beak, he leapt into the harbor after them.

"Hold your breath," he said on the way down. He landed so as to spray as much water around as possible.

Momentarily sheltered by confusion and the high wall, he had time to help Mary into the submarine hatch. Then, thinking of the large harpoon he'd seen in the erstwhile beachmaster, Drin headed, fast and directl, for the harbor entrance. He sprinted through the harbor with a surface-racing tail-stroke, and usee his legs to help him over the shallow spots. This time, he didn't even notice the dirty water.

A look back told him the human primitivists were busy with their colored flags again, and when he ducked under water he could hear the sound of the harbor gate creaking shut. Another look above water showed him that the large ship with oars was underway and pursuing them.

He reached the canal through the harbor wall well before the submarine, and sped to its end. But the massive gate was already closed and locked. He put his beak against it and pressed as hard as he could, and the thrusts of his tail sent waves of brackish brown water back down the channel. The gates hardly noticed.

He surfaced and scouted the channel walls. They were not quite vertical, perhaps widening half a Charter unit over two Charter units of rise, and the cobbled surface provided plenty of claw holds. It would not be out of the question to attempt to climb it.

But first he tried bellowing at the watchmen to open the gate. Not to his surprise, they refused. He did, however, have the satisfaction of seeing their little guardhouse collapse from resonance. Looking back, he saw the submarine enter the channel with the oar ship in hot pursuit.

"Mary, what's your status?" he sent.

"I got the dart out, patched the wound and patched the suit. Hurts like hell. I won't be running around for a while. I'm a little worried about that ram."

"Ram?"

"That rowboat with the solid nose that's chasing me. It's got to weigh a cube, it's moving fast, it's built to bash things, and it doesn't have any brakes. How are you doing on that gate?"

Weigh a cube? That was about eight-times-four as much as his body. Pollution!

"No luck at all," he sent. "Any chance your submarine can ram it open?"

"I'll try the underwater grate. That has to be the weak point."

Drin moved to the side of the canal and watched the humped deck of the submarine flow by him. Its wake grew, then disappeared. There was silence for a heartbeat, than a muffled boom. The gate held.

"Mary?" he asked.

"I'm okay, considering. Might have done some damage. Going to back off for another try."

She did, but that was no more successful than the first.

"Drin, if you can climb out of this, you'd better get going."

The primitivist ram had entered the canal at full speed. Clearly, they were going to try to crush both Drin and the submarine between the ram and the gate, regardless of what damage that did to the latter two. The slaves rowing the ram, he realized, probably didn't know their ship was charging at a locked gate. And its officers must believe, wrongly, that destroying Drin and Mary gave them a chance to avoid reeducation.

But there was no chance to discuss it with them now. Drin threw himself at the canal wall and his legs found claw holds on the rocks under water. Carefully, he heaved himself up the near vertical embankment. But as soon as he tried to put any weight at all on his forelegs, claws slipped on the damp mossy covering of the stones near the waterline, and he tumbled back into the canal. He tried it once more, then saw the submarine break the surface and start accelerating backward at the ram.

"Mary!" he bellowed, forgetting the comset.

"I got us into this, I baited them. I'd rather go down fighting." Despite the brave words, her voice trembled. "Good luck, friend."

He clung half in and out of the water like a paralyzed lungfish and watched the two human vessels collide. There was a tremendous thundering boom as they hit, followed by cracking and splintering sounds. In seeming slow motion, the ram rode up over the submarine and the rock walls transmitted an eerie hollow grating sound to him as submarine's keel scraped along the canal's stone bottom as the combined wreck grated down the channel with scarcely diminished speed like a piston toward the massive gate.

There was too little room for him to remain where he was.   He released his hold, slipped back into the water and swam for the gate. Maybe everything would grind to a halt before it got there.

Underwater, Drin heard a sudden, ear-piercing crack. Pollution! he thought, the hull of the submarine must have broken. He surfaced and looked back. Both ends of the submarine stuck out of the water. The primitivist ship rode further up on one of the pieces and then fell off to the side, gouging its ram into the side of the canal. Its stern hit the other side and, with a great screeching and rending, the keel of the ram snapped, leaving the broken human ship stopped sideways in the channel. Men, some of them skewered by splintered oars, tumbled from the broken vessel like fish from a torn net. The mess ground to a halt just a Charter unit from the gate.

"Mary?" he sent. There was no answer. Flames, from spilled heating fires aboard the ram, or discharging power leads on the submarine, began spreading in the above-water wreckage.

Drin threw himself into the devastation, prying blood-stained pieces of the ram away from the broken submarine hull. There was movement all around him, and he saw that the human survivors were having no better luck than he in climbing the slippery canal sides. Hoping that the time it took would not prove critical, Drin seized the still upright mast in his beak, snapped it with a vicious twist of his body, and let it fall so that its top rested on the dike above.

"CLIMB!" he roared to anyone who would listen.

Some of the astonished humans caught on and began scrambling up the mast to safety above. One was a large red-bearded man - the same one, he realized, that had mocked him from the decks of another ship only weeks ago. They stared at each other in a frozen moment of recognition, but Drin had more than an arrest on his mind.

Ignoring minor burns and lacerations, Drin clawed away the

remains of a lower deck to expose the broken pressure hull of the submarine. It was filled with water. Drin stuck his tongue in and located the cockpit from feel and memory. Mary was not in the seat, but he could scent her blood. He felt around the tiny compartment, using both manipulators. He found her underwater gear, and, presuming success, grabbed it. A few more precious seconds, and he found Mary motionless in a small air pocket near the back of the cockpit.

With both branches wrapped around her, he strained to pull her up and, like a hatchling, into his mouth. With her legs sticking painfully down his throat, he was just able to close his beak over her head. Then he smashed his way out of the wreck, inhaled an hour's worth of air, and dove back into the putrid water. Over-buoyant, he swam down to the wooden grid and held on with his legs.

There was hardly room for both Mary and his tongue, so, with the skill of a contortionist, he managed to slip a loop of the tongue out the fleshy corner of his mouth, leaving the ends of the manipulator branches inside. Drin lowered his head and squeezed water from her lungs. They reinflated on their own as he forced the water from his mouth with air from his bladder. He squeezed again. She moved. Conscious? He hoped she would understand quickly enough not to panic.

He felt her hand pat one of his fingers. It seemed a controlled, understanding, gesture. He turned his attention to his external predicament.

With gloom and debris in the water, and Aurum low in the antarctic sky, he should be invisible from above. He began exploring the bottom of the gate where the submarine had smashed into it. Here and there, an outer buffer of great tree trunks had been smashed to kindling. But nothing behind had broken enough to let him through.

There was purposeful movement inside his mouth. "Drin, I've got my gills on. You can let me out now." Mary's voice in his ear was the best news he'd had since he'd come into the primitivist cesspool. Using his tongue to keep her from bobbing to the surface, he expelled the bubble of air from his mouth, then let her float free.

"How do you feel?" he asked.

"Lousy. No broken bones, I think. Tired. I've still got a little fluid in my lungs." She drifted slowly over to the grate and surveyed the damaged grate. "I guess I didn't put a hole in this thing."

"It appears not."

Trapped. They were both silent.

"Uh, Drin? Can you think of any way we could make them think I did break through? If they think we're already gone maybe they'll open the gate to come after us, or to clear the floating debris "

The grate was too fine for even Mary to squeeze through - it was probably designed with human sappers in mind. His tongue could just fit, but wasn't long enough. But maybe ...

"I could try to blow a bubble with some debris through the grate an out the other side."

"Hey, go for it!"

He did it, placing his blowhole against one of the spaces between the beams of an undamaged section and blew. Some of it escaped on their side, but not much - some must have gone through. They waited for a subjective eternity. He was on the point of suggesting another frontal assault when they heard a hideous, hollow, creak.

They waited. Nothing.

Then another creak. Drin thought he could detect a slight shudder.

"I think they're trying to open it," he said. "You might have jammed it a bit when you rammed it. That's a case of an emotional, spur of the moment action that did the exactly the opposite of ...'"

"Drin, your folk's eyes are built for hindsight. Why don't you stop philosophising and just try to help them open the gate?"

Of course. With a firm clawhold the bottom stones, and not having to fight gravity, Drin could apply his full strength. He waited until a creak signified another attempt to open the gate, then pushed. Slowly it began to move. There was a crack and a grind as something let go. Drin released his hold immediately, and the gate began to swing open on its own.

Hiding on the bottom beneath flotsam from the wreck, they drifted with the current out through the opening. Then, with Mary hanging onto a leg, he swam hard for clear water until he judged they were well over Lord Thet's horizon. Then he surfaced, turned on his back and sheltered Mary between his legs as he would a hatchling, and let horizon-grazing Ember and Aurum do what the could to warm her while he took great breaths through his mouth to rid himself of heat and to pay his oxygen debt.

Mary was quiet for a while - exhausted Drin surmised. So it startled him when she suddenly sat up and yelled: "Look, Drin, contrails!"

Do Tor had finally arrived.

★ ✹ ★

Among all races, when violence is obviously futile, reason is encouraged. For this reason, where there is the likelihood of an irrational physical confrontation, the inclusion of a large Do'utian Monitor is highly recommended. Humans excel where strength is needed in confined places. And, where overhead intelligence and logistic agility are required, the Kleth can make a major contribution - but care should be taken to avoid endangering Kleth individually.

- Planet Monitor's Handbook, Team Composition

...their mating bond is such that individuals become physiologically dependent on each other. A Kleth seldom survives the death of a mate, nor is their any record of one wanting to do so. Efforts to sustain life in these circumstances are always futile and should not be attempted.
- Planet Monitor's Handbook, Medical Appendix

✦ ✶ ✦

The Kleth aircraft met them just over the horizon from Lord Thet's city, on the beach of an uninhabited island dominated by a huge granite crag that gave shelter from the circumpolar wind, and after greetings, Team Leader Do Tor and his mate started unloading supplies.

Mary was exhausted so Drin scraped a deep pit in the sand for her, gathered wood, and lit a fire. Then, despite her exhaustion, and still limping from her wound, she insisted on washing her clothes and body in the frigid polar water, and turned an amazing shade of blue before she got back to the fire.

"D-don't worry," she told him as she shook convulsively under a blanket in front of the fire, "Its-s h-how we get our b-body heat b-back up."

Do Tor and his mate stretched their wings to catch some fish for her and jibbered with amusement as she threw away all the good parts and heated the remaining muscle almost to the point of decomposition on a flat stone she put by the fire. Drin looked forward to having a good long feed later that night, in his own manner, on his way back to Gri'il's beach.

"Sorry late. Assumed you'd just leave Thet and wait for us," the Klethan said in a guttural, sing-song English that was actually lower pitched than Mary's, despite his being less than half her mass.

"We tried," Mary laughed. "Things got in the way. We surface dwellers have certain problems about just flying away when things turn sour."

"Don't understand why primitivists had so much technology."

"Lack of interest on our part. Ignorance of the Charter and evolutionary pressure on theirs," Drin offered. "The best fighters end up in charge, and the best fighters are, more often than not, those with the best weapons. Also, if you can't make it clever, make it big." It would be a long while before he would forget the huge ram bearing down on him. "I doubt that Lord Thet or many of his people even understand why the Charter prohibits development in these areas; they've rebelled against anything resembling a scientific education."

"For humans, there is an inherent contradiction between 'back to nature' and 'no technology.'" Mary contributed, "because human nature is to make and use tools. So what happens is that the primitivists start reinvent the wheel using primitive technology that, per capita, pollutes unmercifully and requires gobs of labor." Mary picked up a stone and threw it out of sight. "So then you get leadership dominance games that the most ruthless win, with slave labor of one sort or another for the losers. That works well long enough for the glandular bullies to start assembling miniature empires, and then . . ." She shook her head. "Allowing this Lord Thet set-up was taking non-interference too far, in my view. But that's up to the council. Anyway, we have our killers."

"Maybe," Drin demurred. "But I don't think this is a one species issue." From a philosophical standpoint, he certainly didn't want it to be Human versus Do'utian, but something more than that, was bothering him. "I'm not sure we have the whole story. In defending his hunting, the human Jacob Lebbretzsky seemed to include the Do'utian primitivists in his defense."

"Do'utians help get selves butchered?" Do Tor clucked. "Strange thing, I think."

"If you think in groups, yes. But that isn't the natural Do'utian way to think." Drin moved his head slightly from side to side in mild negation. "I want to ask Gri'il some questions and learn more about this murdered Beachmaster and his harem. I may have made some unfair assumptions about the last victim."

"Name was Glodego'alah, by the way," Do Tor added. "Left the north pole as a disillusioned student eight cubed great revolutions ago. Not happy as primitivist, either, but responsible. Took care of harem. Good being. We did our homework." The Kleth held its hard translucent wings out in a gesture of pride.

"Oh yes," his mate said, the first words she uttered, surprising Drin. Until now, Go Tan had been inert, folded up. One partner or the other might dominate, but they were always together. Divorce was unknown, as were widows or widowers. Go Ton's contribution was unusually forward, for a subbordinate Klethan. But Monitor couples were known to be more independent.

"Did you bring the Do'utian interface coronet?" Drin asked.

"Not so late, otherwise." Do Tor rummaged in the pile of unloaded supplies and found a glasscloth package the size of a folded human tent. "Here."

Drin placed it in his pouch. Its woven-in antennae picked up and decoded motor nerve impulses - even those sent to absent peripheries. Now, not only could he ask questions of Gri'il; she would be able to answer.

There were also a tent and collapsible kayak for Mary. The tent fit nicely in the hollow he had dug, and she opened it up with its door to the fire. As it resumed its memorized shape, she turned to her fellow monitors.

"This," she said, "is camping. It's what most of us have in mind when we think of going back to nature, or living in a primitive situation. But, as you see, it's not primitive at all. And it's not social - we usually try to get away from other people when we do this. What's happened back at Thet just hasn't really registered with my people. I ..."

"Mary, why should it register with you any more than with the rest of us?" Drin interrupted. "You have no special responsibility for them just because they happen to be human. There is no need to apologize."

"Oh yes, Go Tan agrees," Do Tor's mate spoke up. "We are one civilization on this world. Whole purpose of Planet Trimus. Eight-cubed years of lives meaningless if not. Eyes of Trimus we are. We should have noticed violations before dead bodies appear."

"Any Do'utian can smell that place in currents an eight of the way around the planet. We ignored it." Drin said.

"Th-Thanks," Mary said. "I just ..." She shook her head and made sounds of human sadness, though Drin thought it was more in relief. He flicked out his tongue and wrapped his fingers around her hand, and she rewarded the gesture by squeezing him gently back, and baring her teeth in a big smile.

"We all go to the beach tomorrow, and gain more understanding," Do Tor said. "Now rest."

"You rest," Drin answered reminding him that Do'utians didn't sleep in the eternal days of a polar summer. "I need to eat, feed the harem, and keep my injuries in water until they heal more. I will see you there at the beach. Take care, Mary."

She hugged his fingers to her, careless of her wrap, and his most sensitive organs were pressed into the alien heat and smell of her. He was overwhelmed for a moment, then she released him. "Yeah, you too," she said.

He backed away from the fire carefully, to avoid upsetting anything. Clear, he turned. And as his body turned toward the water, his mind followed, thinking ahead to his duties. His cuts and bruises were beginning to hurt, true. But something in the back of his mind was pushing him, something perhaps as powerful as the instinctual desire to join with the harem that chose him as their provider and their protector. It did not make sense to him that humans - even as degenerate as Lord Thet and his gang - would or could suddenly start preying on Do'utians, even given the sort of general philosophical license primitivism in both species seemed to grant. Something less random and more evil was happening. Perhaps Gri'il could help him.

✶ ✹ ✶

The Planetary Civilization must be permitted to evolve, and experiments must be encouraged, for only through change is knowledge expanded.
　　　　-Article 5 of the Compact and Charter of the Planet Trimus

★ ❋ ★

Aurum stood high above Ember when Drin returned to the harem beach with his mouth full of fish, and the star had moved a dociradian west by the time he finished the simple duty of placing the fish into throats. Once done, he unpacked the neural interface cap and approached Gri'il.

Even now she hesitated, putting her nose to the beach. Despite everything that had happened, her distaste for this artificiality was evident. But then, apparently recognizing the necessity, she raised her head and came to him. He fitted the cap over her.

"It will take a while to calibrate itself. There will be a bit of a delay to start with, but you'll get used to it. Now, just tell me your name, as if you were whole again. Repeat it until the computer in the cap gets it right."

It produced an intelligible "Gri'illaboda" after about six tries, and she got used to it in a few more. Finally, she could speak through the device more or less naturally.

"Okay," Drin said. "I'm going to record this, so why don't we start by having you say who you are?"

"I am Gri'illaboda, co-mate of Drinnil'ib."

Great. Just great. "I am sorry, Gri'il. I am a planetary monitor, and not a primitivist. I care for you, yes - but more as a senior family member, not as a mate."

"You replaced our beachmaster, mated with my co-mates."

"It was not my choice. I did not seek you or them to mate."

She was silent for a few heartbeats. He could hear the waves and the sea birds.

"Drinnil'ib, I was the daughter of Slora'analta and Broti'ilita. Did you know either of those?"

"The historian."

"Who told the old tales of the free seas and made a romantic out of his daughter. I was bored with school. I met a free rover. He took me here, quickened my ovaries ... then took my tongue."

"Glodego'alah?"

"Never. Glodego'alah was a tourist who saw what had happened, fought the free rover for us, then took us here to be safe. But he paid for his charity in a way that happens all too often here."

"Then I am sorry for what I thought about Glodego'alah. We are seeking the humans who killed him, and four others who were killed. Did you know any of them? Did they have families here?"

"Glodego'alah remarked once that harems change masters easily because of such human predation. Their ships come in the channels between the islands and the ice pack where beachmasters gather fish."

Drin nodded. "I came close to be a victim myself on my way back from my initial investigation. It is easy enough for them - I suspected nothing until they shot at me. I would think someone down here would warn the humans not to do this."

Gri'il huffed in derision. "The sea lords don't interfere. They say the humans take the weak and the race gets stronger, and that the inbred softness of civilization is thus cleansed from our blood. But Glodego'alah was not soft."

"No, I'm sure he wasn't. Who are these 'sea lords?'"

"They are the free rovers, the ones who take from both poles what they want. They live like beachmasters at the south pole, then swim north and have all the luxuries of civilization. They are ... the human word is hypocrites."

"And if they don't come back?"

"A harem doesn't stay unmastered long here. A sea lord shows up soon enough to claim a missing master's family. They seem to know, somehow, when one isn't coming back."

Her passiveness disturbed him, but perhaps it was simply adjustment. Early Do'utian history wasn't any prettier than early human history. Less so, in some respects. And the Kleth, of course, were cannibals well into their spacefaring days. Drin shuddered, wondering at his fascination with such things. But he had to ask; it might be important.

"Gri'il, how was your tongue to be taken?" Did she just submit to such an amputation?

"The sea lord who ran off my first mate, said it was traditional. He demanded this after the first mating, then he said he would not take my egg unless I submitted. Also ... I can't explain. I sometimes feel a need to surrender my self, to let the tides of providence have their way with my flesh. At any rate, I did not resist. In my state at the time, he was God."

Submit to mutilation, or die. Such was her natural paradise. What polluting monster would...

"His name?"

"Gota'lannshk." The same ruffian he encountered at Cragen's? Drin hissed in disgust.

"You know of him?"

"We met. Look, Gri'il. Will you come back to the North with me? For treatment."

"We are bound to you. I need to stay with you, to submit to you. And I have the eggs, remember? Or are you so civilized that that doesn't matter?"

The eggs probably shouldn't be hatched, Drin thought. Two fathers. No tests. No family. No birth allocation.

"Gri'il, compulsions are subject to medical intervention. My duty is to try to right the wrongs done so far, if I can, and prevent others from being done. Can you get the others to come?" And how many more such were their out there in those islands. Should they save them all? by force if needed?

"If it is clear that we are leaving, they will come, for whatever good it will do them."

"We'll regenerate their tongues, teach them to speak, send them to school."

"They were hatched out here. Their minds were untrained during the crucial years."

Truly feral. He feared as much. "Still, we have to try. We can find a deserted northern island for your co-mates, and arrange for them to be watched. But what about you? Now that this has happened, can't you see your way back to ..."

"To what? We live with the humans and the Kleth on this planet at the expense of ceasing to live like Do'utians, at the expense of always pulling against our own inner nature. And the stars are too far apart for it to matter. I showed my tail to all of that. Say what you want. I lived. I swam in the wild currents. I did it on the beach. You want me to go back to that northern emotional straight jacked and listen to all those proper titters and I told you so's? I'd rather die!"

And her present state was not a humiliation? But her age-old argument, Drin thought, was unanswerable. The civilization of Trimus was for those who thought it mattered.

"We don't want to tell you how to live. I'm sure your privacy would be respected, and protected."

"Like in a zoo! Drinnil'ib, You rescued us, fed us. Don't you want us? Don't you feel the need to own and protect us? Or in the name of your Compact have you let the humans reengineer your sex."

Drin groaned. He wanted her enough, but he did not *want* to want her. At least not as she was now. The whine of fans reached him before he could find a suitable way to explain that. Mary! Relief flowed threw him. The aircraft settled on its fans, the hatch popped, and Drin walked over to greet his partner, leaving Gri'il with her beak in the gravel.

But Mary was nowhere in sight.

"Mary?" he called, worried.

Do Tor opened the canopy, jibbered to his machine, and the cargo door popped open. Of course, Drin realized. There was no room in the Kleth cockpit for a human, and indeed, it took Mary a while to unfold herself from the cramped space.

"I'm here, Drin."

"It's good to see you!" He explained about the sea lords. "So I think your human hunters have Do'utian accomplices, at least in principle. But things still don't swim well in my mind."

"The strongest, fastest, or most clever survive. I can see that, I guess. You think the Sea Lords were using Lord Thet to cull their herd, so to speak?"

"That seems to fit."

"Well, Lord Thet's gang of wannabe barbarians seems to be only too happy to help. Your people are the most challenging hunt in the ocean, they probably think."

"Brings up the question of whether we have right to interfere," Do Tor observed.

"To save lives?" Drin protested. "Of course we do."

Mary sighed and gestured to the sky. "Drin, there are now many beings out there who can trace their origins to our home worlds, but who have engineered so much into themselves that they look on *us* as primitivists. They could make a problem like Lord Thet vanish in an instant with no loss of life - but would we want that?"

"Those who didn't get killed might appreciate it."

Mary shook her head. "The parts of our natures that lead to this mess could easily be changed, but then what would we be? Death, even random death, may have a justifiable role in society that transcends individual needs. Perhaps, to keep our identity, we need to learn to accept that."

"I think," Drin asserted, perhaps a little more loudly than necessary, "that such issues should be debated by the planetary council and that *our* job is to not let anyone else get killed until they do and decide ... whatever. Now, I have four physically mutilated - and three of them intellectually mutilated - Do'utian women to bring back to where they can be properly protected and cared for. Let's do that and sort the rest out later."

"Agreed," Do Tor clucked. Mary nodded quietly.

"Gri'il," Drin said, "Is there any way the others can be told of how long a journey this will be?"

"They will follow you if I do," she said, coldly, it seemed. "But the hunters will be watching."

"And the planet will be watching them!" Drin proclaimed. "They won't dare do anything."

"I will ride with you," Mary said. "In full uniform. At least they'll know what they're playing with."

Drin didn't remind her of how persuasive her uniform and submarine were at Thet harbor.

"We'll fly cover with loud voices and guns," Do Tor said, spreading his wings. "Aircraft can fly itself, so that makes three above."

"Oh yes," his mate chimed. So it was decided. A convoy North.

✦ ✹ ✦

Drin led the way into the water the next morning with Mary's warm legs and arms comfortably around his neck. They'd fashioned a light glasscloth collar for him that she could grasp and so hold her position in the current of his passage. This was no irritation, but the bulge of an appliance she had constructed to protect her wounded knee was a noticeable reminder of their vulnerability in these waters - many more monitors would be needed to handle Lord Thet and his allies without loss of life.

Gri'il came quietly after him, and as predicted, the harem followed.

It was a fine gray day with favorable surface winds, and light, cooling surface squalls. A brackish current flowed north here from the icecap on the largest southern island, overlying warmer saline water flowing from an inner pole drainage basin, and so the Do'utians had made good time without becoming overtired.

By the morning of the second day, Lord Thet's domain was well behind them, and they glided through the waves half way into reef-crowded tropical waters. A volcanic island with wide black beaches lay to their left, and a reef to their right, but the channel was fairly deep. Drin was just beginning to relax and enjoy the scenery when the human ships appeared.

"Don't think they're hunters," Do Tor sent. "Big Do'utian male right with them, no shooting."

"Can you describe him?" Drin asked.

"One and three eighths Charter unit long. Big white crescent shaped scar behind the blowhole. Do you know him?"

"If it's who I think it is, I've smelled him before. A harem-coveting sea lord with his tail across two beaches. It's time to ask that rogue a few questions."

Gri'il and her co-mates keened as if she were being mortally wounded.

"It sounds like our refugees have smelled him before as well," he continued. "I'd better let the those humans know what we're about. Ready Mary?"

"Gills on." He felt her arms as well as her legs encircle his neck and her hands grasp the collar. She was secure. He dove and, slamming the ocean back and forth with his tail, headed toward the lead human ship much faster than he could manage on the surface.

About ten Charter units from the hull, he broke water again. So did his harem - he'd forgotten to tell Gri'il to stay back. It shouldn't be necessary; but he was uneasy.

"Mary, I'm not sure how much comfort we should take from Gota'lannshk being present."

"Why would they shoot at us and not him?"

"Why is there a sea lord always ready to inherit the harem of a victim? Why did Gota'lannshk seem to know that I'd had a close call with these hunters when we met him at Cragen's?"

"Lord Thet..."

"Mary, I don't want to insult your species, but I don't think that idiot has been running this atrocity."

"Huh? Why?"

"Later. I just hope these people have sense enough to keep out of this." Drin inhaled and boomed as authoritatively as he could, "Human ship, we are Planet Monitors escorting citizens on an official mission. We need to ask your companion some questions. Please do not interfere. I say again, do not interfere."

Mary waved at them and smiled.

The report of the harpoon gun reached him first, then Mary's scream and the sharp, deep pain in his neck.

"Look out," Do Tor yelled over the radio link.

The taste of blood was in his throat. He dove and heard a sharp smack on the water over him. Instinct said to head for the very bottom, but Mary, if she were still alive - he could no longer feel any pressure from her legs - wouldn't survive that. Despite the pain, he pushed water hard and got about eight-squared Charter units away from the ship before he surfaced again.

"Mary?" he called. If those polluting, suicidal, feral idiots had killed her...

There was no answer. Oblivious of his wound, he turned back toward the ship, rage building.

"Do Tor, I can't see behind my head. What's happened to Mary?" Did the Kleth follow him?

"Drin. Long spear in your neck. Went through Mary first, through her leg. Not necessarily fatal wound, but suggest you make for nearest island. Go Ton will go with you. West, Drin, now. I've called aircraft down. That ship will not fire again. Go!"

As if to contradict the Kleth, the harpoon gun fired again and the lance slapped the water beside him. He could hear warning blasts from the aircraft and Go Tan squawking at the top of her lungs, telling the human ship to stop shooting. In the name of eternal repudiation, the murderers would bay for this. He started swimming toward the ship.

He felt, more than saw, a Do'utian charge under him directly at the human vessel.

"GRI'IL, NO!" he bellowed hopelessly, much too late.

The impact boomed out, sound reaching him underwater before through the air. Then, beneath, he heard the creaking and cracking of wood and the screams of humans underwater.

"Drin!" Do Tor screamed. "Get to that island, now. I take care of this. I will mark them. They will not escape, not melt into primitivist population. I mark. Go, now, save yourself. Save Mary."

"Drin," a soft voice called. "I'm awake. It hurts like hell, but if you have to go back for her, I understand. I can take it."

Reason returned. "Mary. No. I'll have to trust Do Tor." There was no way Gri'il could have survived that impact. No way that he would have. And the eggs... it was better that way. Perhaps Gri'il had known that. But his wound had little to do with the effort it took to push himself toward the island.

A whistle and some kind of explosion sound behind him. Then another. He could hear loudspeakers. Killing for killing - perhaps they would understand that. Then, somewhere from the back of his mind, between the currents of pain and grief, a thought formed in an eddy of cold fear. Gota'lannshk had disappeared when the shooting started. To where?

The island was a long swim on the surface and he gagged on his blood by the time he got there. Go Ton was waiting at water's edge, alone, with a med kit that must have weighed as much as she did.

"Come on, just a few steps further, above the tide line," she urged.

He did that, then he was on his belly, his tail still in moist sand. Go Tan fluttered to the top of his head, out of sight. He heard the buzz of a bone saw, and the shaft of the harpoon soon tumbled to the ground. There was a yelp, quickly stifled, from Mary. Then a numbness started spreading through the wound. Soon he felt, as if he didn't know what had happened to him, that all that was wrong with him was a stiff neck.

"Now, Mary," Do Tan said, "I know it looks awful, but I think it best to leave that piece in your leg alone until help arrives. Human aircraft will be here in eight-fourth beats. Might do more harm than good if I try to remove it now."

"I understand," she said, "this sounds ridiculous, but right now I feel okay, except my leg is dead to the world. I'll be all right as long as I don't look at it. Can you help me down?"

"Not alone. Lieutenant Drin, can you lend a tongue?"

His tongue still worked; the barb had not gone in that deeply, perhaps in part because Mary's leg had slowed its entry. He reached back, and between the three of them, they were able to lower Mary down to the sand.

"Where's Do Tor?" she asked. Pollution! She'd forgotten, Drin realized, and he couldn't warn her with his tongue extended so far.

"He's with the aircraft cleaning up the mess with the human ships," Go Ton responded, shakily. "He should have everything well in hand and be back with us soon."

"You've been too busy helping us to check!" Mary said. "I'll contact him, let him know we made it and find out how things are."

"Please do not do that," Go Ton pleaded.

Just a little further, Drin thought. There! Mary was safely down, and he could speak again.

"But, I know how much he means to you ..." Mary started, oblivious to the danger.

"That's *why*, Mary," Drin interrupted, "for the sake of providence, think!" The Kleth team had taken the ultimate risk for them, and Go Ton's position was precarious. She would live as long as she believed her mate was alive. But if everything was not fine with Do Tor, that would effectively eliminate Go Ton as well. "We need Go Ton just now."

"Oh!" Mary said. Everyone was quiet for a heartbeat. Then Mary continued, her voice with a certain forced steadiness. "Go Ton. Uh, that human garbage doesn't have any weapon that can hurt Do Tor. He'll be fine."

That human garbage shouldn't, Drin thought, have had any weapon that could have hurt him or Mary. But here they were.

"Drin, I am stiff-winged on Do'utian first aid," Go Ton said, firmly changing the subject, "but I think the spear should come out of you now. It is the sort that works its way in deeper every time you move, and without Mary's body holding it back ..."

"Do it." Before the anesthetic, Drin could sense how close the barb had worked itself toward his central nervous column. He had arteries and blood to spare, but didn't want to stop breathing just yet.

"If you could roll on your side..." Go Ton asked. He complied, then lay silently, feeling little tugs and tears in his flesh and tried to imagine one of Go Ton's tiny thin horny arms deep in his flesh with knives, cutting a passage for the barbed spearhead.

Then the Kleth said: "Mary, need help. The strength of your arms."

Using the discarded shaft of the spear as a crutch, Mary hobbled around behind him, patting him on the beak as she went by.

A little later, he head her say "oof," felt a sharp pull, and saw Mary fall backward into his field of view again - her arms bloody up to the elbows, her hands clutching the cruel barbed spearhead. Go Ton remained behind him; little tugs and pulls continued for another eight-cubed heartbeats.

"Now that's all closed as well as I can do it," Go Ton said

"Thank you," Drin said, and rolled slowly back onto his belly. "Did the harem follow us here?" The thought of them reminded him of Gri'il. He shut his eyes and let the empty feeling pass.

"Yes, they're huddled together in shallows behind you," Go Ton answered. "They seem very sad, beaks in sand, but are unhurt, I think."

Drin was thinking that Do Tor should have been back by now, and searching his memory for any kind of convention for handling the worst case situation. There would come a point when, if the news were bad, Go Ton would have to be told, and nature would have to take its course. To do otherwise would be to not respect the decision her people had made to not change this part of their genetic make up. Perhaps the best thing would be to wait until she asked herself. If ...

The challenge roar echoed off the lava cliffs and caught them all by surprise.

In an instant, before he even realized what it meant. Drin's heart doubled the strength of its beats and he could feel the effects of various body chemicals, not greatly different from those that hit him when he fertilized the feral eggs. That primordial insult deserved an equally primitive response. But he made himself stay still, and without moving his injured neck, he swiveled an eye to the direction of the noise. Far down the beach, a big, scarred male.

"Same Do'utian we saw with the human hunting ships," Go Ton said from above.

"Gota'lannshk," Drin rumbled, in no shape or mood to play primitive beachmaster games. "His beak is dripping with this. Tell that idiot to stay away from us, before I kill him!"

"Drin," Mary whispered, almost inaudibly, "he's bigger than you, and with your wound you'll kill yourself before you get to him. Try to calm down. Think. If he inherited Glodego'alah's harem, and he was connected with the human hunters ..."

"*Precisely*, Mary. A lot easier to get Lord Thet's people to eliminate his rivals than fighting for a harem on the beach the old fashioned way. These murders were no game of survival of the fittest, or even of macabre chance. Those polluting idiot sea rovers carefully selected the hunting victims and no doubt led Lord Thet's ships right to them. Lord Thet probably lost a few selected men as well, just to keep things even, gain birth allocations, and reduce the number of his political rivals." Drin's anger increased. He should turn the murderer into snail meat. His breath came faster.

"So," Mary said, "the whalers get their hunt, their flesh, and think they're just playing by some tough rules. But it's all fixed ahead of time. Premeditated. Drin. Stay down, please. Drin? Drin! Give me your gun."

The Do'utian sea rover bellowed again and blind rage started working its way through Drin. The nerve of that cow stealer! He heaved himself to his feet, oblivious of the wound.

"DRIN!" Mary screamed. "Give me your gun! Drin. Your gun! Now!"

In some small corner of his consciousness, Mary's words got through. Somehow, as he began to rock back and forth on his legs, he sent his tongue into his pouch and retrieved the weapon for Mary, almost absentmindedly dropping it on the sand next to her. That popgun was never, he thought with a last wisp of clarity, meant to stop a charging Do'utian.

He got a whiff of the challenger, ripe with arrogance. He heard his cows keen and smelled their fright. Dimly, he remembered there were things one was supposed to do in beak-to-beak combat, things that used the opponent's charge against him. Ways to use the tail as well as the head to put the other on the sand, but that all seemed very fuzzy and far away just now. All he wanted was to charge and bite the throat.

Hardly even aware that he was doing it, Drin lifted a clawed front leg, dug it deep into the sand, and bellowed. The sun was high; it was a good time to taste blood.

The other began its charge. He stomped forward to meet it. Somewhere behind him he heard a series of sharp, high frequency sounds began at regular intervals. He didn't care, his body was aflame, producing heat many times faster than he could lose it. He didn't care. It felt good. He felt the wind of his passage build up, giving him some relief. Somehow, both hind legs moved together while both front legs hit slightly apart. The beach shook beneath him. He fixed his eyes on the other's neck, looking for an opening, looking for where cycle of its charging stride exposed the throat to Drin's beak.

But its neck kept getting lower to the beach. Its charge seemed to become unbalanced and slow. His opponent screamed now in protest and its scent changed from challenge to fear and danger. It keened and shrieked and wavered from side to side.

With the danger call, a bit of consciousness returned to Drin, and he swerved at the last heartbeat, avoiding a collision that could have ripped open his stitched up insides an left him to bleed to death.

The sea lord collapsed into the sand in front him, plowing a furrow two Charter units long with its gaping beak. He passed by the hulk in an instant and into an eerie silence. The bellows and the sharp sounds had ended; only the surf and the thunder of his own mad rush sounded on the beach.

Burning inside, Drin exhaled gales, bent his path into the sea, and let momentum carry him into the cold water, sliding forward until it covered him. A very gentle bend of his tail brought his head back to the shore.

The drama was not over. The fallen sea lord groaned and snapped at sand. Its right foreleg was covered with blood and bent at a wrong angle. Its hind legs pushed sand uselessly, trying to propel it somewhere. Then it used its tail to turn itself over, trying to roll to the cooling waters of the sea. Once, twice it rolled. But, as Drin settled himself into the life-giving cold water, the sea rover stopped rolling. Its tail rose majestically and thudded into the sand. Once, twice.

At the last, it threw its tongue at Mary, falling far short."Dirty human cow," Gota'lannshk screamed at her. Then ... nothing.

Heat death.

Drin lay in the shallows panting. Fiery pain shot through him. He could taste his own blood again; some of Go Ton's handiwork had come loose. He saw Mary prone, the shaft of the harpoon still projecting bloodily from her leg, her elbows in the sand, his gun in her hands, still aimed at the sea rover. She must have put a hundred bullets in his opponent's knee, but now she was shaking and moaned. He knew that killing a Do'utian over this was the very last thing she had wanted.

He wished to comfort her, but he was tired. Very, very, tired.

★ ❈ ★

His next awareness was of a hotness on his neck. He opened his right eye and looked back. Mary was there, flattened against his neck, gently calling his name.

"Mary," he managed to say, softly as he had ever said anything, "I'm awake. I'll be okay."

She was apparently having trouble breathing, but turned to his eye and said, "Oh, Drin. Oh, Drin. It's -it's so hard to get my arms around you." Despite her appearance, he somehow knew she was happy.

Noise and smell intruded. The sky over the island beach was filled with both aircraft and Kleth. The death smell of Glodego'alah was there, among the smell of many beings, and the sound of many voices, Kleth, human, and Do'utian. He recognized Do Tor's and Go ton's among them and took a ragged but deep breath of satisfaction. Everyone had come through, and like rational, civilized beings, they were all discussing what was to be done next.

THE TRIMUS CHRONICLES: NETWORK

Neither forcible reeducation of citizens who have chosen to leave civilization, nor the effects of the unchecked expansion of their low technology communities is consistent with Trimusian values. Therefore, the Trimus Planetary Council hereby approves and directs the transportation to Aurum III of such residents of the Trimus natural reserve regions who do not voluntarily option to accept and behave according to the environmental and social restrictions of the Compact and Charter of the Planet Trimus. The Aurum II planetary bioforming project will be redirected toward that end.

—Signed 4704 TF:
Bo Flor, Kleth/
Karen Olsen, Earth /
Gori'allolub, Do'utia

The severed head of a Kleth scientist, displayed with other evidence in a transparent case in the lobby of the presentation dome, set the mood for the gathering in the Trimusian Capital, Triapolis. Lieutenant Drinnil'ib of the Trimus Planet Monitors looked at it with forensic curiosity and over half a macroyear's experience. The eyes were unusually far apart, almost half a doci, for a Kleth, and the two notches in the Kleth's crest signified a warm weather birth; a congenital feature, if Drin remembered. A wonder of the universe that that tiny skull had contained a brain as powerful in life as his own. The plumage had been black, with the sun-bleached tips of a field worker, or avian athlete.

Drin settled himself down on a free pad. A human about one-sixth Drin's length, probably Councilor Karen Olsen, sat on the edge of a pad three aisles down. A fellow Do'utian male had settled in comfortably far behind and to his right; it was Councilor Gori'allolub, Monitor General, smelling grim. His tail hung over the standard charter unit length pad. Likely eight-squared and six doci's. No one, Drin thought, cast votes based on size, but, somehow, the big bulls often rose to the top. Drin waved the tip of his own, somewhat shorter, tail in respectful greeting to the other Do'utian. Other humans and Do'utians occupied other pads, but no Kleth were to be seen. Such meetings were not their style.

The ready tone echoed across the roomy dome soaring three charter units above him. On Trimus, humans got their pronounceable language, Kleth got their convenient octal numbers, and Do'utians got room to breath. Drin blinked to look at the sonic after-image and sensed the different textures of the surfaces; hard bright arching ribs above with deep black between. When he opened his eyes, for all appearances the dome was now transparent, and he was eavesdropping on an Aurum III biological team, eight-squared days ago, near a bioforming station on a northern island. The sensors had been set up to monitor animal behavior in the station area—and they may have done just that.

A human and two Kleth were in the area.

"So they're coming *anyway*," the human, biologist Theric Soames, remarked.

Drin judged the inflection of Theric Soames' voice as hostile, and swiveled an eye toward Councilor Olsen, a firm advocate of resettling the primitives. She showed no reaction to this opposition, but then Drin wouldn't have expected her to show surprise as freely as her daughter, his Monitor colleague Mary, and many subtle changes in humans were mysteries to him. But he knew there was substantial human opposition to resettlement, both from fatalist liberals willing to let things evolve as they would, and hard-beaked conservationists like himself.

"I knew it but I didn't want to believe it," Soames continued. "The council is going to turn two centuries of work, a whole new planet, over to irresponsible children."

"We not design Aurum III from start for primitives," a Kleth remarked, looking up from her seedlings. Ko Kor was her name, Drin remembered; wide eyed, smooth crested, and gold tinted.

"No. But we adjust. Some chance now," her mate answered. That would have been Sha Ton. Drin knew the head; the rest was a large, nearly human length, male whose sun-frosted black coat gave him an almost spidery look.

"It's premature," Soames said. "We still had a lot to learn from our original ecological design."

"Like Kleth monkey-bats and Earth pine cones," Ko Kor boomed in accord. "If works, maybe help reforest Southern Islands on Trimus after primitivists gone. Monkey-bats good eating, too."

Drin sympathized. He still felt outrage what the polluting primitivists had done to some of those islands in the areas of Trimus that were supposed to have been left alone.

"Oh, yes," Sha Ton concurred with his mate. "Lunch time. Got some for Theric too."

The Kleth leaped into the air and with strong wing-beats sped toward the station.

"Hey, wait a minute," Soames yelled. "Stay out of my food; I'll get it later."

Desperately? Drin wondered.

The station, a geodesic dome, was tiny by the majestic Do'ution-compatible standards of the capital city, but it was meant only for Kleth and human. A circular patch appeared in a pentagonal panel halfway up. A loud, startling, crash came next, faithfully reproduced.

Sha Ton back-winged in surprise and hovered over the collapsing building in the smoke.

Another hole appeared closer to its top, with even a louder noise. There were sparks from severed power leads and a fire started. Debris flew and spots of grass started steaming here and there.

And, for no reason anyone could see, Sha Ton's head fell off. His wings continued to beat once, twice, then his body, no longer knowing what to do, simply fell through the hole into the fire.

Ko Kor screamed and launched herself after her mate.

The human grabbed for her and got a leg in his hand. She slashed a claw at it, knocking it off.

"My life is in there!" Ko Kor screamed and flew at the building, diving into the flames.

The human stared at his bleeding arm. A biologist, Drin thought, should have known better than to try to keep half a Kleth team alive. Soames vanished from view and the scene showed smoking wreckage for a minute, then faded to gray.

If there were any clue in this, Drin didn't recognize it. He gave a low rumble of frustration, pushed his massive frame off the pad, and turned to face the Councilors, already discussing the crisis. The human Councilor, Karen Olsen, looked at him and opened her mouth as if to say something, then appeared to change her mind, shaking her head. She nodded to Drin and left, giving Gori'allolub a respectful pat on a leg as she went by; friends on opposite sides of a very complicated issue.

The Do'utian Councilor dipped his beak to the departing human and approached Drin.

"Lieutenant," the Councilor intoned with full authority. "I know your views."

Drin dipped his beak in assent. There was no need for Gori'allolub to tell Drin what low tech population pressure was doing to the reserved areas of Trimus, nor of the reluctance—misplaced in Drin's mind—to reeducate the polluting idiots.

"But I also know your intelligence and your dedication to our civilization. We felt it best that a Do'utian be in charge of the investigation. Also, for impartiality's sake, it does not hurt that the most likely suspect be pursued by one of similar bent on this issue. The focus must be on the deed, or accident, not the politics. Your answers will have more credibility among the opposition. There must be a solution that strengthens our unity, not divides us."

"Agreed."

"The human, Soames, has disappeared. The rest were evacuated. You will be the first Do'utian to visit, in person, a world built in part for Do'utian settlement. That is an historic responsibility."

And an historic adventure, Drin thought. There was no elevator down to Aurum III; it spun too slowly; so he would command the first Do'utian landing-craft built in several macroyears. A tantalizing fore-scent of virgin beaches and unhunted pack ice wafted through his mind.

"I am ready for the challenge."

"Good. The schedule for resettlement of the human and Do'utian primitivist populations depends on your success." The Councilor hesitated, then asked, "Is your life complete?"

So the Councilor thought he faced more than normal danger. Drin raised his beak, and opened it slightly; a Do'utian ready for anything. "Nothing of consequence is undone."

"That is best. In such a cause, sacrifices are sometimes needed. Those are troubled waters, Monitor. Go quiet them if you can."

Lieutenant Drinnil'ib touched his beak to the floor, accepting the duty.

★ ※ ★

The base mass unit of Trimus shall be the "dom," the mass of a cube of water one doci-charter unit (1dc), 10^{-2} charter units (cu), (8^{-2} cu base twelve or ten) on a side, at maximum density. Equivalent units are: Kleth, 102 eggs; Earth, 3.68 (base ten) kilograms; Do'utia, 1.07 10^{-5} (base twelve) cube. Subordinate units, such shall be derived from basic physical formulae. A cue (charter unit of energy, for instance, is one $dom\text{-}cu^2/beat^2$.

—Compact and Charter of Planet Trimus, Technical Appendix

The English prefixes "macro" and "mini" shall have specific meanings in the octal numeric system of Trimus. Macro shall be used

for an exponent of three, and mini for an exponent of minus three. For larger triads, the prefixes di (2), tri (3), and so on may be added and the last syllable dropped. Thus the prefix for 10^6 shall be "dima," and for 10^{-6} shall be "dimi." This is exactly analogous to the Kleth suffixes Y* and Ӱ, as used in "no Y*" (10^6), and "no Ӱ" (10^{-6})
    —Compact and Charter of Planet Trimus, Language Appendix

Gradually, pronounceable Kleth and Do'utian words—or direct translations such as "cube," from Do'utian for cubic tail, or no no, from Kleth for 10^{-11}, penetrated Trimus English. Also, some human decimal and even more ancient duodecimal words survived, such as "century" (144 years) or "dozen" (14 of anything) that worked in other cultures continued to be used.
    —Go Zom's notes on the Compact of Trimus

✷ ✾ ✷

Spacecraft work was painstaking, but experience had shown that a second set of eyes, and a mind that swam in different seas, often saw things other minds did not. Also, in the tradition of Do'utian space voyagers, Drin intended to know his ship. It was, in essence, a steam rocket with an exhaust velocity of eight-cubed charter units per beat. Water stored in the great tank that also served as Drin's quarters. It was pump-fed through antihydrogen mass converters to make steam; each converter a porous bed of very high temperature refractory alloys that surrounded an annihilation chamber.

The *Egg* contained half a minidom of antihydrogen ice, distributed among three eights of electrostatic dewars. He intended to check the quintuply redundant isolation and feed systems on each of them. These systems had to store the antihydrogen and deliver it to the annihilation chamber in near perfect isolation from the world of ordinary matter. But near-perfect, for Drin, meant a leakage rate that would be fatal to his Kleth and human partners. Do'utia was young for a life-evolving world and natural fission reactors were an occasional and unremarkable feature of its geology. Scale and opportunity had dictated that Do'utian space flight had been nuclear powered from the beginning, and experience made their designs the best in the known universe, if the criteria were performance.

But he had to meet human and Kleth safety needs here, and wanted to be absolutely sure.

An underwater hatch cycled, clanging in the back of Drin's consciousness, so he was not completely surprised when human Monitor Mary Pierce swam up beneath him and pulled herself onto his back. "Welcome, little one." Out of view to even his swiveling, bifocal eyes, she was a nice warm spot on his neck. "Our ship looks very sound so far."

"Oh it's good to see you, Drin. What a relief!"

"How did the negotiations go?" She had just returned from duty with the team informing the largest of the human primitivist communities of their imminent relocation, and trying to secure their voluntary cooperation. It didn't take a marine biologist to tell him the short answer was "not well."

"Not well. One self-styled Lord Thet is still having the time of his life and doesn't want to budge, and his primitive empire is growing despite everything. He even objected to our taking some people he'd enslaved back with us."

Unlike Kleth and Do'utians, who, unless maimed, could eat off the sea and fly or swim around the planet, humans needed technology for transportation. And their primitivist alpha males controlled all the transportation from their stinking settlements. Eccentrics and idealists living alone or in small groups on the tropical islands around the inner Pole had been captured, and, having abandoned their links with Trimusian civilization, had found themselves having to play slave or starve.

Drin fumed. "That idiot has three percent of the human population of Trimus and is producing thirty percent of the effluents—untreated sewage!—in an area that's supposed to be completely free of such things. One can't even swim near his area without having tongue stunk, eyes stung, and starving for lack of anything uncontaminated to eat!"

"They're certainly a much worse problem than the Sea Lords," Mary sighed.

"Bah! Reeducate those thoughtless, live-for-today hedonistic buccaneering beachmasters too!" he grumbled. Human degenerates were one thing—he could look on them from an analytical distance, but mention of the renegades of his own species touched a nerve. Slavery was mild compared to what the rogue beachmasters had done to their often unsuspecting harem recruits. "What do they think will happen in a few macroyears when this mindless interspecies Petri dish we are creating on Aurum III boils out into the rest of the universe?"

"Drin, some feel we've solved too many problems for our own good on Trimus. Eternal lives of cyberservant-supported study and art just aren't stimulating enough for some of the people our biology produces. There needs to be an outlet for them, but we shouldn't have to live with their consequences. So, according to the Council, they get their own planet, to relearn all the lessons the hard way. Speaking of eternity. I could lie on your nice soft blubber forever, but," she climbed to her feet, "I need to prep the upper decks for me and our Kleth partners."

"Yes. I'll do the visual on the hull while you check the penthouse."

He helped her up the ladder, dove below, through the waterlock and into the sea. It was a warm day near the inner pole, the great crescent of infrared Ember hot under the disk of gold-tinted aurum.

It was so enervating that he lost concentration and almost missed it: a clogged exhaust vent; a dark spot in audio where where the others shined like regular rows of stars. The ship hadn't reported it.

"System B, code 73147," he sent immediately, ordering a wholesale system swap. Meanwhile, three beats of his tail got him up to the fouled vent.

It looked almost like a spiderstar nest; the seaweed and muck inside hadn't grown there—someone or something had deliberately filled the vent with debris.

"Code complete," the ship confirmed. We have a blocked vent, ordinal 3472 . . . "

"I have it and am cleaning it," Drin interrupted. "Why didn't your predecessor see it?"

The answer came with cybernetic speed; "My predecessor was instructed to ignore it by an authorized maintenance simulation command that stayed in the command register, and so didn't show up in the discrepancy checks."

Drin growled at a frequency that caused the hull to resonate. "What's the status on the other command registers on the A side?"

"Clean now."

Drin hated himself for what he had to ask next, but the logical suspicion had to be removed.

"Check the source of the anomalous command. Code 72537, Commander only. Check against Planet Monitor Mary Pierce for code, voice, and date."

"The code matches but not the voice, and the date was 124.2." So someone other than Mary had gotten Mary's access code and, ten days ago, inserted a highly technical and innocuous command that allowed whoever had clogged the rocket vent to do so undetected last night. "Any other 'ignore maintenance data' commands active?"

"None."

Someone, presumably someone opposed to resettlement of primitivists, had tried something subtle to delay their mission. Or scare them out of it. If they knew Mary's code, they might have access to other mission information. Are we going to be controlled by this? he asked himself.

Also, even if he could convince headquarters to let them launch, his Planet Monitor's judgment said that it would not be a good idea to go right on schedule. Someone was after them. Best take the initiative.

"Tell Mary to start the final prep, with a hold at three eights. We're going to take off as soon as we physically can. Also, don't let this change off ship. Send data that simulates business as usual."

Drin sank to the pad on the bottom of the tank. He slipped his interface head band on over his ears and eyes in a quick motion. Vision fields cleared and it was as if all the ship structure around him had vanished and he was lying on a platform at the bottom of a bubble in the sea.

That was a little too unnerving, so he adjusted the sonic contrast up a notch until the *Egg*'s ribs and upper cabin became detectable as a sort of transparent gray ghost. A simulated control panel floated in front of him, and he imagined a simulated tongue flicking out to touch the various ethereal controls. This human innovation bothered some Do'utians, but Drin had always liked it—with this, in an emergency, he could react almost as fast as a human.

"Clear here," he announced.

There was a whine of pumps and then a roaring sound that reminded him of being directly under where Go Stohn Falls plunged a dozen charter units into the ocean. The ship stopped rocking as it lifted up on a bed of steam and the thrust feedback system damped out all motion. Then the pressure went up like he'd just dived twenty charter units instead of two. Full acceleration.

"Okay, Mary?" he sent.

"Yes . . . I'm . . . fine," she answered, though obviously sounding like she was in discomfort. Well, it wouldn't last. Windstream noise peaked, then began to fall as they left the atmosphere.

The engines gulped water. His effective depth rose rapidly as the water level in the tank around him fell. His hearts increased their beat and his tail tip flicked nervously. This was not a stately elevator ride.

A call came in; "*Trimus Egg*, L2 traffic control. Are you safe?" A Kleth voice, not a computer. Of course! It was Do Tor.

"Do Tor, Lieutenant Drin, Greetings. Can we dock early? Or should we modify our trajectory?"

"No traffic, clear to dock. We were supposed to warn you to hold launch because Do'utian protest group in the area. Moot now. How you knew?"

"We had an external anomaly and we decided we'd be safer up here. The question is how did they know?"

"Drin," Mary's voice joined them from her station in the conical cabin of the spacecraft, "That may be my fault. I had a human partner on the negotiation team, really opposed to resettlement. We shared quarters so he knew my key. I'm sorry, I feel rotten about it. My stupid mating instincts."

Another Monitor opposed to resettlement Drin thought. But where did that lead? Connections here, connections there. To what?

"Instincts not stupid by definition," Do Tor offered. "And instinctual behavior not human-only. Elsewise Ko Kor would have waited to tell us what happened before completion of fate."

Completion of fate, Drin thought: another Do'utian philosophical concept which had percolated throughout Trimus culture. The Kleth could not conceive of continuing life after the death of a mate, but could contemplate prolonging death for a sufficient purpose. They told the tale of an ancient Zan Zor who avenged her murder by feeding herself slowly enough to her children that she was able to name the killer of her mate to visitors four days later.

The water surface dropped past him and down into the grate below; what little they needed from now on was in bladders tanks that would work in zero acceleration. If things went according to plan, he was done with swimming until they reached Aurum III.

★ ❀ ★

The inner system of the K2 star, Aurum, is dominated by the "brown dwarf" Ember. Trimus, of course, is a satellite of Ember. Two small terrestrial worlds, perhaps tidally ejected outer satellites of Ember, share Ember's orbit.

Aurum II is a small world at the L4 resonance point with a strong magnetic field and a resulting hot exosphere that precludes a dense atmosphere.

Aurum's third planet, at the L5 resonance point is about half the mass of Trimus, but denser and smaller and so has similar surface gravity (0.97 Do'utia, 0.47 Earth, 0.81 Kleth) It rotates slowly, once every five Trimus days (15 Do'utia, 7 Earth, 10 Kleth) and so has almost no magnetosphere. Prior to bioforming, it had a very thick carbon dioxide atmosphere and a surface temperature near the boiling point of its sterile oceans despite being warmed only by Aurum. Since bioforming, the average surface temperature has stabilized at just over the freezing point of water and the atmospheric pressure at 1.32 Standard Trimus Pressure (2.4 Do'utia, 1.7 Earth, 0.74 Kleth).

Aurum III Settlement Guide (Draft), Introduction.

★ ❀ ★

On approach Drin viewed the orbiting ring of equipment that had done most of the physical work of bioforming Aurum III. Aurum System was a deliberate backwater among local galactic culture, but for eight squared Trimusian years it had been the one of the most active industrial nodes of the Galaxy, importing quadrocubes of oxygen and spewing out trimadoms of carbon dioxide ice. They'd built a space power facility as large as that of any major transportation node and the attention that attracted down-current, Drin thought, might eventually end their solitude. But for now, with the bioforming job almost done, the machines were surplus and the power system waited for starships that didn't yet know it existed.

Meanwhile, two Kleth scientists had been killed down there.

Aurum III's relatively low mass and extensive atmosphere made for a reasonably gentle maneuver of about twice Trimusian normal gravity. The *Egg* flew broad end first into the first wisps of haze at six times eight-squared macro-units altitude. Its engine exhaust formed a relatively cool layer between the ship and the atmosphere, pushing the hottest part of the entry plume off of the bottom of the ship.

Gradually, his weight built up as the exhaust of the *Egg*'s engines was pushed back into a pad of gas in front of them. The ship tipped its nose down ever so slightly giving it just enough negative lift to counteract the centrifugal effect of their passage around the small planet.

He got heavier and heavier, until he was definitely uncomfortable.

This, he thought, was what a trip to Mary's Earth would be like. No, thank you. To think that her people had evolved in such a field!

Just when he thought that this was approaching his limit of uncomplaining endurance, it started to let up. He watched the horizon tilt back toward the base of the *Egg* and felt his weight return to almost normal. Terminal velocity. He looked down through the hull and the engines, rendered insubstantial to his viewscreen-covered eyes, and saw the breakers surrounding the target island. Then he made out the charred ruins of the bioforming station.

That hint of scale was all it took. Involuntarily, he groaned. This was exactly like the simulation and it wasn't at all like the simulation. He knew he really *was* falling from a fatal height. Stare *up*, stare up, he told himself. A roar of rockets and a shock of heaviness and pressure hit him. The ship groaned and creaked as it tilted and the rockets roared in compensation.

His beak opened and an involuntary death-wail emerged from his gaping mouth.

Then, almost suddenly, they were quietly floating in an alien sea. Drin spouted in relief as pumps began flooding the tank with minimally filtered external water, for ballast and in case they would have to leave quickly. He sampled the new seawater, and although it was filtered, he got a whif of a strange smell-set and began, almost unconsciously, to try to deconstruct it. He quickly noticed the lack of the human pollution that had diffused to every corner of Trimus' oceans, but there were other differences.

Drin knew that some minor changes had been made to the species mix that had so far proved successful on Trimus, for instance, Aurum III had no real hot climate zone and lacked warm-water sea life. Nor, due to the dense atmosphere and high axial tilt, was there much glaciation outside of the highest polar mountain ranges. So there was little of anything fetid and less of the ice-melt taste.

But what was *that*?

"Lieutenant Drinnil'ib okay?" Go Ton wanted to know, presumably responding to the wail.

"Just a traditional new-planet-challenge," Drin covered. Well, *he'd* used it on every new planet he'd landed on. "Everything's fine except the there's something funny in the water." What *was* it? "Be right up." Drin slipped off the headband and swam to the top of the rising surface. The three others were at the rail, ready in their field gear; Mary in a sleek gray and white amphibious 'second skin' coverall, Go Ton in a loose bright yellow coverall, matching her plumage while Do Tor was in a less conspicuous sky blue.

"Something dangerous?" Mary asked.

"I don't know. I can't identify it."

"Maybe when you get out, it will get clearer?"

"Much as I want to get out of this can, we're going to have to be very careful from here on out—help is a long way away. I suggest you take the aircraft ashore with Go Ton and Do Tor and make a first pass at the station ruin. I'll hold the ship in readiness in case we have to leave quickly."

"Sure." She reached toward him and he flipped his tongue toward her and held her hand momentarily. Then she looked right at him, something she had never done before, she briefly stroked the upper surface of her second finger, almost as intimate a gesture as could be made from her species to his. Then, without saying anything, she let go, waved, and bounded up the catwalk to the upper part of the *Egg*.

Drin drew his branches back into his beak and in the privacy of his mouth, touched the Mary-anointed finger with the hand of his other branch. Had she been a Do'utian woman, the gesture would have been an invitation to quicken her ovaries, risk her life, and merge their heritages.

She must know. Did he dare discuss it with her? What did this mean when they were so different biologically? She was three centuries old now; not much younger than him, and perhaps, having experienced everything in the normal bounds of behavior was curious about what might lie just over the line.

As he was.

But what shame he would feel if one like Councilor Gori'allolub ever found out that he had considered exchanging such sensual intimacies with a human. He shuddered; his tail would grow no longer at that! No, no, *no*.

✦ ❋ ✦

The mathematical model of convergent evolution has itself evolved independently among most of the spacefaring races. Despite wide variation in biological form, the common laws of physics determine which tool-creating behaviors won't work and thus constrain the set of reasoning and future-imaging abilities that produce technology. So too did the consequences of competitive struggle induce certain

*necessary similarities, which quantitative sociologists like to call
evolutionary attractors, in the games logic of resource territoriality,
group cooperation, and bargaining behavior.   This theory of
fundamental common behavioral motivation underlay the Trimus
experiment in multispecies planetary culture.*

—Go Zom's notes on the Compact and Charter of Trimus

★ ❊ ★

"Here's what we found," Mary told him. She sat straddling his
neck, leaning forward with her chin resting on the top of his head.
"The station ruins were already being overgrown with ivy, but there
clearly was an explosion. Go Ton found the detonator right next to the
blackened remains of Ko Kor's body. Play the recording."

The *Egg* sounded a tone and the screens at the top of his tank
shifted their image from the sea to the outside to the ruined bioforming
station. The ivy had overgrown parts of it, but otherwise it looked just
as it had at the end of the earlier video record. Their view, recorded
from Go Ton's camera zoomed into the dome through the gaping
holes in its top, and after scanning burned benches, empty cages with
their doors swinging open, ruined gestation vats, it steadied on the
carbonized remains of a Kleth, and a small blackened box. Go Ton's
hushed voice narrated.

"Memory of Zan Zor, she let flames consume her while she searched
for this. She *did* try to tell us, and the idiot rescue party missed it!"

"Oh, yes." Do Tor added in an unaccustomed here and now second
voice. "Possible bomb blew off a piece of dome that took head off."

Drin couldn't confirm that from the record, however he couldn't
dismiss it. A freak shrapnel accident? A fragment of dome panel, viewed
edge on, would be below the threshold of the recording's resolution.
The orientation, however, would have had to be just wrong. And, even
if invisible to one sensor, it should have been visible to others. Maybe
if the piece was small enough?   Drin reviewed Go Ton's recording
again, in slow motion. The scorched, partly legible labels of the cages
caught his eye; Canis __pus? _rsus midden____is? A piece of the
dome roof lay in the burnt wreckage *inside* the dome.

"Aircraft ready," Do Tor's voice announced.

Things were stable here so it was time to go see for himself.

"Coming," Mary answered. "See you outside, Drin."

He finished packing his pouch kit, released the ship to itself and
dove for the tank door.

Once out of the ship, the newness of the Aurum III seas assaulted
his senses. The smells of species were clear and distinct, like the notes
of a major chord compared to the white noise of Trimus' oceans. It
reminded him that ecological control needed to be reestablished here

before a random pattern of adaptive radiation took hold—one in which the planned human and Do'utian components might not fit so well.

It also puzzled him that there were still a couple of notes in this simple olfactory harmony that he could not identify. Then he recognized one of them as not dissimilar to the human swordfish he had enjoyed so often on Trimus. Of course, he thought. Its diet would be slightly different here and its excretions likewise.

He had a lot to learn, and looked forward to it.

Free of the spacecraft propellant tank, Drin stretched his muscles and shot through the water with enormous, powerful, tail strokes, closing his eyes to shield them from the pressure of his passage. In front, his bony nose cleaved a sea that felt almost as dense as flesh from the violence of his speed.

Out of breath, he shot for the surface, and with a mighty and well timed tailcrack shot out of the surface, reaching a full two charter units above the wavetops. Oh, the exhilaration of it! Oh, the freedom.

He expelled his old air in mighty bass note, and felt the reaction push him back like a steam rocket.

"Gesundheit!" Mary radioed from the aircraft, a double teardrop in a rounded delta wing hovering on its wing fans only a few meters higher than he had leapt.

He twisted in mid air to take the impact on his back and protect his legs. The tremendous splash scraped his back clean and no doubt stunned a lunch's worth of fish.

"More care, Lieutenant. Aircraft not submarine capable," a worried Do Tor honked.

"Oh, no," his mate added.

"Wow! How old did you say you were?" Mary laughed. Then stopped abruptly. "Drin! The ship!"

He bent to the right and looked back.

A great hole had suddenly appeared in the rounded upper dome of the tank, just below the conical cabin, only a doci or two above the waterline. Then as he watched there was a flash of steam and another one appeared next to it. The conical cabin, deprived of support, began to sag into it.

The aircraft accelerated, banked and started to turn back toward the ship.

"No!" Drin roared. "Do Tor, ditch! Now! Take the aircraft into the sea!"

"Say WHAT!?" Do Tor protested at first.

"Dive!" Drin shouted. "Get that egg-polluting thing under water!"

For no reason that Drin could see, a part of the aircraft's wing fell off before it knifed down into the waves.

A cone of air over the dying spacecraft, blasted into luminescence by gamma radiation, was now much brighter than distant, cloud-filtered Aurum. Just as he dove after the aircraft, he felt an enormous sting near the base of his tail. A piece of the ship? Or had something had bit him. But what?

No time for that now. He doubled back on himself and slammed water behind him,and sprinting toward the sinking aircraft.

The bubble canopy was filling rapidly with water, but his comrades seemed all conscious, with their heads above the water level. The impact had torn away the wings, but for that, the aircraft seemed intact. He dove alongside, matched sinking rates, twisted, and grabbed the machine between his front legs. Then, cradling it much as an Earth-otter might cradle a shellfish or a young otter, he rose back to a depth of about half a charter unit. The bubble in the canopy expanded and a Mary nodded at him as if to say, "we're okay."

The sky above the ocean was insanely bright and filtered down as a hellish blue-white. There should be, he thought, no reason that anyone should suspect that they survived that blast. For avoiding another attack, that might give them some breathing room, but for rescue, it could be a problem.

✳※✳

Sentient omnivores were designed into the Trimus ecological system from the beginning and size limits were engineered into its subsentient carnivores. There were no big cats or U'Ulatan Spear-tooth packs on land, no great white sharks in the oceans, no deathspores in its skies; nothing large, numerous, or vicious enough threaten unarmed members of the three sentient species in their own element. The birthrates of some large herbivores were lowered as well, and a certain amount of culling by traditional hunting methods was a design expectation.

Planet Monitor's Handbook, Ecological Appendix

✳※✳

Mary could pack twice her mass for long treks without complaining. Do Tor could fly with a burden almost as massive as he was. Drin's folk, however, did very well to manage their own bulk on land, and even his finely honed, athletic, Planet Monitor's body would have been quickly worn down by a burden only one-fourth his own mass. And after eight squared days in near-zero gravity, about the best he could manage comfortably for long periods was about one eighth more than he weighed.

Therefore, because that eighth was easily eight times more than Mary, Do Tor, and Go Ton combined could carry, Drin carried *everything*, including Mary. Absolute size matters.

Besides, there wasn't that much left to carry. A medical kit salvaged from the aircraft. The core of its cybersystem and its communications equipment. Emergency tents and blankets. Dart gun ammunition. Containers for boiling liquids. A rotary generator. An analyzer.

All the electronics were powered off. The first thing that had occurred to all of them was that electronic noise was one common denominator with respect to whatever had attacked the bio-station, the spacecraft, and the aircraft. Another common denominator was location, and they were making a reasonable effort at changing that before powering anything.

Do Tor had suggested a cave. Drin had replied that that made sense, but it had better be a big one. So Do Tor and Go ton were off looking along the banks of a deep river on the other side of the island.

The forest was cool and moist; the trees wetted him as he pushed through them, following a small creek. Aurum was haze dimmed and the chill polar wind kept him comfortably cool. He would need to eat well in a dozen days or so, but for now the enforced abstinence was good for him. The smells were the smells of wild wood; Earth pine with its sharp needles, broad olli'ulstican leaves, light and bright with a fruity bouquet, stolid aspen. The animal community came with a breeze from some nearby trail: nimble six-legged squirrels from Kleth, a whiff of Earth dog, running free. The ripe droppings of the carrion-gull from his grandparent world. The smells were familiar, but in a new, free, clean environment.

In fact, he was feeling unreasonably good, given their situation, except for his back.

"Mary, could I ask you something very personal?"

"Sure."

"My back still itches where something bit me after the ship blew. Would you scratch the scar?"

"Okay." She yawned. Then he felt her skitter down his rolling back past the equipment pallet to the base of his tail. She went immediately to the right place, which surprised him. It should be well healed by now.

"Drin," her voice was much sharper now, "I don't want to scare you, but there's something still in there, and it's pretty deep."

"Oh?" he rumbled and stopped, then bent his head back in a painful contortion to look. There was indeed a deep long gash in his blubber, still oozing. Pollution! He should do something about that. It was time for a rest anyway, Aurum had come out from its cloudy veil, the wind had slacked, and he needed to stop generating body heat and let his temperature back off for a bit.

"I think we have the med kit. Do you want to try to dig it out now? I could use a rest, and I won't feel much until unless it gets below the fatty layer. What is it?"

"It looks like a silvery wire. Maybe some kind of monofilament."

"Pollution!" Drin lowered himself to his belly and held himself motionless. Every movement he'd made for the last hour had probably worked the thing in deeper. "Talk about vicious sabotage! No wonder Soames didn't surrender. . . .   Look, the forceps in the kit are solid diamond, they should be able to handle it, even if it is monofilament. And Mary, remember that what looks like a horrendous wound to you may be a minor nick to me. So even if whatever it is cuts in deeper, please keep your fingers away from it!"

"Roger that."   After lots of "umms," "ahs," and "uh huhs," she declared victory. "Okay, I have it. Long, thin, silvery thing." She held up the forceps. Drin could see nothing.

"You'll have to bring it closer for me."

"I'll put it in a sample jar and tape you up, first."

Drin grumbled as she squeezed fluids from tubes, tugged here and there. Then Mary was in front of his left eye with a shallow clear diamond sample jar. He sent a branch of his tongue out to take it.

The lens of Drin's eye was almost as wide as the jar, and evolution in and out of water had given him the focusing ability and retina to take full advantage of that aperture. With the fingers on the other branch, he removed the lid, stuck the forceps in, and moved the filament around.

It didn't seem to be a single strand, but something rather more complex. And, just on the limit of his vision, there appeared to be nodules or grains of some kind. He managed to isolate one, lift it up, and shake it. For a moment, it caught the light just right, and it looked like a net of some kind.

"A spider web?" Mary asked, her voice soft with wonder. "What kind of spider? What kind of web?"

"Possibly monofilament," Drin guessed, "a fullerene, or a string of some kind of nanites. We'd need more equipment to find out, but I suspect from the video of the attack that, all spread out, the thing is a circle about a quarter charter unit in diameter. If it lands on something, the nodes work their way through it, pulling the filament along between them."

"Organic, or Mechanical?"

"Or organomechanic. No polluting way to tell just now." Drin put the lid back on the sample jar. "I'd guess from what we've seen that it makes short work of hard composites and metals, but gets bogged down after a few eighth-docis in soft wet stuff. Like me."

"Or sea water?"

"That's what you and I are, mostly. Seawater and pollution. Well, we have a clue."

"But," Mary asked, "Is this something a fanatic saboteur could concoct at a bioforming base? Why both the bomb *and* the spiderwebs? Or did they come from somewhere else?"

They spent the rest of the journey to their new cave home in deep thought.

* ✳ *

For environmental reasons, Kleth power transmission technology had spread throughout the Local Worlds long before the founding of Trimus. Superconducting waveguide tubing for far infrared produces no external fields, can be strung long distances under ground or water, and carries information as well as power. A sudden line break may produce a transient high intensity beam, but standard connectors shut down the minimagnetron arrays instantly when a break is detected.
Planet Monitor's Handbook, Technical Appendix

* ✳ *

The cave was too small, Drin complained to himself, as he scraped his back returning from a futile trip to the ruined station some days later. He couldn't turn around in the partly submerged lava tube except just inside the weathered out, half submerged mouth, where the black sand floor rose almost to the widest part of the tube. The gentle solar tides of Aurum III rose only a doci or so, but on the nearly level sand of the tube, it made almost a charter unit of difference in where the estuary shoreline fell, cutting its floor area in half at high tide, making the place feel even more claustrophobic.

Someday he would excavate a more comfortable channel and create a larger dry area, but today his mind was on a different technical problem. They had equipment, they had a source of power, but somehow during the explosion at the station, the rotary generator's output lead had been damaged, leaving bare waveguide and no way to get the power out. Without power, they had no way to call for help or warn anyone about the nets until someone came in range of their personal communicators. And once their batteries gave out, they would be, effectively, stuck in the shell age.

"Mary?" Drin called, softly lest the echoes in the confined space deafen him.

An awful buzzing racket ensued, then a cloud of dust and debris fell from the roof and roiled toward him. He backed up, getting his tail in the water again. He felt, then heard, a solid thump and saw a largish rock roll out of the settling cloud of dust. Then there was a smaller thump.

"Hi, Drin." It was Mary, grinning, clothed in volcanic rock dust, wielding a vibrosaw they had salvaged from the biostation ruins. "In one fell swoop, ahem, I've made a back door for me, a front door for the Kleth, and a chimney. A few more days of work, and this place will be habitable."

"I am glad we have *some* good news. I couldn't find any usable connectors in the ruins."

Mary's teeth disappeared. "Nuts."

"I think," he offered, "the next step is to check the wreckage of the *Egg*."

"I guess. Drin, I keep thinking I should be able to do something with what we have."

Drin looked away in negation. "I can't see how. Wave guide power transceivers need infrared wave scale dimitech, or maybe minilithography, and the best we have in our tool kit is a miniwaldo set. I hate to think of how long . . ."

"Okay, okay, let's go on an *Egg* hunt." She ran to the water, splashed in up to her knees, made a shallow dive, and surfaced halfway to the cave mouth, and started pulling herself back to the shore, laughing. "Actually, I should get a couple things together first. Can you wait a bit?"

"Mary, I think there's going to be more residual radiation than you should see. Especially if we get stuck here for years. You should stay."

She slumped. "You're right as usual, Lieutenant. Look, Drin?" She shook water off of her head, hair flying.

"Yes?"

She pressed herself warmly against the side of his head and murmured. "Come back, huh?"

Drin touched the tip of his beak to the sand beside her. Two could play this game of inappropriate courtship signals, he thought. She laughed and kissed the top of his head.

Then he backed out into the wider part of the cave, turned and swam out into the river.

Once in the stream he sounded briefly, then sent a blast of steam into the air. Do Tor and Go Ton soon appeared overhead, and he told them what he intended and asked for some air cover.

✴ ❈ ✴

Aurum III is a world of exaggerated vertical scale, above and below water, its volcanoes reach over four macro-units above sea level and not much less than that below to the mean ocean floor. The main mode of crust cycling, as with many smaller hot-core worlds, is sublithic thermal deconstruction: new eruptions covering older shields deposits, weighing them down, hydrostatic readjustment taking ancient layers down below the mantle, where they decompose, releasing their gasses. Thus many volcanic plateaus are surrounded by deep trenches and hot springs.

—Aurum III Settlement Guide (Draft), Geology Supplement

✴ ❈ ✴

The marginal trench was a dive beyond even Drin, but the *Egg* had touched down just landward of the edge of the island shield, and he hoped to find at least some debris there.

Again, what was that smell? An Earth species, certainly, but not one he could place.

He broached and scanned the air. Do Tor and Go Ton were circling overhead like a pair of Do'utian diving gulls looking for floating carrion and the black humor of that analogy made him chortle. He would have said something, but they were conserving communicator power - no one knew when they would get to charge them again.

A few beats later, Drin's sense of location told him that he was over the wreck, and he sent a single spout skyward, a prearranged signal to let them know everything was fine. Then he dove down, and down. The water was cold and stagnant, and illumination was only a matter of some shadows being less dark than others. He started chirping, and a fuzzy sonar scene formed below. Lava pillows, large spiral-shelled shellfish from Kleth, occasional small fuzzies, and, there, he found it, about eight-squared charter units down and left. The half shell wreck of the *Trimus Egg*.

It astounded him that so much had survived, but gammas and pions traveled too far in mere air to make for a concentrated explosion, and near-field heating may have slowed the mixing rate. Still, as he drew near, he could smell the carbon and metal ash of materials heated to their kindling temperature.

He was silent, and as the sonic images faded from his perception, a faint blue glow remained.

So, the remaining structure must be still radioactive, almost five days after its exposure. He sent a tongue branch into his pouch for a radiometer.

And backed water immediately when it started glowing red-orange.

A fear began to develop in him, a suspicion. Nervously, he ascended a bit and swam directly over the hulk. The radiometer was non directional, but he could use his body to occult the source; in effect locating it by seeing which way his body's radiation shadow pointed. In his shadow, the detector dimmed to a dull red, then as he got out of the way, went back up to orange.

Several trials, turning in different directions, show him that, as near as he could tell, it was a point source. There was only one possible explanation; at least one of the antihydrogen dewars had survived and must be leaking, still trying to feed antihydrogen to a converter. How?

He descended to bottom and sunk to his belly in the detritus ooze. The radiometer went almost down to black, and he released a bubble of relief. He had time to think.

Of course, the converters! Their walls were tungsten an eighth of a doci thick, and they surrounded each Dewar in a cluster. It was a safety feature designed so that in case one of the clusters was breached, the resulting radiation would not damage the others.

He'd known the things were diamond-tough, but this was unexpected. Not only had the engineering actually worked, it had worked too well! It would have been much better if everything had let go when the ship was hit.

With the cold deep water as a heat sink, the solid state electron heat pumps would have much less work to do, and the Dewar's emergency power supply might last this long. But when it gave out, the antihydrogen ice in the core would start to evaporate, react with the inner chamber walls, and evaporate more antihydrogen in a runaway reaction that would cause the dewar walls to fail from radiation damage. Then the dewar would collapse instantly under the water pressure, causing all the remaining antihydrogen to be mixed with matter. Not in a fizzle of several minibeats, but, essentially, at once.

That could happen, he realized, at any time, or be set off by any shock wave, or perhaps a disturbance. But they still needed the power converter. And, since the remaining dewars would eventually fail anyway, it would probably be better to set them all off deliberately, at a known time.

Their supplies had included some command-fused explosives, he recalled, stored in one of the cargo lockers at the unfueled waterline. Before he could talk himself out of it, he took a hand lamp from his pouch, crept up to the hulk and began to circle it, looking for the locker. Crazily, despite the fact that the upper two thirds of the spacecraft had been vaporized, enough of the bottom of the tank had survived in places to allow one to imagine that nothing had happened!

He found the locker about a third of the way around the hulk. Very gingerly, he worked the manual release, and was rewarded by an intact storage hold—a virtual treasure trove, considering their circumstances. There were the explosives lockers, vibro drills, floodlights, diamond coated fiber line, an inflatable cargo raft, and a Do'utian beak shovel. .

He permitted himself a slight purr of satisfaction. The shovel was a simple tool that would let him dig and move many times the amount of mass he could move with his tongue. The invention of such tools had played a role in Do'utian civilization comparable to that of the horse harness for humans. The DCF line was thin, light, high tensile strength, and just about indestructible. Best of all, the floodlights, of course, had two each standard power connector splices!

Carefully, he unloaded the raft and set the rest of his treasure in it. He vented an explosive locker and withdrew four charges and put them in his pouch. Using the DCF line, he tied the beak shovel in three places so it would hang below the raft and tend to keep it upright.

Then he inflated the raft and sent it toward the surface loaded with his treasure.

Drin went around the exposed underside of the hull with his radiation meter, hoping that he could find the leaking dewar and place the charges on the hull just opposite it. But after several minutes, he realized he would have no such luck, and would have to go into the wreck.

He put the radiation meter in his pouch—he would have to do this as fast as Do'utianly possible, and looking at the meter would only waste time. With the charges in one hand and the light in another he went up over the torn rim of the hull. Where?

He flicked off the light and in a couple of beats, saw a faint cone of blue. Don't hesitate, he told himself, and swam directly to it. The floor grid was still perversely intact. Did he dare risk raising a panel? He wasted time in a frustrated near panic about that before it occurred to him to see if the charges would fit through the holes in the gridwork.

They did, just barely. He activated them in sonic command mode, getting a confirmatory blink on the end of each. Then he forced them through the gridwork, letting them fall below to the bulkhead just over the converters and dewars, each hitting with a nerve-rattling clank.

As soon as the last one fell through, he pushed himself up, swam gently back over the rim and away from the wreck until he was several charter units clear, then abandoning himself to justifiable terror, he sped for the surface.

A charter unit from broaching, Drin bent his course parallel to the surface and located the beak shovel hanging from the raft, then raced for it, surfaced and looked toward the sky for the Kleth.

"Drin? Drin!"

He rolled his eyes to the cargo raft itself. Do Tor and Go Ton were calmly seated on the left pontoon, wings folded, their horny feet brushing the wavetops.

"Good hunting!" Do Tor congratulated him.

"Oh, yes." Go Ton added.

"Monitors, we need to leave quickly. Some of the antihydrogen dewars survived the nets . . . "

The Kleth wings popped out in unison.

". . . and may implode at any time." Drin dove under the raft, grabbed the beak shovel, surfaced and put it in the raft. As he opened his beak, he got a strong taste of the strange sea life he'd smelled earlier. No time to investigate now, he thought. He considered dragging the raft for a moment, then changed his mind, dove under and surfaced beneath it, so that it draped over his broad back.

The Kleth had taken to the air, and were circling Drin as he made best surface speed toward the island.

"Is your friend coming too?" Do Tor asked.

Drin swiveled an eye back along the surface and saw a large, white, erect, fin knifing along beside him, about three charter units to his left. Underwater it looked to be an Earth fish with a conical head that was unusually wide across. It had several gill slits, instead of the usual one. Also, the mouth wasn't in the usual place. There, Drin thought, that slit below the head must be it.

An alien?

If so, it was a large one, almost half as long as he was. And why the Earth smell?

It decided to move in to investigate him. It closed rapidly. It opened its mouth.

Drin's afterbrain took over. His foreleg, muscled for carrying half his weight around on land was already in motion when the great grayish-white fish opened its mouth. The thing, which seemed originally intent on striking at Drin's nonexistent gills, started to change its target.

Drin's claw, without any conscious control from him, missed the head, but still caught it the thing just behind its gills, and the next thing he knew, he had the front third of it painfully clamped onto his leg while the rest floated away, spewing fluids into the sea.

After seeing a demonstration, Mary, Drin remembered, had likened a blow from Drin's foreleg to striking something with a huge serrated axe.

"Mary calls them sharks," Do Tor called.

Them?

A quick look found three more fins, and a ping illuminated four. One of them headed for the rear half of their companion, and two headed for him. Drin sounded, heading straight down as fast as he could, shaking off the head of the first shark from his foreleg about halfway down. That got the shark's attention long enough for him to get well away.

The wound in his leg was deep and painful. How, he wondered, had a mouth in that clumsy position been able to do *that*? His leg bled.

Out of nowhere, another shark appeared and started diving after him. Drin sent his tongue into his pouch and pulled out his gun. Then he jackknifed and faced the thing, waited until it was almost on him, and put an explosive bullet into it.

He had to weigh ten times what the sharks did, and individually, they were no match for him. But he knew that, collectively, they would easily wear him down before he could reach the safety of land. Was there any way Do Tor and Go Ton could help him?

His afterbrain, responding to minute water pressure variations, slammed his tail into another of the creatures before he realized what was happening. It floated stunned in the water.

Bait.

He quickly jack-knifed back, nipped the shark in two, stuffed the back half down his throat for a long overdue meal, and held the polluting front part distastefully sealed inside his mouth. Then he headed for the surface as fast as he could, counting on the sheer speed of his ascent to protect him.

It did. He shot out of the water to an altitude of about a charter unit, and almost hit circling Do Tor.

"Cover me with your guns!" Drin boomed. Then he twisted on his back and struck the water with a stinging maximum impact. Two or three sharks floated senseless on the surface. Drin snapped them up and headed directly over the wreckage of their spacecraft, nipping heads off as he went.

"I count three eights of sharks," Do Tor called. A shot rang out. Two eights and seven, now, Drin hoped.

"Three eights six," Do Tor corrected his optimism, as if reading his mind. Several more shots rang out and even more sharks appeared.

"Fine!" Drin roared in frustration. "I'll take every one of the polluting things in the whole polluting ocean with me."

He arrived over the wreck, filled his lungs as best he could on the fly, and headed *down*, expelling the gory mess in his mouth to distract any followers. It seemed to work; they congregated over the wreck for the leavings and he couldn't detect any of the beasts on his tail, but he didn't slow down to check more carefully. About ten charter units down, he bent his course back to the raft, and broached in a long low arc, barely clearing the waves, and turned his comset on. It was time to use the batteries.

"Monitors, Lieutenant Drin. I'm going to detonate the rest of the ship, soon. Get set for a big wave. Tell Mary."

He reached the raft and saw no sign of sharks. He grabbed the emergency light with one branch of his tongue, the coil of DCF line with the other, and pulled them back into his mouth. Afraid to try to save anything more, he headed away from the site as fast as he still could. Exhaustion and what was probably the onset of radiation sickness were slowing him considerably. He was having to spout much more frequently than usual. Fluid in his lungs. And he was pissing torrents.

Do Tor and Go Ton were pacing him overhead.

"Do Tor, Go Ton," he sent, "best help Mary prepare. The wave will likely put the cave under."

"Monitors, Mary, I think I'm set for anything. Suggest you stay with Drinnil'ib."

"No, Mary. The air won't be safe here. They'd best go. I'm not fragile, and I intend to get through this." He didn't mention the sickness. "Do Tor, get out of here. Orders. I'm going to detonate it now."

Without waiting for an argument, he sounded. He thought furiously; he had to be in the water to send the sonic command but he wanted to be out of the water when the shock arrived. He might have one good broach left in him, he thought, and he would have to time it just right. He tried to calculate, but it was too complicated, distances too uncertain, and he was too tired. So he guessed and sent the command when he was at full speed up, halfway back to the surface.

With one last, desperate, slam of his tail he vaulted above the wave tops. He seemed to hang in the air forever while nothing happened, then, just before his back touched the water again, three ripples went by under him, extremely fast, deceptively small. He'd saved his hearing, he thought as he plunged in, by less than a fraction of a beat.

Drin surfaced again, looked back, and almost wished he hadn't. A huge dome of sea had grown behind him with incredible speed, and the nearer part was transforming itself into a wall of onrushing water almost eight-squared charter units high.

Drin spouted once more and filled his lungs as best he could and rose with the wave

It was like being in the spaceship at launch again. He was lifted up and up as he tried to swim down. He couldn't stay under, and his head came out of the water on the slope of a huge hill of liquid. The wind howled like the worst part of a Coriolis storm. He could see Do Tor and Go Ton in the distance racing away, and his sense of level told him he was looking down on them.

A glance at the island confirmed that. The wave, he estimated, would inundate all but the highest peaks.

Then he was sliding down the hill of water at incredible speed toward the island. He pushed his legs forward to slow himself, spreading the webs between his claws.

And found himself standing on an almost glass-smooth wave, toes out of water. He didn't dare fall. He couldn't make himself breath.

With his eyes on the side of his head, he had nearly seven eighths of a sphere of vision, and processing this, the physiologists said was what most of his massive forebrain did. It was usually a blessing, but just now it enabled him to see the top of the wave, far above him, start to curl forward and break into white foam. Behind and above that a column of dirty steam rose up to the cloud deck like a comic-scale ring-shelf plant, and likely far beyond.

Drin's wave was headed toward a steep volcanic cone on the end of peninsula stretching out from the island. Instinctively, he tried to lean away from it, and his path actually bent slightly. The feeling of having even that little bit of control over what was happening to him unfroze his mind. He was headed too far inland to skate around the outside of the cone, but the saddle land connecting it with the rest of the island was low. He bent that way.

It was actually a short cut, he thought with some grim humor. The mouth of the river of their cave was on the other side of the gap, just toward the main part of the island.

The water ahead of him rose up between the main island and the cone—the wave was being funneled between the two. Its speed slackened and Drin settled from his feet back onto his belly, still sliding down an advancing slope of water, still in control.

He shot through the gap in an instant, then cubes and cubes of water crashed down on him, twisting him this way and that as his weakened and abused muscles strained and strained, trying to hold himself together. Finally it abated, and he let himself roll with it.

Eight cubed charter units from the island, what remained of the wave had passed by under him, and he found himself floating in what seemed to be a more or less normal sea.

He tried a gentle tail stroke to send him landward, but it hurt too much.

His legs seemed to have fared better than his back, however, and he was able to begin paddling, Mary-fashion, back toward the cave, letting his tortured back muscles rest.

Even this far out, he could see the devastation: only one tree in ten still standing, those leaning, the beaches covered with debris, the river choked with fallen trees and reduced to a trickle.

From this side of the peninsula, he could see that a huge bite had been washed from the base of the volcanic cone leaving a hard lava core to jut out at an impossible angle toward a side vent that was no longer there.

His eyes went to the beach again; there seemed to be more of it than a minute before. In fact . . .

He looked behind him. The water was rising there.

Ignoring his pain, he swung himself around and began swimming with as much speed as he could manage, away from the beach.

He rose higher, and higher and felt the wind build up again. He did not look back a moment, but kept struggling up the wave. Finally he sounded directly into it, then emerged again, unable to stay down. But he felt himself falling; he had passed through the wave before it had formed a crest.

He let himself drift around, totally exhausted, spouting pink with every breath, and watched the incoming wave hammer the island. He floated for subjective ages, fading in and out of coherence. Finally, with a great effort, he reached into his pouch for his gun, and brought it into his mouth.

If the sharks came now, he was done. He estimated the things could chew at him for hours before they got to anything definitely vital. But he wouldn't suffer that. As a last resort, he could still put an explosive bullet in his forebrain and not experience his own undoing.

With such cold security achieved, he recovered some psychological energy, and began to paddle himself toward the river mouth. The sky above was a strange blood red; Aurum was peaking below the cloud deck, lighting it from below creating a strange scene of crimson lit billows and gray shadows. Their sun had almost completed its slow journey to the horizon and would hang there several days before it started up again in this world's arctic summer. From the shore, an Earth dog howled the way Drin had never heard one howl before, carrying clearly over the waves. The sea, reflecting the sky, seemed to be made of blood.

Drin fought the remaining current with his legs, pulling himself slowly upstream.

He keyed his comset. "Mary?"

No answer.

"Do Tor?"

Nothing.

"Test?"

Nothing. The unit was dead; probably from having been left on too long, since no pounding that left his pouch intact could possibly have harmed it.

Of course, there had been the electromagnetic pulse of the explosion.

He put it back in his pouch; he'd assume a power problem for now.

He rested. He moved forward a few more charter units. He rested. He moved. He rested.

Had he come upstream far enough. His sense of position told him he had, but the landscape looked completely unfamiliar; the channel seemed to run too far south.

Where was the cave?

He scanned the north shore, across a field of freshly deposited sand.

There; a rough arch of lava sticking out of the sand. The lava field behind it looked familiar, too. He opened his beak.

"Mary?" he groaned, thinking it probably sounded more like an acoustic fog warning than a name.

"Drin, Drin!" her high pitched voice came echoing back, seeming to be from a million miles away. Then her frosty blond head popped out through the hole she'd cut in the top of the cave.

"Drin!" she screamed, sounding much closer now.

Her hair was matted and dirty. She had angry red marks on her face, and she limped as she ran toward him on the sand. A hand was heavily bandaged.

With a last, gigantic, effort, he struggled a few steps onto the sand to meet her, and fell on his belly, completely spent.

She threw herself against his head and tried to hold herself there, repeating his name over and over.

He opened his beak slightly and slipped the branches of his tongue around her, holding her to him. They stayed that way until she seemed to regain her composure.

"Drin, we got through it. I broke a finger and wrecked a knee. Do Tor has a hole in his wing, and Go Ton is trying to patch it with one hand and guard our prisoner with the other, so I have to get back and help. Then I'll be back with the med kit for you. And Drin, for whatever crazy kind of sense it makes, I love you. I have to say that, and say it now before anything like that ever happens again without my having said it. I love you."

Drin couldn't think of anything rational to say on that subject, but he was suddenly aware that his mouth was sore from the things that had rattled around inside it.

He let go of Mary and took them out and spread them before her.

"I found some connectors," he said.

She waved and arm at the devastated island around them, started laughing and seemed unable to stop. What was so funny? Drin thought. They *needed* the connectors.

★ ✳ ★

In seeking the explanations of things that happen, create many models before discarding any. Understand the difference between a fact and an assumption. Do not project your rationality on what may be the result of an irrational act or non-rational happenstance. Learn the differing motivations of the other sentients.
            —Planet Monitor's Handbook, Forensic Methodology

★ ✳ ★

The prisoner, Drin decided, was one of the most abject and miserable human beings he had ever encountered. Theric Soames was so tight, surly, and touchy that conversation was impossible. Mary didn't want to use drugs, but they had to find out about the nets, and find out soon. So she had asked them all to leave. She wanted to continue the interrogation human to human, without drugs.

"Trust me, please," she told Drin. So he assented to their return to the privacy of the cave.

There was plentiful dead wood all over the island now, and Go Ton had started a large fire. For one of the few times in his life, Drin was welcome for the warmth. Do Tor sat on a log near him. He was restive from not flying while his wing healed, and Go Ton was being exceptionally attentive while she was around, which was not always. Go Ton was the only one of them physically fit enough to collect food for them. Incredibly, she managed.

Drin regurgitated a salmon skeleton and cast it away.

"How do you do it?" he asked.

"Made net from the line you brought. Put across river bed near new rapids. Collect fish."

"Your energy is a marvel. I should be able to help myself in a few more days." "Day," especially here in eternal light of high arctic summer, still met a Trimus day to them and not the leisurely rotation of Aurum III. But for some beings in the mists of the future, Drin reflected, that would change.

"You realize," Drin remarked to his Kleth partners, "that there is nothing that validates our Trimusian culture more than to plant a secondary colony. At this point, we stop worrying about whether our ancestors came from Do'utia, Kleth, or Earth. We are now all from Trimus!"

"Oh, yes," Go Ton agreed. "But we can never be same, so always tension between three and one. So Mary insists on us stay away while she interrogates Soames. Does human-separate things maybe we should not see, but she does *them* for Trimus."

"Oh." Drin rumbled. Emotionally, his attachment to Mary, despite his best intentions, was approaching that of a bull for a harem cow. This was utterly, totally unreasonable, yet what Mary might be doing to induce Soames to talk tasted like a polluted stream to him. But perhaps his Kleth friends could help here. Go Ton's perspective was interesting and comforting.

"Go Ton, what do you think the English word 'perverse' means?"

"Deviating from what is considered socially acceptable. Definition relative, not absolute."

"How much affection can there be between different species before Trimus culture considers it not socially acceptable?"

Do Tor flapped a bit of wing, indicating to his mate that he wished to take over the conversation. Go Ton emitted a low coo of consent. "You and Mary?

Drin hesitated a long time. "Yes," he finally said.

"No shame in that to me. Touch friendship natural for both your species. Not for Kleth."

"Oh, yes," Go Ton added. "But we're progressive Kleth. See how much Do Tor lets me talk?"

Do Tor flapped a bit again, then made the sort of hiccoughing humor sound of his people's laughter. "Trimusian Kleth," he said, "are considered perverse, by traditionalists on Kleth, because of the very name Trimus. On ancient Kleth, one doesn't speak of three. Know you why?"

"No. Of course I am curious, but you do not have to tell me."

"You have told us dangerous secret so we tell you one. Our nests hold three eggs, one from each of three pairs. Two eggs one sex, one the other. Everything fine for seven or eight days. Then nest is too small. While parents away, a choice is made, and two eat the one."

"Huh," Drin rumbled, "You have seen my people's beach manners. We are all part of nature. The fight to live selects the strong."

"No fight," Do Tor corrected him. "Sacrifice. The one who is to die chooses self by not defending. But sometime not."

"Oh, yes." Go Ton added. "On old Kleth, for every six eight-cubed couples, one triple. Great perversion. Parents flee or be killed. Sometimes two triples get together and pretend to be three couples. Considered witches, demons if discovered in old days. You and Mary not perverse. Are interesting. Three Kleth is perverse."

"But essential, at the start, by what you say." Drin remarked.

"Big question, hard for Kleth to discuss, hard to study. Nothing recorded, but two-egg nests usually fight, then one wins and both die. No one talks about it. Our third nestmate was intelligent being, like anyone. No biological difference. Do Tor and I start life by killing and eating our nest mate. Instinct, not decision, but we remember. Our genetic engineers can change this, but the result isn't Kleth. You can tell Mary," Do Tor said, "No else, please."

"I don't judge you." Drin said. "You are my friends. I will not speak of it to others."

"Good. So we not tell others what you and Mary do."

Drin's recharged communicator asked for his attention before he could think of a reply.

"Yes, Mary?"

"I'm bringing Soames back. He freely admits that he planted the bomb in the bioforming station, arguing that it was philosophically justifiable to prevent the inundation of Aurum III with transplanted primitivists. He remained resolutely silent with respect to who else on Trimus was party to this effort to sabotage a Council decision.

"But he emphatically denied having anything to do with the nets, and claimed to know nothing about them. He seemed genuinely surprised when he saw their captive sample, and pointed out that it had come as close to killing him as anyone. I suppose you'll want to talk to him."

"I certainly do. And, Mary?"

"Yes?"

"Did your mother have access to your codes?"

"Drin! Karen Olsen is the architect of the resettlement policy! Yes, she's the alternate custodian of my personal files, but there is no way . . ."

"No offense, little one, I don't think she is a suspect. But we might have to worry about anyone close enough to her to have access to her files, as your roommate did to yours."

"I see. She's not like me, that way. She hasn't been active, that way, that I know of, for some time."

"Very well. Warn her if you trust her. Mary, do you have your gun handy?"

"Yes. Why?"

"Do you remember the burnt labels on the cages in the bioforming station?"

"Uh, Canis something, a type of dog: those little harry carnivores with the high pitched yap that we keep as pets. The other one was Kleth I think. If it were Earth life, the genus might have been Ursus, which would have been a bear, and I don't think they would . . . oh. The howls."

"Someone," Drin rumbled, "has clearly revised the ecology of this project to make it hostile to settlement. I was trying to think of what might be the equivalent of sharks on land."

★ ❈ ★

While what our Trimusian pioneers did was almost radical, it was done for a very conservative reason. The pioneers of all three species were dedicated to the idea that a stable interspecies culture could be created without significantly reengineering the brains and endocrinological systems of its participants. They did this in full knowledge that most of the galaxy and even their own homeworlds would eventually look on them and their descendants as living fossils, but they were comfortable with that destiny, and so far, we have been able to sustain it, with varying degrees of dedication.

—Go Zom's notes on the Compact of Trimus

★ ❈ ★

"Now," Do Tor shouted from aloft.

Drin released the water wheel by taking his left foreleg off the radial beam, and it started turning.

The general purpose line wrapped twice around the rim of the lava stone flywheel on the same pine log, went down one side, twice around a groove carved in another smaller stone disk, and back up again. That disk was attached to their generator's input shaft.

He watched the lash-up turn nervously, the flywheel axle rested on four magnetic bearing casters, salvaged from a cart in the ruin of the station, that looked too small for the job. It bumped and clattered around, but didn't look ready to break.

The waves had moved sand around capriciously, and exposed a rapid drop of almost a charter unit that necked down into a sort of natural shoot, producing a flow of three to four macrodoms at a speed of a couple of charter units a beat. They had cut the curved paddles from a huge hollow xo tar bin log, the spokes from wave-felled aspen, and everything was held together with construction glue salvaged from the ruined station, and DCF. The generator told them it was putting out four eight-squared cues per beat.

The power line ran back to the cave to their dearly purchased power splice, to a communications modem they had salvaged from their net-wrecked, irradiated, ditched aircraft, and back to the aircraft's transmitter, sitting under a mesh antenna retrieved from the ruined bioforming station. Drin knew the transmitter worked because his comset lock light said it found the carrier, but he couldn't listen in.

That couldn't be helped; Mary's call had to be encrypted, but it was frustrating.

The log looked like it was trying to work its way to the right as it rolled. Drin grabbed a discarded branch in his beak and gave it a shove back to center. The green wood began to smoke from the friction, and the stench was awful, but things seemed to turn more smoothly. They'd have to shim the stone pile under the caster bearings as soon as Mary was done. Then they could recharge the vibrosaws and the comsets.

After a minor eternity, the lock light went out.

"Mary, I need to make some adjustments," he called.

"You've got about ten minutes for lightspeed delay. Then we wait." "Drin," her voice was soft now, "If I don't get a call back in a couple of hours, I guess we can assume we'll get hit by the nets in the near future."

And they could also assume a dishonor polluting the highest levels of the Trimus Council, which would make a mockery of everything Drin believed in.

"Roger," he replied in low, disheartened tones. The whole damn universe smelled wrong, he thought as he finished shimming the mount. That should about do it; he let the wheel run again.

A movement, almost behind his tail, registered at the limits of his peripheral vision. What? He turned to get a better look. What the polluting hell was that? A carnivore of some kind?

As it reared up at the sight of Drin turning, and it looked big, even to him. The legs, covered with brown fur, looked almost as massive as his own. With his length, he probably out-weighed it by four-eights, but on its hind legs, it reared taller than him. Its head was maybe only twice as big as Mary's, but most of that was a pair of heavily muscled toothy jaws that could probably crunch even his bones. Polar bear? But weren't those white?

Well, two could play this game. He bent his sore back slightly, lifted his tail as a counterbalance, and reared up himself, his beak rising to almost half a charter unit above the ground. He opened his beak wide enough to swallow the beast whole and waved his huge claw-tipped leg at it.

It stood still for a moment, claws floundering dumbly in the air, then yielded the display contest with a high pitched grunt, dropped to a four legged stance, and bolted in apparent terror.

Drin rumbled with laughter for a moment, then froze as it scurried right into the cave.

"Mary!" he bellowed. "You've got company. Carnivore. Get your piece ready."

She screamed. There were low growls, but no explosions. Drin was on all fours immediately and galloping to the cave as fast as he could through the still wet alluvial sand. He roared a desperate challenge.

Mary screamed again, and her loud pure high note augmented by awful dissonant screeches from Do Tor and Go Ton. The carnivore wailed itself, as if in pain.

Then Drin was under the arch. He smelled blood.

The cave and the equipment were a mess. Soames was moaning; something was wrong with his arm. Then the thing turned to face Drin, and despite the difference in size, it charged him. Of course; he'd cornered it.

Drin whipped his tongue at it, branches curled into a heavy ball of cartilage and ligament, and hit it square in the head, sending it sprawling into the communications unit.

It had already been wrecked, Drin told himself, as he got his gun out of his pouch.

The thing was back on its feet and charging before Drin could bring the gun to bear. He couldn't snap his beak with his tongue out, and he was, just then, too off balance to hit it with a claw.

He tried to swing his open beak at it, missed, and it was under him, at his throat, biting incredible deep for its small mouth. Drin groaned in agony, but finally rocked back enough to raise a front leg.

Then it was over. The upper half of the carnivore slammed into the ruined comset again, as fur, bone, entrails, and general gore splattered everything else in the cave, including Mary, Theric Soames, Do Tor and Go Ton.

Drin gasped. He was pumping rivers of blood onto the cave floor from a throat artery.

He looked at Mary dumbly, thinking it might be the last time he would see her. She was busy, using only one arm, giving something to Soames. Do Tor had the vibrosaw. Mary grabbed the man's arm just below the joint. He looked at Drin as she held the torn stump out for what was apparently to be a crude surgery.

Drin tried to croak something, but Go Ton was talking to him trying to get his attention.

"Your ventral heart, Drin. Quiet it. They teach you how. Concentrate. Quiet it."

Yes. Think of deep, ice-cold water. Long endurance conditions.

"Good. Now, somehow, you have to stay on your feet while this mess I work on."

Somehow, in the cave's wreckage, Go Ton had found the medical kit. The Kleth waded through the visceral garbage to get under him. A spray numbed his throat.

Drin realized he was woozy with heat. The charge to the cave, the fight, short as it was, with the carnivore. But if he fell now he'd crush Go Ton.

Cold Deep Water . . . negative buoyancy, standing. Drin locked his leg joints under him and let every other part of him go distant and quiescent. He stood, he endured.

How long? The dead alien flesh scattered around was beginning to smell. Finally, tugs on his outer hide told him Go Ton was closing the wound. At the last, a spray and a feeling of tightness. Smart fiber artificial hide.

"Done now," Go Ton declared. "Be more careful. Not enough for a wound that big again. Can lie down now, Go Ton will work on Theric Soames."

Drin backed away from the gore and settled into the cool sand. Unconsciousness came quickly.

★ ✳ ✦

Do'utian medical treatment offers several unique challenges to human and Kleth care givers. Foremost of these is the sheer size of the dose needed to do anything to a Do'utian. The principal means of providing Do'utian internal medicine is to use secondary vectors, biologically engineered bacteria that, when introduced into the Do'utian bloodstream in a dormant form, revive, multiply and give off the appropriate drug as a byproduct. Dosage is controlled by the preprogrammed number of replications allowed to each bacterium.
—Planet Monitor's Handbook, Medical Appendix D

★ ✳ ✦

Drin watched Mary clumsily wipe the grease from her face with her right sleeve while holding a hunk of blackened meat. Go Ton had told him the two bones of her lower arm had snapped rather cleanly, and the surface wounds were deep punctures more than tears. With their limited medical facilities, recovery would be long and painful. For now, single branched Theric Soames was less disabled.

"Give it up, Soames," Mary argued. "I'll grant your ideals, but other peoples ideals count, too. It was a hard decision, and sorry it didn't go your way. But your conscience can't dictate to everyone else."

Soames now stared at the dirt. "I'm not ready to admit . . . betray anyone else. I set the bomb. I hoped it would at least scare people into delaying things long enough that the political people could force another vote. I didn't want to hurt anyone. I tried to save Sha Ton's life."

"Huh?" Mary said. "Sha Ton wouldn't have lived."

"No, maybe she *would* have lived, if this egg sinks." Drin replied, realizing after he spoke, that the Do'utian idiom he'd translated might not mean much to his fellow monitors. A fertile egg sinks. "Never mind. Do Tor, what do you know about the Kleth that died, Ko Kor and Sha Ton."

"Besides being victims, not much. Deaths obviously incidental to attack on project."

"If Kleth are mates from the beginning, wouldn't they be born at the same time? In the same weather?"

"Oh, yes." Go Ton answered

"Ko Kor's crest was notched, but Sha Ton's was smooth." Drin observed, "the implication being that they were not born at the same time or place, and thus not nestmates. But they were listed as nestmates. Why? And one had followed the other in death, like a nest mate. Why"

The heads of both Kleth snapped up in unison and stared at him. Go Ton's hand found her mate.

"You have seen what we could not." Do Tor finally said in an apologetic and formal tone, and in a respectful proper English that Drin was unaware the Kleth could speak, "We would never consider it because of our fear and denial of those few who do not share our first guilt. We shall check, but the records are very private. We shall need Council approval."

"Oh, yes." Go Ton chimed, very softly for her.

"Monitors," Drin rumbled. "I think Sha Ton's husband and sister are safe on Trimus, as were the brother and wife of Ko Kor. As parts of a triple, they would be expendable because they could die without killing anyone else, or continue to live if one or the other of them died."

"Oh, yes," Go Ton added. "And the conspiracy would keep their dirty little secret unless they betrayed the conspiracy. Lock in. Was too perverse for me, a Kleth, to think of. Observant, suspicious, Drin had to spot difference in crests. Rest is reason."

"Okay. I knew what they were, we were all part of it," Soames admitted, adding "I thought I could save her before whatever was happening set off the explosives."

Do Tor lifted his wings slightly, a Kleth indication of irritation.

"But she did not want to be saved," Do Tor stated. "She had something more important to do."

"The cages," Mary said, at last. "Canis lupus, big gray, and hungry. Ursus middendorfis. Of course, the biologists had to be in on it. Wolves, bears, sharks, all enhanced, and none of them part of the official bioforming plan. What about the nets?" Mary asked. "Something to cover up the evidence?"

"I think Soames gets credit for too much." Do Tor said in the low resonant tone that indicated Kleth contempt. "He didn't know about nets, he was in open when they fell. Could have been *his* head. If he knew Sha Ton not going to die for mate, he knew for what she *was* risking her life. So that's what he tried to stop."

"Damn you, I was trying to save her life, bird brain!"

"Monitors, remember. These are criminals! Cheat Charter; cheat Council; cheat each other too. Sharks keep Do'utians primitivists out, wolves and bears keep anti tech humans out. Leave world for Kleth. Sha Ton was a rebel all her life, and I think wanted a world safe for Kleth triples. You wanted world for humans and not Do'utians - so you planned to bomb the baby wolves and bear. But the nets came and Sha Ton saved them for her partners back on Trimus before the electrical fires set off the explosives—if she didn't do it herself to save the conspiracy and hide tripleness. In a way, with her death she fulfilled a destiny she evaded at hatching, and perhaps that is how she saw it.

"Also, Earth birds, per unit mass, have best brains in whole strange universe. Compliment accepted."

And deserved, Do Tor, Drin thought. But if Soames really didn't have anything to do with the nets, were they an accident? A wild card of fate. Or did someone back on Trimus know about them, someone placed highly enough to hide that knowledge and use it?

✱ ✵ ✱

We who founded Trimus had a reverence for the past and our own natures. Perhaps this was nostalgia, or ancestor love, or the sensing of a dead end in the ultimate quest of the genetic engineers to fix everything. If we were clever enough, we thought, we could show, by the three sentient species living together under a single law, that much of this change was unneeded; that we could preserve much more than others thought and still live at peace with one another. We knew we would have to work at it, but celebrated our common ability to act with reason over feeling. No one thought it would be easy, and we gloried in the challenge of these lofty heights.

—Go Zom's notes on the Compact of Trimus

✱ ✵ ✱

With Aurum again so near the horizon, sky was again blood red. It could not simply be the low sun, Drin thought; there must be a lot of dust in the air.

"A volcano somewhere?" he asked Mary as they walked toward the river.

She laughed. "Of sorts. Drin, you guys, you just don't think about consequences, because, most of the time, you're too big to suffer ordinary consequences."

"Consequences?" What did she mean . . . oh. "I see. Sea bottom turned to dust from the spacecraft explosion? Look, what would the consequences have been if I hadn't made a controlled detonation?"

Mary seemed to giggle and sob at the same time. "Controlled?"

"Well . . ."

"Drin, sometimes you just don't have very good judgment about things on my scale."

They had reached the generator wheel. Drin was moving very slowly now, and looked at the river below the wheel. There were fish in Do Tor's net, he hoped. He had to recover his strength, or the infinity in front of them might not last another day. The mission. Drin examined the transmitter; it's input line, which had been attached to the ruined modem back in the cave, was a standard connector. He had trouble thinking; were power supplies standard? If not, they should be.

"I think if we could connect the generator directly to the transmitter, we might be able to send a digital signal. On and off, by interrupting the connection."

Mary patted him. "I'll go back and salvage a connector so we can patch them. Meanwhile, maybe you can eat something?"

"If it swims into my mouth. Which is not that unlikely, if I put myself in the right place." He yawned in imitation of a cave, with his tongue, branches and hands as bait. Mary laughed, and then she was off.

Drin turned to the water and slid in. He had a moment of exhilaration as the weight left his legs. Freed from that demand on his energy, Drin's body fed more blood to his head. His back still ached, but days on land had left those particular muscles alone, and while they protested, a few easy movements started to warm them up a bit, and what had felt so devastating seven Trimus days ago now seemed a nuisance. He let himself drift downstream. He hunted. He ate.

The wolf smell hit Drin as soon as he hauled himself from the water near the transmitter. No more good feeling, his protein starved muscles burned with the pain of their reimposed burden. He should stay in the water for another day or two, but duty called.

He looked around. A large rock, maybe an eighth of a unit tall, stuck up from the sand about two thirds of the way from the cave to the river. The wolves were around it growling. From time to time the end of a large tree branch swung over it.

Mary? Drin pulled his gun out of his pouch, and felt a warning buzz along with the usual activation signal; only ten rounds left.

He keyed his comset, and got a warm up signal. Pollution! He hadn't turned it back on since the recharge - - too far gone, mentally, to check. It was on with checks complete in less than a beat, but that didn't do any good about the past. "Mary, I'm back. Is that you in the wolves?"

"Drin," her voice was shaky, "Drin, I'm out of rounds, but they don't know that, so they're being cautious.

"I'll try to get to you, but I can barely move."

"I don't dare run to you. First thing I show any fear and they'll be on me."

"Where are the Kleth?"

"Go Ton's looking for you. Do Tor's watching Soames. We got worried."

"Sorry. My comset was still on recharge. Do Tor, forget Soames, we need some firepower."

But it was Soames voice that answered. "Too late for Do Tor to forget me. And if Go Ton tries to help, I'll blow his head off."

Pollution! What had happened in there? At least Go Ton was, apparently, still alive. Best leave that problem to Go Ton when she returned.

"I'm coming, Mary. Not very fast, but I think I'll make it."

"Okay." She replied. Drin saw the stick jerk down and heard a yelp.

He heard wings overhead, and through his tongue out and made the monitor sign for silence. Go Ton alighted just ahead of him.

"Heard, Lieutenant," she said.

"Load trank; you'll have to take him. Good hunting."

"Loaded. Front door, full speed. Good hunting, Drin."

The Kleth leapt into the air and gained altitude. Eight charter units up, she stooped, buzzed the wolves surrounding Mary sending one yelping away, then headed for the cave mouth at a speed that only Kleth reactions could envision.

Meanwhile Drin got close enough to shoot at the wolves.

"Mary, I'm in range. Can you run?"

"Like a deer. Of course, that's breakfast for these things."

"If you can spiral in toward me instead of running right at me, that should keep you out of the finder range and give me a clear shot."

"Got it. Regards to Mom." She, Drin realized, didn't expect to make it either.

"Mary Pierce. For whatever it means, I love you too. Now run while I can still stand."

The stick descended once more, and this time Drin heard a howl. Then Mary sprinted from behind the left side of the rock. Three wolves were right after her.

In a fraction of a beat, Drin shot once, and one went down. But the others didn't seem to notice. He shot again, and a second went down but the third lunged at Mary's leg.

It got a shoe in its face, and a bullet before it could recover.

Four more wolves leapt over the bodies of the fallen.

Drin pressed the stud down and five rounds went before he released it. Three wolves down, one stumbled over the other two, and was joined by four more. Drin had two bullets left.

A roar of frustration left his throat, as he shot one, getting one wolf in the midst of a leap at Mary. Too close; the bullet could just as easily have locked onto her.

The wolves stopped and looked at him.

He roared again, this time putting a little anger in it, and stepped forward. One of them yelped, and they retreated, milling around, sniffing their dead.

Mary sprinted to about three charter units of him before the wolves realized Drin wasn't going to charge them. Then they came after her again. She tried to run faster and tripped, struggling though the soft, wet, sand. Drin moved, slowly painfully forward, but he was too far away.

Suddenly, for no apparent reason, one of the wolves screeched and started biting at its own rear leg, apparently biting it off entirely. The whine got the other's attention and they milled around yelping and sniffing bodies.

Something hissed in the sand beside Drin.

"Mary, NETS!"

"I hear," she gasped struggling toward him.

The front part of a wolf's head fell off, leaving a blood-spurting howling horror. Compassion used Drin's last bullet as Mary reached him.

"Get under me," he said and turned toward the river. His fight and flight glands were in full gear, but they had almost nothing to work with; his muscles were burning their own tissue, slowly. He felt a vicious sting on his back.

Mary scrambled under his head. The water was eight squared charter units away, the antenna, its mesh reflector an ironic reminder of what was falling on them was within six eights.

The mission. They should try to save it, the transmitter, and the generator.

The tip of his tail burned. Amputated.

"Mary, where do these polluting things come from?" he groaned as he staggered on.

The question was rhetorical, but to his surprise, she answered. "Not Trimus, we think. Do Tor took our sample apart while you were gone, with the med kit. They look grown, not designed. But it could be that's what we're supposed to think."

Another sting on his back.

"Are they dispensed? How do they move?"

"They're very light absolutely, but still much denser than air. They wouldn't reflect light like light sails, unless there was stuff between the membrane that burned off in aerobraking."

Four charter units to the equipment. A net brushed a leg, slicing deeply. He stumbled a bit.

"Watch it guy," Mary said, forced calm in her voice. "Uh, they could reflect radio waves, just like our mesh antenna. As long as the radio photons are bigger than the mesh openings."

Radio waves, like any other electromagnetic waves, exert pressure, Drin thought, and the nets were very light. And the mesh was actually about the same size as their antenna's.

"Do you still have the connectors, Mary."

"Yes."

They were at the equipment and the nets hadn't hit it yet. "I'm thinking we can levitate or deflect them with enough power."

"That sounds a lot better than me trying to carry this stuff with one arm. I'll try to get the flywheel going."

Drin's first reaction was the he should do that and she should make the connections. But on the end of his tongue, he had two hands available, and she didn't.

The lines to the cave; he would have to cut them sharply and cleanly to put them into his connector, but he didn't have a tool. He cast his eyes quickly around the machinery for anything he might use. There was nothing.

A net might do the trick, but ironically, there wasn't one handy just now. Or was there?

In his back.

He opened his beak and looked at his gun. It had a diamond barrel, with a raised fixture for attachments on the end. He bent around and looked at one of his fresh new scars, put the gun barrel in, pushed his flesh aside, then pushed the barrel down, in, twisted it and pulled it up again. It hurt, but not enough.

He did it again, and this time was rewarded with the feeling of having surgery without anesthetic. He couldn't help groaning in pain, but when it was done he could see, glinting in the horizon reddened light of the now-rising Aurum, the thread of a net.

He grabbed the output line, pulled what he hoped would be enough of it back from the direction of the cave, draped the collapsed net over the cable, and gently sawed back and forth.

It cut through the glass cord sheath like a diamond edged vibroblade, and he stuck the cleanly severed end into the connector. A net burned the top of his head slicing the sensitive area around his blowhole. Shaking, with weakness and pain, He repeated the procedure with the other cable.

"Mary," he called, "turn it loose!"

The wheel creaked, the generator telltales went on, the wheel went faster. Drin tried to think; power, lightspeed, the constant of To'ictillig, photon pressure—it all blurred.

A net hissed into the wet sand behind him. He moved nearer to the dish and looked up in to the gray, deadly, sky. Aurum peaked through the cloud cover again and its low golden glow caught a net glinting far above him. He backed away, but then noticed that it seemed to slide away.

He lost sight of it, but then saw a brief plume of steam where it must have hit the sand a charter unit away. He caught another brief plume further away. One hit the wheel and hissed.

"Drin, I think it's working," Mary shouted over the noise of the wheel. "The nets are avoiding us like we were in some kind of force field."

Drin lay down in the cool, wet, sand and started taking long deep breaths, too exhausted to even reply. Soames, Do Tor and Go Ton, the nets embedded in his hide and all the other problems; even Mary faded in relief. Safe for the moment, his body reclaimed him.

✶ ✺ ✶

A day later, Drin felt much better; his meal had worked its way to the rest of his body, Go Ton's trank rounds had easily subdued the slow moving and suprised Soames, Mary seemed her old self again, and Do Tor thought he knew what the nets were.

"The webbing is a thin diamond alloy tube only a few thousand atoms across," he said, "Not quite monofilament, but when it is very hot, it cuts almost as well"

"Oh, yes," Go Ton added as Drin grunted his own ironic concurrence.

"High temperature but not much heat," Do Tor continued. "Water, flesh, wet wood, and sand stop it in a doci or less. But it goes easily through bone, plastic, glass, composite. Nets receive, transmit, or reflect radio waves at fairly high efficiency, depending on what the nodes that connect the webbing do. Possibly Ember is radio-bright enough to push them away, so they don't fall on Trimus."

Net falls, Drin remembered, had occurred a few hours after use of high powered communications.

"Then," he speculated, "the deaths were not a crime at all, but an accident? They seem too convenient."

"Can't tell if they are artificial or naturally evolved, but they seek miniunit radio sources—what we use. They could be deliberately attracted."

"By who?" Drin asked. But it was becoming all to clear. All the threads had a common connection, one he wanted to reject, that he didn't dare voice.

Before anyone could answer his question Mary's comset beeped for attention. Who?

"Hello. Mary Pierce here, go ahead."

"This is Spacecraft *Trimus Compact*, on approach. Captain Loren speaking. You should see us shortly to the west. We have an ecological team, Councilor Olsen, and Gori'allolub aboard.

Drin's beak went to the sand at the omission of Gori'allolub's title. Whether the others noticed it or not, that immediately told Drin the worst of his fears had been confirmed. He would almost rather not be rescued.

They saw the spacecraft first, a tiny teardrop against the gray clouds. Then a single heavy sonic boom rattled back and forth from the cones of the nearby volcanoes. A slipstream roar followed the boom, and finally a crackling torrent as the spacecraft engines scaled up to full thrust, allowing it to settle gently into a billowing cloud on the sea beyond their river mouth.

★ ✷ ★

Macrovirus is a name applied to various self replicants which, absent anything sapients would recognize as intelligence or ability to communicate abstract ideas, nevertheless have evolved the ability to travel between stars and feed. Five are known to be spreading in this part of the Milky Way Galaxy, and only one poses a significant threat to a prepared population. But, in surprise, all are dangerous.

—Planet Monitor's handbook, Off-Trimus Section

★ ✷ ★

The great Do'utian, Gori'allolub, did not lower his beak, and presented himself with the presence of a beachmaster. That, Drin thought, presented a memorable contrast to the circumstances of his speech. In sadness Drin, lowered his own head as Gori'allolub spoke.

"So I must take full responsibility, and ask for gentle treatment of Theric Soames. I believe, and continue to believe, that transport to Aurum III simply delays confronting our problem and needlessly sacrifices an entire world. To do this in a way that flowed in the direction of strengthening the Compact required risking the lives of dedicated people, lest our network became known before it was too late. Now, I must make amends and attempt to do something that will allow the future to face the problem in accordance with the wishes of the majority of the Council, including my most intimate friend whom I have wrongly betrayed."

"Two Kleth dead, even if tripled," Go Tor spat, angry as Drin had ever seen him.

"Gori'allolub has resigned from the Council," Councilor Karen Olsen added, unsteadily, it seemed to Drin, "to take charge of the biological reengineering effort. Even though I supported resettlement, I should have recognized the depth of his opposition and done more to achieve real compromise. So I take some of the blame and am staying here with him until the job is done."

She gave a tight smile, and when she did so, her resemblance to Mary startled Drin. Most intimate friend, Gori'allolub had said, yet on opposite sides of a hard political question . . . was this possible? Drin's beak opened as he tasted the wind—as if he would find an answer there. And there was an Earth strangeness to Gori'allolub's smell.

"Now to more pleasant things," Karen Olsen nodded to Drin. "There is a Do'utian slot on the Council open. The Kleth and Human members have voted to nominate Monitor Lieutenant Drinnil'ib. I think there is little prospect that the Do'utian members will veto this."

"What!" Drin blurted, then quickly put his manners together, and touched his beak to Karen Olsen, "I mean I am honored. But politics? I do not swim in those currents."

The Councilor laughed. "None of us do, at first. But you have the needed dedication to the Trimus Compact and Charter, a far better education than most, and a considerable popular following from your, shall we say, exploits."

"Oh, YES," both Do Tor and Go Ton sang.

Drin dug his nose almost a doci into the sand trying to think of something to say.

Do Tor came to his rescue.

"Excuse. I assume we are now safe from nets, but would like more than assumptions."

Oh, yes, Drin thought.

Karen Olsen nodded. "Very safe. We saw what you did from our satellites, and have the spare Aurum III comm maser deflecting the stream to Aurum II for now."

"Why are they here?" Drin asked, "A macrovirus, I know. But using the term explains nothing."

"We think the nets were initially attracted by the electronic noise at the start of bioforming activity, almost a macroyear ago. Unfortunately, a scientist involved with resettlement opposition found the nets and saw a way to cover the tracks of the conspiracy. They kept the nets a secret and used Aurum III's satellites to lure them here."

"Knowing the Ko Kor, Sha Ton, and I would get killed?" Soames whined.

"Sacrifices are necessary burdens of office," Gori'allolub said. "You chose the risk."

"And our investigation?" Mary asked quietly. Drin could sense incomprehension in her voice.

"You," Gori'allolub stated, "were expected to be delayed, to discover the external threat too late, but not the conspiracy, nor to counter either threat quite so effectively. I badly underestimated your abilities, Drinnil'ib." Gori'allolub added. This time he did tip his nose slightly. "That all four of you would survive sabotage, three net falls and two antimatter containment loss events defies reasonable prediction."

The tone of Gori'allolub's remark suggested that Drin had done Trimus a disservice by staying alive. With a start, he realized that this must be just what Gori'allolub felt, and that below the reasoned discipline, the ex-Councilor smelled not unlike a bull chased from his harem.

"I meant you no personal harm," Drin hissed politely. "You assigned me to seek the truth."

"I asked you to quiet trouble waters, not roil them," Gori'allolub growled. "Now, I must apologize for putting myself above the Council. As I am sure you know, exile is an insufficient apology for causing useless deaths."

"Gori'allolub?" Karen Olsen asked.

Did Gori'allolub want lure Drin into beach combat? In his present weakness, Drin would surely lose and the huge Do'utian could eliminate the others by "accident!" Was that the problem with the other's smell? Had he taken chemicals to disguise such a challenge scent until too late?

"There is only one sufficient apology."

"No," Karen Olsen protested, "Time heals all such wounds."

"Silence." Gori'allolub snapped. There was a whiff of challenge, but Drin forced his beak down.

"I will not fight you, master." Drin stated, fighting down his own challenge instinct.

"Do not become too human, new Councilor." Gori'allolub hissed, "or you will lose the people's support. Think of Trimus as a tripod, not sphere mapped with three regular identical colored areas, and you will do much better. No, you do not smell disguised challenge. I have ingested chemicals that will sterilize any sharks that eat my flesh. Karen, if I have failed you, I did so for a higher loyalty; just as you failed to support me in Council for a higher loyalty. So our fun was meaningless. Now, I am going for a swim with the sharks that I helped to bring to this world."

With that Gori'allolub turned and began walking in a measured, dignified way, toward the river.

"Gori'allolub," Karen Olsen shouted, "No. You don't need the Council. I will love you here, give you joy. We can still swim together. Gori'allolub, you are my life!"

Mary stared at her mother, mouth gaping. Drin's head fell. So Gori'allolub himself had drifted in the same strange currents that tempted Drin. How little he really knew the great one. But he knew this much; now only the balm of the most hideous sacrifice would lay

Gori'allolub's pride to rest.

"He has no other choice, Councilor." Drin told Karen Olsen quickly, "to still be a Do'utian and honor his commitment to Trimus. Providence ends all life eventually; let him go now, in balance."

"Where is you medical kit," Karen quickly asked Go Ton, "show me the anesthetics."

Go Ton held the case open and indicated the row. There were hypos and dart gun ampules. Karen took one labeled "Do'utia: Male"

"Mary," give me your gun. Mary complied." Drin understood and made no move to stop her—it would make no difference to Gori'allolub's honor if others forced the pain blocker on him.

Karen loaded the gun, and gave it to back to Mary.

"You know what you're doing, monitor. Shoot."

Mary leveled it at the Do'utian's neck. The acquisition light blinked and she shot. The dart knew to find its way to that same area of thin hide that had caused Drin so much pain with the bear wound. Gori'allolub ignored it, but now he would be able to contemplate his dismemberment free from the distraction of pain.

Mary faced her mother.

"Mom, I understand. I wanted to tell you that I have been thinking of having the same kind of relationship with Drin. I don't understand, really, the fascination I have for it. But It's something really basic. I don't feel bad about it, and I think I can handle it. And let go if I have to."

Councilor Karen Olsen nodded and laughed in a way with which Drin was not familiar. Higher pitched, a different feeling. "After five centuries, Mary? You think you can handle it? Then consider this." She took a hypo tube from the open kit. Drin could read the label; general pain blocker, human. "It was a really fine perversion and I am not *quite* done with it." She stabbed her arm with the injector. "Wait, Gori. It is only my life at stake now, and I will not leave you."

The big Do'utian hesitated but a moment, then resumed his march to the sea, the sharks, and his completion. Drin understood. The old one was leaving all the affairs of Trimus, including Karen Olsen, behind him as a defeated bull leaves his harem to another without looking back. Should he say something?

"Mother," Mary cried, "you're not a harem cow or a Kleth mate! Human beings don't do that. How can we respect their identity if we don't respect our own?"

"You don't know, child." Karen Olsen snapped, and without a further word, fled after Gori'allolub.

It was a life versus a reputation, and Drin could not remain silent. "Councilor Olsen, he used you. He used you to get Mary's codes to try to endanger our lives. He used her communications with you to send the nets at us, twice. He's not worthy of this loyalty!"

At this, Gori'allolub did turn and roar in rage. Councilor Olsen stopped and backed away from the two Do'utian bulls. Drin's hearts began pumping at combat strength, and he took a step forward. So they would both die.

Then, with the slow majesty of one winning a hard fight with himself, Gori'allolub turned back toward the sea.

Karen Olsen looked at Mary, shook her head, and set out again after Gori'allolub.

"No!" Mary shouted and ran after the Councilor. Drin saw that Karen Olsen was too far ahead to be caught by her daughter.

But not by Drin. He shot his tongue out to its maximum length and just managed to wrap both branches around the fleeing human woman, who struggled briefly, then collapsed and sobbed in his grasp as Mary ran to her.

And with that one gesture, which he would remember for the eternity ahead of him, Councillor-to-be Drinnil'ib crossed the line from enforcing the choices made by others, to making such choices for them. He resolved that he would try to do so responsibly and reasonably, for Mary, for Do Tor and Go Ton, and for all the Trimusians in his wake.

THE TRIMUS CHRONICLES:
FINAL REVIEW

I have lived to see the language of a small, off-the-flightway, island on a most unlikely, high-gravity, thin-atmosphere, ultraviolet-blasted planet become the native language of beings whose ancestors came from normal worlds a hundred light years away. I have also seen Kleth base eight arithmetic replace the base twelve and base ten systems of Do'utia and Earth because it is reasonable. And I have seen our public architecture soar, of necessity, to Do'utian scale. So there is much that is unique, improbable and precious about Trimus! But that Trimus speaks English is what I think of whenever I fancy that the evolution of history follows any ordained pattern.
  —Go Zom's notes on the Compact and Charter of Trimus.

✳ ✳ ✳

It was all the Do'utian Councilman and Monitor Commander Drinnil'ib could do to keep his only slightly overweight mass of muscle and blubber calm on the reserved audience pad in the cozy, by Do'utian standards, Trimus University auditorium. Everyone had said that his "Memoirs of a Planet Monitor" was a solid, if unexciting, favorite for the non-fiction award, but his tail would grow no longer with a display of eagerness.

The Human master of ceremonies, Richard Moon, was a bright,

new, humorist with a bushy blonde mane around his head who'd won the non-fiction award last year. He, Drin remembered, won it for "The Flying Whale," an account of balloon-borne anthropologist Doglosha'idn's gargantuan adventures above the Kleth-settled outer pole of Trimus. Richard Moon was saying something intended to be funny, but Drin's attention was elsewhere.

His friend and frequent partner, Monitor Lieutenant Mary Pearce, sat on the edge of his pad, and playfully nudged his head back and forth to distract him. Was his agitation that obvious?

He nudged her back, gently. It would take six of the tiny humans, laid from foot to head, to equal his length. But in crowded places, she was much more mobile and, for her size, surprisingly strong. She moved his massive beak with relative ease—the genetic heritage of a high-gravity planet reinforced by the rigorous Monitor training regimen, Drin reflected, glad for something to distract his thoughts. The waiting was torture.

Mary's touch comforted him and, in an exotic way excited him. In the privacy of his mind, he let himself savor that. They both had open, curious, minds, a deep affection for each other having saved each other's lives more than once, and in the course of these years together—had touched in ways that more conservative Do'utians would find difficult to accept. His worries about this were getting increasingly easier to handle—but he was careful, very careful, on what he let beyond the beak.

Drinnil'ib had no wives, no beachhold, and played the rogue in Do'utian society—however, his people could easily smell the difference between his contentment and the unbeached bull looking for a challenge. Something, or someone, was filling that role in his life—and the scent of that made the Do'utian men he dealt with a little less defensive, especially those who fancied themselves minor beachmasters. His problem was with uncowed Do'utian women who hinted from time to time that they wished to join his nonexistent harem. Drin avoided mating however, having had nothing but bad experiences in that part of live. If his feelings for Mary helped him avoid that, so be it. It was a private matter.

At last the crowd hushed and the award presenter, noted critic and personality Zo Kim glided in over them and settled with what passed for dignity in a Kleth—a couple of precise beats with his jet black wings and a firm two point landing with barely a hop. He was alone—a Kleth that liked to live on the edge. By reports, his mate, Bi Tan, was still on the outer pole, working on her next romance. She was well known for not carrying a comset, for reasons both Kleth and writers might understand.

Highly agitated, Zo Kim approached the master of ceremonies.

Moon wasn't laughing now, though. In fact, as far as Drin could tell, the human looked honestly horrified. Was he refusing to give the presenter the envelope? Drin stifled himself—that might be *his* award. Zo Kim's review of Drin's book had been scathing, as had been his review of Moon's. The stylistic pollution of this posturing pundit had been tolerated by the community because he could read so much, and at least distill the current of content with some accuracy between ill chosen adjectives. After two centuries, toleration had become a kind of grudging, institutional, respect. Perhaps Moon, despite his demeanor, was simply tweaking the tail of the too-pompous critic.

"You know, and I will know *now!*" Zo Kim shouted at the human, lifting himself off the stage with a flap of anger to be head high with the human.

Cut the comedy, Drin thought, *I want to know too!*

"Very well," Moon answered, barely audible, his posture one of defeat, not challenge. What, Drin wondered, was wrong? "It is your right to know. I was told of Bi Tan's end by . . . someone I trust, I did not see it myself, but . . . I have no reason, myself, to doubt the report. But that, of course, does not mean the report is true. There may be a mistake. Zo Kim, I suggest you don't be convinced without seeing the body."

"You try to hide this from me just so that I can live long enough to present an Award? For some mediocre Monitor's stinking salacious pandering sadography?"

Sadography? Okay, Drin thought, so he hadn't pulled any punches about the time a primitivist harpoon had gone through Mary's leg into his back. Occasional violence was a fact of monitor life, but something totally outside the experience of most citizens of Trimus, and he had not quite been prepared for either the reaction, both in interest and in vituperation. But, wait a minute—had Zo Kim just said that he'd won? The tip of Drin's tail lifted off his mat in anticipation.

Zo Kim snatched the envelope from poor Moon's hand, tore it three times with the incredible quickness of the Kleth, and threw the pieces like so much confetti out from the stage. Now Drin was on his feet, hearts both pounding. Pollution! Why this? The hall resounded with rumbles, whistles, and gasps.

Then, in one horrible second, Zo Kim's behavior made sense to Drin, like the sonic image of an iceberg resolving itself right in front of him where he'd been expecting a school of fish. Bi Tan's end? Someone had just told Zo Kim that his mate had died. In the Kleth and their close relatives, the death of a mate triggered an involuntary, emotional loss-driven process where by the remaining mate could both defend and feed its young, for a day or two. It happened whether they had young or not—Kleth were mated for life from hatching and could not mate again. It was as if the two were one organism, but in Zo Kim's case . . .

"Drop dead!" a human voice yelled. Someone else probably hadn't figured it out, yet. Drin located the voice - a black-bearded man, short even by human standards, but stocky and strong looking. Gorman Stendt—Drin knew him by reputation: an author of heroic human space adventures who illustrated them with intricately detailed working models of imagined alien technology, working aircraft, war machines, cities and space stations, all rendered at micro scale and floated or crawled around you as you listened to the narrative. He had an unlinked cybernetic system at his farm, eight-squared macrounits out of Trimus City, so each new work was a genuine surprise. His manners, Drin surmised, must have suffered from his isolation.

Zo Kim had recently excoriated Stendt's historical novel concerning the first Kleth-Human contact as chauvinist, over detailed, and boring. Its length was over four dimacrobytes and Drin had not had time to experience it yet—so Zo Kim may have been right—not that that mattered anymore.

Drin touched his beak to his mat. This was tragic. And suppose the Zo Kim's information was wrong? Or worse—false? Drin's professional interest was triggered by the thought, and he fixed an eye on Richard Moon. Pretending to be reluctant? He discretely slid his tongue out of the corner of his mouth, slipped a branch into his ventral pouch and triggered the alert on his comset. Mary, Do Tor and Go Ton, and any other monitors present would feel the low frequency signal and start paying attention, if they weren't already.

"You and your spies and your claque can drop dead!" Stendt yelled at Zo Kim, still apparently ignorant of what was happening to him.

"Right on!" a Do'utian woman added.

"Shut your beak!" another human yelled—Drin couldn't tell if at Zo Kim or his detractors.

This shouldn't happen here, in public, like this—a spectacle utterly at odds with the Compact's goal of interspecies amity. Perhaps he could delay Zo Kim's demise—move it out of view.

"Silence!" Drin finally roared."Zo Kim, things may not be what you think! Hold onto that thought. You are not complete, you and Bi Tan have things to do. At least let the monitors investigate this rumor—you have enemies. It may be a lie, and if you let yourself believe it, you'll kill her, too."

The whispers hushed, as from perches, chairs, and pads, the audience realized what was about to occur. Stendt and the others, Drin thought, would wish to call their words back the rest of their lives—for drop dead was what just what Zo Kim was about to do.

The Kleth leapt to the podium in a single bound, already visibly trembling. The need for a Kleth to die when his or her mate died, and whatever assistance he or she is given, was normally a very private matter, not a public spectacle. But there had never, ever, been anything normal about Zo Kim.

"No, you phony. I know, now, that Bi Tan is really dead," Zo Kim declared, shaking with an almost manic intensity. "Richard Moon is incapable of credible fantasy."

Despite everything, a scattering of dry spouts, laughs, and chatters filled the hall. Zo Kim would go out like Don Giovanni, Drin decided. Unrepentant.

But Zo Kim had a surprise even there. "I suspected for days now, but hung on in the balance as my body prepared itself—it will end quickly now. Well, everyone, whatever little merit she had as a mate or an author matters not now. Bi Tan was mine and, observe everyone, my destiny is to go with her." Zo Kim's wings raised in an unbalanced, almost involuntary spasm. He would not fly again. "I note that while there are a di-oct and one of Bi Tan novels, there are none of Zo Kim. So she will fly higher in history despite my superior wit and literary sense. What irony!"

Zo Kim's head jerked from side to side. The Kleth's wings went out and in, restlessly. "What irony! My body has begun to prepare itself to feed the nestlings we never had because of Bi Tan's career. It is now far too late for me to join the debate about engineering this out of our species, so please watch the effects for a while with whatever curiosity you may possess." Zo Kim gave a horrid little cackle, both high and low pitched. "Become edified as I become putrefied! Consider it as performance art! I will have my fame, too!"

Did self-digestion trigger self-loathing? It might make some evolutionary sense, Drin thought, as an abandonment of all urge to self preservation. With such analytical thoughts, he tried to put some emotional distance between himself and the awful thing happening in front of him.

"Yes, friends, it looks painful and it is," Zo Kim continued, his dry intellect seemingly unaffected by what was happening to his body, "but the pain is curiously comforting. Drinnil'ib, you sterile, clinical, mannered, murder detective: look, learn, and put a little sense of horror of this in your next one. Eh?"

Drin rocked forward on his four powerful webbed claws digging into his pad, speechless now.

Zo Kim's wings snapped in and out, and his head back and forth. "What a show, everyone! But I am getting bored now. Will someone help me end this? Someone with a little style? Do Tor and Go Tan, your execrable contributions to Drinnil'ib's mindless horror at least had the minor virtue of being interesting. Would you? Please?" This was followed by some almost intelligible Kleth dialect.

Drin rolled an eye toward Kleth Monitors Do Tor and Go Tan, frequent collaborators in real life as well as popular history. In fiction, Go Tan swam in the currents of classic Kleth air-battle, sounded in multilevel free-verse, and had achieved some minor success, at least in terms of the number of downloads from the Trimus net. Enough success, it seemed, to attract Zo Kim's withering attention.

Go Tan, characteristically ignoring her own treatment at Zo Kim's beak, had earlier fumed to Drin about the extremity of personality defect required for a Kleth to be personally rejected by even its own mate. Even being apart for a few hours was risky for Kleth; living apart was a fatalistic, almost nihilistic, act—and Drin was seeing the results of it now.

Do Tor, seated with his bright yellow mate, had been silent about Zo Kim's dying insults, but now he lit about half a charter unit from the dying critic and came no closer.

"Calm down, Zo Kim. Shouting and fighting makes it faster and worse. You need to clean your nest one last time. Could you say something good about The Last of the Air first?"

"No!" shouted Zo Kim, his crest snapping erect.

Do Tor simply stood there. Kleth had different feelings about suffering. And death.

By the compact, Drin thought, Do Tor had reason to let Zo Kim suffer, but this was unseemly—the Kleth monitor was cutting his tail for a transitory revenge. How long was this going to go on? There were tales in legend of Kleth who had, by force of will, lasted as long as a Trimus week. Drin slipped his tongue out the corner of his beak and down into his ventral pouch. The hand on the left branch of his tongue found his gun and changed the load by feel—self guiding darts, short ones for Kleth. He could double check the gun's audio display in a second when he had it out.

No, it wouldn't do. Zo Kim was alone on the stage, and he could probably lock on from here and deliver the euthanasia—but probably wasn't good enough in a crowded room.

"Mary," Drin said softly. "Get your piece. It wouldn't look—right— if I did it."

Mary nodded and raised her many-curved body with ever-fascinating, seemingly boneless fluidity. She drew her gun from her belly kit, loaded the nerve poison clip, and sprinted toward the stage. She seeming almost to fly, though her feet had to strike the aisle every half charter unit or so.

But Zo Kim himself broke the impasse. "I can't say anything good about it, Do Tor, because I haven't read it! Have mercy—I cannot fly. Look, the stage below me is stained! Isn't that interesting, everyone? I am leaking! I am becoming very digestible, right before your eyes!"

Someone actually laughed—indigestible was a word Zo Kim often used to great effect in his critiques. He was clearly in agony with this morbid not-pain, but his brain would be the last thing affected, and he would probably be able to critique the process almost to the last, cutting and ironic as if by some unconscious mental reflex. Drin shuddered.

A putrid smell reached Drin. How long, he thought, could we, the arguable intellectual elite of three species who together have traveled the stars long enough to reach halfway to the core of the galaxy, sit here and watch this?

Finally, Do Tor acted—apparently, the lack of a negative review was enough. With breathtaking quickness, his mouth was at Zo Kim's offered throat. The latter shuddered, made one last reflexive flap of his mottled brown wings, and was still.

Mary reached the stage as someone belatedly told the curtains to close, and over her Monitor's comset Drin heard Do Tor say, softly, "Tastes very sweet."

"Richard Moon," Mary called. Yes, of course, Drin thought as the fog of horror lifted from his brain, standard procedure called for an interview with whoever told a Kleth that their mate was dead, though obviously it had been the last thing Moon had seemed to want to do.

The shocked audience started, on its own, to leave their seats, pads and perches for the clean air outside, as silent as the dead themselves. Death was rare on Trimus, and when it happened it was almost always a fatal accident in some remote area, or the very private suicide of someone who had come to feel their time in the universe was complete. But this was unprecedented—the most private moment one could imagine of sentient being turned into an awful public spectacle. An accident? Zo Kim was unloved, but this? Who would wish this on anyone?

"Richard Moon?" Mary repeated, somewhat louder.

Now Drin was fully alert and looking around the room. Their erstwhile master of ceremonies was nowhere to be seen. Drin's award, if indeed he had won, was so many scraps of paper polluting the stage in front of the curtain and the first row of empty seats. Why? In the name of the Compact, why?

★ ✳ ★

In an example of the theory of random evolutionary drift, the style of technology on all three worlds developed filigrees well beyond the requirements of survival, some being inexplicably weird to members of the other races. To make Trimus work; to have common meeting grounds and shared cultural endeavors, we had to go back to basics in our common forums. Also, what would the point of having the three species cohabit a world if they were engineered and constrained by their technology to the point where they were no longer the three species? So, Trimus city was designed to be simple and almost ascetic even by their current standards. Use of robotics was strictly limited, transportation within city limits is by foot or wing, and buildings were designed to stand on their own, without requiring active support elements.

　　　　　—Go Zom's notes on the Compact and Charter of Trimus.

✴ ✳ ✴

Drinnil'ib's Trimus City office smelled of the sea, as well it should—a deep pool took up the western third of the hexagonal room and connected to the main canal. That, in turn, looped through city from the North Sea from Miller's Beach to Dori bay, carefully arranged to let the Zom current which impinged on the bay flow through and keep it clean. Clean, neat, ordered.

Not ordered enough, Drin thought. He grabbed a crate of pollution effects samples from the misnamed protected regions of the south and moved it from under the main wall screen to the storage shelves and made a note to turn it over to Do Tor and Go Ton—he would have to delegate more and the Kleth monitors were more naturally suited to monitor the pollution of these ad hoc human settlements in the protected region. He grunted. Some protection they had given them— crawling now with human primitivists and Do'utians playing old time beachmaster.

He noted the mother of pearl century plaque with its silver 144 on the wall—a human decimal word for a Do'utian's milestone rendered in Kleth base eight. It was in itself a symbol of the principles of Trimus he held sacred.

The office had been his for over a century, since he'd risen from Monitor to Monitor Lieutenant. He'd stayed there as he was promoted to Monitor Captain, and finally elected to the Trimusian Council and given the Monitor portfolio with the title of Monitor Commander. A human might have requested a larger office, or a Kleth a higher one. But for him, his length of tenancy of this artificial beach was a psychological reward. It would take a bomb to move him. Unfinished business was stuck in the corners, some of which was probably as old as his occupation of the office. It would have to remain unfinished for a few more weeks, he realized. Pollution! That mess on the awards stage was contaminating everything in his life.

The ceilings were as high as he was long—high, almost a charter unit, and the arched windows in the southern three walls let in plenty of light during the day. But the surpassingly clever aspect of the office was that the southeast windows faced Ember directly, and its infrared glow fell on photovoltaic panels on the northwest wall, powering the office and the human offices above him. Those were much smaller, though still big enough to allow two Do'utians to visit in reasonable comfort.

Luxuriously spongy soft living carpet covered the entire room—no need for pads here—and it even ramped down into the sea door. Maybe he should go for a swim. Get some exercise. Write his reports with the currents cooling his brain, and download them later. He looked longingly at the sea water.

Someone was coming—he wasn't really sure how he knew. Perhaps his subconscious recognized a change in the pattern of ripples in the sea door. But such a small disturbance . . . a child? No, a human woman broached the surface, and gracefully pushed herself up with her forelegs to the normal, for tailless humans, upright sitting posture. She opened her sea mask.

"Mary!" Of course. Doing things the Do'utian way as much as she could, to surprise and please him. Humans typically used the corridors, not the sea doors. But Mary loved being atypical. They'd been acquaintances for almost two centuries and partners for the last two-eights.

"Surprise! I just finished checking out a sub," Mary said as she pulled off her flippers. "Mom says Gori'allolub is concerned about Zo Kim's death."

Drin dipped his beak in respect to the Council President. The fact that the case had the Long One's attention made it all the more urgent. That Mary's mother, Councilor Karen Olsen, was playing an active role in affairs again was also good news—she shared her daughter's inclination toward his species, and, over decades, became too attached to one whose honor had come second to other loyalties, and she had been devastated for years by the former long one's belatedly honorable death. Did Mary, at her core, understand the difference between a useful partnership, and human mating, or the Do'utian beach, for that matter.

"Does that make sense?" Mary continued, "Surveillance will turn him up sooner or later."

"A murder," Drin rumbled, anguished, "may have been committed in plain view of eight cubed people, including you and the Councilman Commander of Monitors, and us just lay there like beached gluttons! Yes it makes sense! Besides," he waved his tongue at the evidence boxes, "I don't seem to be able to get anything else accomplished with this cow unbirthed!"

Mary giggled. One of the things that made her an easy partner was that she didn't mind Do'utian beach language—there were a few human female monitors that, once they understood it, felt offended. And as for the few Do'utian women in the monitor force . . . Drin shuddered and lowered his beak at the thought. Many of those felt he was getting too familiar with Mary—to the point of compromising his position. But as long as they were discrete, most people didn't object.

"So I've got the sub ready," she said, back to business. "The connection with Richard Moon seems to be with the Do'utian writer,

Gonikli'ibida. Which suggests we head North."

Drin's head came up at the name. She was a relative, and not all that distant.

"She's a mutual friend of both Bi Tan and Richard Moon—to judge by the number of collaborations in the data base, and she was working on a the second volume of a collaboration with Bi Tan on the weapons industry of primitivists."

Drin nodded. A significant number of bored humans had fled the north to live "primitive" lives in natural reserve lands and waters in the south. One group had fallen into a dictatorship under a "Lord Thet" who seemed to have empire in mind and was busily trashing all the environmental restrictions and reinventing the wheel of human history. It was not surprising that a conservative Do'utian like Gonikli'ibida and a radical Kleth like Bi Tan might find common cause in documenting "Lord Thet's" efforts and their dangers.

An effort to exile Thet and his followers to a freshly bioformed world in the Aurum system had run afoul of outraged biologists and conservatives who had deliberately sabotaged the ecosystem of the new world to make it dangerous for settlement by primitivists. Drin had played a leading and ultimately tragic role in overcoming the conspiracy, but the ecological damage had been done, and any resettlement program was octades in the future. Meanwhile human Monitor agents were trying, with mixed success, to attrit the colony voluntarily. Meanwhile Thet was out of control, restrained only by threats of violence that, occasionally, had to be validated.

"Yes," Drin added, "I know they were having a hard time with getting editorial support because of how Zo Kim panned the first volume for being too wishy-washy and boring." With some justification, Drin thought—he'd read the first volume. But the word had to get out somehow.

"I have a hard time with that." Mary shook her head. "A Kleth publicly deriding his mate's work."

Drin nodded. A "Kleth Divorce" was common vernacular for any mutually destructive parting of the ways. "Zo Kim found pollution in *everyone's* work. So if it's murder, and Zo Kim's reviews are the motive, we'll have literally a million suspects, given how long Zo Kim has been cutting away at people's artistic efforts."

"Yeah. Well, anyway, I'd rather pursue *that* lead than try to locate Bi Tan."

Drin nodded slowly; the body of Zo Kim's mate had not been recovered—indeed, she might be still alive, working away in isolation, unaware that her mate was dead. If so, the approach to her would have to be sophisticated—and delayed as long as honorably possible.

One didn't run up to a solitary Kleth and spout "We've been looking all over for you! Uh, . . ."

Drin had no desire to view a repeat performance of Zo Kim's death. If Bi Tan were still alive, the Kleth would handle it, in privacy, with dignity.

Drin had attended the death of a fellow monitor whose mate had been killed in the line of duty with Do Tor and Go Ton. They silently offered him a drug to lessen the initial shakes, and left him alone in his office to close the couple's affairs. A few minutes later, he'd invited the group back to say his farewells, and nodded to Do Tor. The Kleth were so intelligent that one sometimes let float loose the fact that they lived twice as close to death as a human or Do'utian, and had attitudes toward sacrifice, pain, and the eating of flesh that were so *different*, that the other two species instincts sometimes seemed mere variations on the same theme.

Handled properly, Bi Tan, if still alive, could make whatever statements she needed to make painlessly, finish her business, and depart with her dignity intact.

But Gonikli'ibida came first. The outward subservience of an intelligent Do'utian female was a fragile behavioral artifact, founded as much on fear as biology. Given a cause, a Do'utian woman could do anything to achieve her ends; however horrible, anything. It was their saying that the cow defends her children not to her death, but to yours. Gonikli had no children—but she was an author.

"It's an old Do'utian family," Drin said. "Relatives of mine. Their place is on the south coast of Droni island, near the Innil Glacier. Actually, it's not far from my birthplace. My sister lived with them. Part of . . . Doglaska'ib harem." By a face-saving formal arrangement only, Drin added to himself. Memories. His sister Bodil'ib had died in a fall on the glacier, almost eight-squared years ago, of a broken back and internal injuries before adequate help could reach her. He'd learned about it while at Monitor training. Officially, her life had been incomplete and she had struggled, courageously, against the end. Her life was less incomplete than most knew.

He hadn't been there for her. He'd mated, imprinted, then denied it and left as if he were a human. It had seemed so reasonable, so *Trimusian*, at the time.

"Are you feeling okay, Drin?" Mary asked.

★ ❋ ★

Trimus orbits tide-locked to the brown dwarf, Ember, that supplies half its insolation. The other half is supplied by the K2 primary, Aurum, about which Ember, its associated satellites, and the Trojan worlds revolve at five and a half Trimus light-minutes' distance. Trimus' atmospheric pressure was engineered to be similar to that of Do'utia and Kleth, about one and a quarter that of Earth. Average

surface temperatures range from one and an eighth times the freezing
point of water on the inner pole to just over freezing at the outer pole.
It has extensive icecaps and continental masses at the east and west
poles. Random volcanic isles and impact crater rims spot its oceans.

The north polar area of Trimus is dominated by an ice cap,
partly over a number of large, volcanic islands and partly over sea.
Volcanoes are more common in the north due to the thinness of crust,
a product of tidal distortion as well as the complex orbital resonance
involving Clinker (Ember's third major satellite) and distant Aurum
that results in Trimus' one-sixth-radian libration. A volcanic island
arc circles the ice cap at the top of the inner hemisphere, well north
of the Trimus arctic. Following bioforming, a north flowing current
became established which moderates the climate along this arc—the
seas there are usually free of heavy pack ice.
　　　　—Planet Monitor's Handbook, Planetology supplement.

✶ ✹ ✶

The Polar Sea was Drin's element. As the temperature dropped his
metabolism increased and he brought his sustained speed up to half a
charter unit per beat. Northward, northward. Mary's submarine kept
pace beside him. Now and then he would sound deep, turn and fling
his tail at the water five or ten times until he had to shut his eyes against
the slipstream. Then with one mighty, convulsive twist, he'd broach
like a rocket, shooting almost two charter units above the wavetops.
From there, he'd scan the horizon for signs of food or distant land.
Then he could either knife into the water to pursue a fish normally too
fast for him to catch, or slam flat on the surface, scouring the parasites
from his hide.

His monitor comset, of course, could tell him exactly where he
was—but that didn't feel like seeing for himself. His was a spacefaring
race and hungered for the wide view as well as the deep.

Once, just to show her submarine could do it too, Mary followed
him into the air, using its buoyancy tank exhausts like jets to nose it
over smoothly into the water.

It was on one of these leaps that he saw the wind ship; a cloud of
sails scudding north.

Once they were under water, he let loose several blasts of sound
and watched the sonic image of the water-air interface shimmer as the
parts of his brain that actually "saw" interpreted the sonic information
gathered by his ears. There was an oval bump about eight cubed
charter units east of them. A check with the locator aerostat showed no
electronics at that position. A renegade whaler? This far north?

"Mary, look out for a primitive ship almost due east of us, possible
poacher, about point four. No comset, or any electronics."

"Roger, I have it at point-three-seven pi radians from north. Small single hull, just under two charter units. Wide beam. I don't think it's a whaler, Drin."

"Lets hope not." He and Mary both still bore scars from an unlucky harpoon shot from an earlier encounter with a ship from Thet's south polar sea colony. Ignored by Trimus' mainly complacent civilization of philosophers, recreationalists, and artists, it had recruited disaffected, hostile, or bored humans until it had become a behavioral problem. He and Mary had been given the job of cleaning up one of its nastier messes—humans hunting Do'utians with harpoons. "But we'd better check it out."

"Let me lead, guy. Stay out of range, okay?"

As their relationship had progressed, Drin found Mary, more and more frequently, talking cow-to-calf. It was something they would have to discuss—sometime later. Despite the minor humiliation, her suggestion made sense, particularly since some of these primitivist humans would resist non-human monitors. But he had a suggestion of his own.

Pollution! Make that an order—he was senior.

"Mary, out of range shall be about a charter unit under the ship for me—and relay your voice through your sonar—I can handle the frequency shift. And you stay in the sub! They can see you easily enough through your canopy, and it's solid diamond, which you are not. Also, let's get Do Tor and Go Ton involved now."

A macrobeat later, as Drin and Mary paced the ship below its horizon, the Kleth's contrails traced a white vector toward their destination.

"Weapons not visible," Do Tor sent, with an "oh, yes" echo from his mate. "But two decks likely below what we see."

"You stay in the aircraft, too." Drin sent back. "No heroics."

"Roger, stay in aircraft. Heroics depend on situation."

Any other monitors would be treating him with beak-dragging deference—a danger in this situation. But Mary, Do Tor and Go Ton had been through too much with him to be awed by his new status; they'd spout before he wandered onto the wrong beach, thank providence! Two turns of Trimus ago, Drin thought, I was waiting to receive a literary reward. Chaos and pollution!

"Ready when you are," Mary sent.

"Let's go in," Drin ordered, vacated his lungs in a big steamy cloud, then sounded deep and headed toward the ship at an energy spendthrift charter unit a second, his undulating tail and body shoving water efficiently and purposefully behind him. He closed his eyes to protect them from the pressure and relied on the deeper, but fuzzier audio image, illuminated as much by the noise of Mary's submarine as by chirps of his own voice far above the range that she could hear.

They were below the small ship in minutes. Drin stuck a hand out of his beak and gave her an okay sign, and watched her sub shoot toward the surface.

Mary hit them with her loudspeakers. "Sailing vessel, this is Monitor Lieutenant Mary Pearce. You are unregistered and in an ecologically sensitive area. Be advised that hunting large life forms is prohibited in these waters, and that I have back-up immediately available. Please state your business."

Mary's use of her rank surprised Drin. Was this the same woman who, three years ago, had undertaken an interrogation in the tropics by walking up to another human completely naked and saying, essentially, "Hi, I'm Mary." Well, she swam in colder waters now. As they all would until the council decided what to do with the primitivists—and, somehow, did it.

"Mary Pearce?" the response came. "Should have known that by the way you ran that ship of yours up to me, lee side, smart and pretty. Yohin Bretz a Landend. Harbor pilot, 'till Lord Thet decided his mistress's brother should have the job. Got this as a consolation prize."

Drin released a bubble with his tension. This rustic human sailor had guided them through the harbor on their first eventful visit to Thet's city state, and lived there all his adult life. In spite his wildly different values concerning technology and sentient relations, Yohin had been a competent professional with a sense of his duty. Drin wondered how many of these wooden ships might get stuck in the polluted mud flats of that choked river delta Thet used as a harbor and a sewer, now that Yohin was no longer on the job.

"Yohin!" Mary cried out with relief. "Tell me you're not poaching, please."

"Not poaching a thing, don't think so anyway. We take enough fish to eat. Small ones—nothin' the size o' your fish man friend. Say, he your backup today?"

Rustic, but no idiot at all, Drin thought, laughing to himself. Still, he stayed under the boat, hiding his chirps in the random ocean noise while slowly building up a sonar image of the lower decks. Cabins it seemed. No metal in contact with the hull.

"Now there, Yohin!" Mary laughed. "I'm supposed to ask the questions. No guns on board?"

"Got a rifle. Another consolation prize from Lord Thet—after what you folks did to his guard, he decided to get a little more advanced. Shoots good, too. Don't think it would bother the fish-man though, and I've got other ways of catching fish. Hell, the way Lord Thet's going he'll just be another Trimus city in less than a century."

Drin had heard and seen enough below, it was clearly a passenger vessel. He flicked his tail and, rounded the hull, then slammed the ocean aside twice and shot two charter units out of the water. The decks were clear of anything suspicious as well. He dove in and surfaced beside Mary taking care to minimize the splash.

The humans seemed to appreciate his athletic show—they were pointing and some of them clapping. At the rail of the ship was the lanky, thatch haired human male he remembered; the man made a motion with his head that might have been surprise, or a greeting.

"Mr. Bretz a Landend, Councilor Drinnil'ib, Commander of Monitors." He pitched his voice low to carry clearly through the sea noise and the walls of the vessel.

"Well met, Commander. Impressive jump there. Getting used to you folks now."

"How so."

"Running tourists out of Trimus City since I left Thet. And, Lieutenant Pearce, I am registered—but I left the gadget on the dock. This is wood, wind and sail here, no compromises."

Mary laughed. "Drin, I don't think they're any threat to us. Yohin, do you still have slaves?"

"Yeah, but they can't be slaves up here, so they're crew. Recruited some more. Look up in the riggin'"

Drin looked too. A human, heavily clothed, waved down at them. Did he remember the face from their adventure at Thet? Do'utian's didn't forget, he told himself, that was what all the extra brain mass was for. But connecting memories in real time was something else— and he'd gotten a lot of patterns stored in his two gross of Trimus years. Then he looked at the side of the ship. It had two eights of ports all along the deck below the top deck, and there was a human face in every port but two—and those were Kleth! The ship was loaded with tourists! He even recognized some of the people from the awards event—Gorman Stendt's black beard and the wild red hair of Nelle Yvle, the humorist. How embarrassing!

"Mr. Bretz a Landend," Drin rumbled, "Next time, take that one polluting gadget with you. Then we can get to you if you need us, and we won't bother you when you don't."

"Look, fish ma—Commander. That's like being half pregnant. When *I* say I'm wood, wind and sail only I mean—hey, Mary Pearce what are you doing?"

Mary had emerged from the hatch behind her canopy and was pointing a marker gun at the wooden vessel. Drin barely heard the snap above the sea noise, but he saw the dart planted just above the waterline.

"You're marked now, Yohin," Mary shouted. "I've tagged you with a transponder, and your customers can't arbitrate because it's not your fault."

Yohin scowled and shrugged.

"By the way, where are you headed?" Mary added.

"Hot Springs Island. Landfall tonight, if we don't have any other delays." Yohin replied, ignoring the dart. The volcanic island was about midway from Trimus City to their destination.

Drin's ear comset tone sounded. The Kleth wanted to speak to him.

"Hot Springs Island was last place Bi Tan seen," Do Tor told him. "Writer's colony there."

Interesting. Bi Tan with Richard Moon, Gonikli, Gorman Stendt, Yohin and his primitivist crew. But knowing where a Kleth had been seen two eights of days ago was about as helpful as knowing where a cloud had been. Kleth were naturally prone to flit wherever they pleased, and eight to the eighth years ago they had developed aircraft to do it farther and faster. Bit Tan or her body could be anywhere on the planet or in nearby space. Gonikli would be much easier to find.

"Good to see you again, Mr. Bretz a Landend," Drin said. "We'll be on our way now." Drin sounded without further ceremony and resumed his course northward.

He was soon joined by Mary's submarine. "What's bothering you?" she asked.

"Memories," Drin answered. "Of several kinds. From recently, and . . . from my youth. I'd rather put you in their wake until I understand them better myself."

Mary looked at him and put her hand on the inside of her canopy. Drin slowed and sent his tongue to her, grasping the plastic with the hand on the right branch while pressing the hand on the left against the canopy opposite her. He felt her warmth through that. Sometimes, words were not needed.

✶ ❋ ✶

The culture of Trimus should be looked on as a three-legged stool, not a mystical fusion. The three intelligent species maintain their separate identities under and supporting the overall planetary unity, as codified in the Compact and Charter of the Planet Trimus.

✶ ❋ ✶

"Drin, it's—it's awesome."

The Ib family complex was built on a great beach of black gravel now well above the tide line.They were approaching from the north, and the banded half-disk of Ember, lit gold by distant Aurum, rose a quarter of the way to the zenith over the snow-capped volcanic cones behind the great Do'utian domes as if it was just another, greater, dome. Mary rode on Drin's neck, holding on to the thin, but virtually indestructible, decorative sash that Drin wore to show his office. On this beach, for politeness' sake, everyone's status should be clear.

Drin nodded. By ancient Do'utian standards, the Ib family estate buildings were respectable, but hardly awe inspiring. But, excepting some of the government buildings at Trimus city, they were among the largest on the planet. Drin blew a little steam in an involuntary spasm of humor—he remembered that there was a tacit agreement among the Do'utians that no measurements be taken, lest it lead to beach-status arguments. "Their branch of the Ib have lived here since the founding. The small white stone dome in the center is older than anything still standing in Trimus city."

"Small? It has to be twenty charter units across! Drin, the Ib in your name—is it?"

"My great grandfather was a second son. If he had been first, and my father had been first in the subsequent line, I would be master of that. But," Drin paused for a short laugh, not entirely free of wistfulness, "there are at least a hundred Do'utians on this planet with a closer claim. The flanking domes are fairly recent; they replaced older domes that fell in a quake eight-cubed, three eight-squared, seven-eighths and two years ago. The more modern hexagonal structures house employees and a small replicator factory."

"How many live here?"

Drin had to think. "Doglaska'ib is the long one, and has been for nearly seven centuries. He has a harem of five including Gonikli'ibida, though this is attended more by his son and heir, the master Borragil'ib. Two bachelor brothers maintained offices there, but they live in Trimus City for the most part. There is a child in residence and Borragil'ib 's widowed sister. Uh—" it was uncomfortable for Drin to admit the next—"a cousin, a returned primitivist, and two of his beach harem are staying there too, temporarily. So there may be a dozen in residence, but our ways are such that two or three are all we're likely to find here. This complex will house three-eights comfortably, and there have been larger gatherings. Their cybernetic system maintains the place between visits."

"They have an artificial intelligence in this place?" Mary sounded horrified, Drin thought, at what she clearly thought was a violation of the values and possibly the Compact.

"We aren't in Trimus City anymore, Mary. The domination of one mind by another is not abhorrent in Do'utian culture, and this is perhaps the most Do'utian place on Trimus. The computer is a tool, technically subsentient."

"First Yohin, then this. I'm getting a lesson in the gray areas of slavery law today," Mary remarked. "An uncomfortable lesson."

"A stool without legs," Drin remarked, referring to Go Zom's famous metaphor, "would be uninteresting."

"You guys don't use stools," Mary countered, and laughed to take the edge off.

It was, Drin realized a purely Trimusian thought. If the Ib beach hold represented the foot of the stool, then he and Mary were where the legs joined the stool.

For all its timeless stony magnificence, the complex wallowed in technology to a breathtaking extent—a Do'utian settler from eight macroyears ago would not have felt out of place. They passed through a magnetic suspension barrier on their way in and Drin shivered as the field stabilized liquid barrier scraped anything loose on his body from him as he pushed through it into the delicately perfumed water of the complex. He had to pull Mary's submarine through the barrier; it propelled itself by pushing water with electromagnetic fields, and the barrier interfered with that process.

The ramp from the sea door was covered by a transport carpet composed of microcilia that pushed him up and into the entrance chamber without his having to move a muscle. Mary's eyes went wide when she found that the water of the sea door had seemed to solidify to let her walk from the submarine to the solid surface with wavelets lapping on either side of her. A smart nanite jell, Drin assumed.

Drin had grown up with all of this, but it hit him with waves of nostalgia whenever he returned from the open sea, or even the comparatively ascetic environment of Trimus City.

No one had come to greet them, but this was not unusual in Do'utian society.

"Smooth currents to Dag Doglaska'ib," Drin greeted his uncle and host, knowing the system would relay the greeting. "We've come to talk to Gonikli'ibida, Monitor duty, I'm afraid. There's been a questionable death."

"Smooth currents, Commander Drinnil'ib," a disembodied Do'utian voice said, as if the speaker were standing near Drin. "Ibgorni speaking for the house. Doglaska'ib receives your message, and bids welcome."

It was as if the long one himself were speaking, Drin felt. Ibgorni's mind had grown in Drin's absence—perhaps more than even he could take comfortably.

"Gonikli'ibida is in residence," it continued, "but outside now. We offer you the yellow sector in the south dome. Does the Lieutenant wish to stay with you or have her own quarters?"

Mary looked at Drin, and he had a quick decision. Which would cause more gossip? To send Mary away halfway across the huge complex when everyone knew that they lived together in the field would look like he was being overly sensitive. Drin opened his beak just enough for Mary to see him give the okay sign.

"The Lieutenant," Mary spoke, "will stay with Commander Drinnil'ib, facilities permitting."

"The appropriate facilities will be in place by the time you reach the sector, Lieutenant. Commander, Borragil'ib has been informed of your presence and wishes smooth currents. He also intends to feed at midnight and asks if you would join him."

"Tell him the honor will be mine." Drin dipped his beak slightly as he said this.

"Borragil'ib?" Mary asked.

"The first son. Dag Doglaska'ib is very ancient, and while physically sound his mind explores uncharted seas these days, in intense concentration. Borragil'ib is of my generation, and is still intrigued by the organization of things." Drin headed for the corridor to the south dome, its opening artfully disguised by holo dust. Halfway through he realized Mary wasn't with him.

He turned and stuck his head back through the insubstantial but opaque curtain. "Shall we?"

"Uh, Drin, this is just going to take some getting used to."

What was troubling her? Holo dust was just standard Do'utian interior decoration, Drin thought, the technology was twice as old as Trimus, at least. Then he realized—

"I'm sorry, Mary. I forgot you don't see at audio frequencies. Don't worry, It's just well-managed dust." It must have looked to her as he were sticking himself through solid rock.

This time she shook her head, gave him a nervous little giggle."You guys are so huge, so elemental, so natural; and things are so basic at Trimus city, we forget to think of you as having such a technological heritage. It doesn't fit the image somehow."

"There are branches of us, as there are of you, that are minds with no use for organic bodies, or even individuality." Drin shuddered, slapping his tail against the side of the hall. "They are out there, and I think they watch us now and then—like we watch the lungfish."

"I think I can handle the holo dust," Mary said, "it just surprised me a little." She followed the rest of him through the curtain. "Lungfish?" she added, shaking her head.

★ ✳ ★

Borragil'ib spotted a Stingsnake, grabbed its neck with one branch hand in a lightning whip of his tongue, stuffed the long, thick body into his mouth, and pulled his hands in after, until only the flailing head of the poisonous beast projected outside his beak. Then he severed it with a judicious nip.

Drin had to admire his cousin's technique. The Stingsnake was the largest Do'utian sea predator brought to Trimus, and its bite on the tongue could fester. A human would get a painful puncture, but the air breathing aquatic vertebrate's venom had no effect on them. Did we make our oceans too safe? Drin wondered. Perhaps we need a little something to fear out here—besides each other.

Smooth, slim and sleek Borragil'ib feared him, or rather feared the questions he came to ask. His cousin swam with a classic grace, nowhere near matching Drin in strength, but still seemed to slip through the water as fast on half the effort.

They talked to each other in the old sonic images language, symbols related to each other in two dimensions rather than just by linear grammar. When Mary had asked about this, Drin had reminded her of English sentence diagrams. She had nodded. "Very well," he'd said, "substitute symbols for the phrases, nouns, and verbs. Then add a few more lines. It's complicated, and not necessarily any faster, but it handles a lot of subtleties. It's especially good for mathematics."

What Borragil'ib's images told him was that Gonikli'ibida did not want to talk to Drin, and the family did not want Drin to press the issue.

The family? Drin imaged the long one.

Borragil'ib imaged a black sphere, a symbol for the unknowable, and a warning not to press that issue.

Gonikli's research into primitivist weapons?

The symbol of challenge was associated with Drin's inquiry and Gonikli'ibida's reluctance, and this tied to response-to-challenge.

A description of Do'utian psychology, Drin wondered, or a threat.

Kleth and Human were difficult to describe in these chirps and whistles, but there were conventions. Drin shot his tongue at a passing fish, grabbed it, and stuffed it down his throat. Then he composed the symbol for human (the symbol for a monkey-like Do'utian vertebrate plus the symbol for thought) and modified it by talking-of-others-deeds-of-words, and related it to the dead Kleth (a now non-thinking thinking flying creature), related those to the dead Kleth's maybe dead mate, and tied the human and the dead Kleth to Gonikli'ibida with friendship bond symbols. Finally, a question symbol was tied to the human's position symbol.

Quickly an image returned negating Gonikli'ibida's connection with the death.

Drin sent one negating that image, and another asking simply, "where is Richard Moon?"

Borragil'ib broached for a breath, dove deep, and returned with the smell of a house-snail trailing him. He showed Drin a picture negating Gonikli'ibida's knowledge of the human's position, and associating Drin's questions with challenge again.

Drin questioned the need to defend Gonikli'ibida from questions.

Borragil'ib raised the image of honor challenge.

"No," Drin replied in the definite, linear logic of English, "I do not challenge your honor."

"You swim in Do'utian seas now, Commander. Seek your

information elsewhere."

"Your protests have now convinced me that Gonikli'ibida is somehow more connected in this than in being a way to find Richard Moon. I am bound by my duty to learn what that connection is."

"There is none! She is an artist and wants to be alone to think. She does not know where Moon is. Leave it at *that*."

"Very well," Drin said, smelling challenge. People as thoroughly civilized as the Ib would not be involved in beachmaster duels. But they had political influence that, if anything, could be more deadly. It was time, Drin thought, even at his level, for him to dip his beak. Perhaps Mary or the Staff back at Trimus City would have some ideas.

★ ✳ ★

Death is a common denominator of Trimus, our philosophy was to not extend individual consciousness indefinitely by cybernetic means. Some still might go elsewhere for this, and so cease to be Trimusians. But death does not come from physical aging—Do'utians do not die of old age, and the human and Kleth had engineered that from their genes long before their first contact—but from accidents, or from choice. Humans and Kleth enjoy risk, and so had a median life span of just over three centuries (503 turns for Kleth, 472 for humans) at the time of founding. Do'utians who don't have accidents at sea simply get longer and stranger, usually refusing to communicate or eat after seven or eight centuries. We revere the cycle of life, but, as intelligent tool-makers, on our own terms.

— Karen Olsen, "A History of Trimus"

★ ✳ ★

The facilities that Ibgorni had contrived for Mary at the spur of the moment included a pool of warm water, tiny by Do'utian standards, but a convenience they easily understood. It was not quite as long as Drin, but in it, Mary could swim several body lengths, sound, and even spout after a fashion; the warm moist air from her lungs quickly turned to steam in a room temperature meant for Do'utian comfort. She was swimming vigorously when he arrived back at their room, perhaps a little bit overfull from a night of hunting and feeding that had, he thought, gone a way to quiet Borragil'ib's itchy-tailed hostility.

In the hot pool, Mary had no need of the artificial skin she normally wore to protect and insulate her, and Drin examined her anatomy with his usual discrete fascination. Mary, several times, had told him that it did not bother her in the slightest to be examined in this manner, and that, truthfully, she liked the attention, and if he were curious about what she felt like, that would be fine as well.

Drin's curiosity did not reach that threshold of intimacy yet.

Raising his tail for leverage, Drin reared up, put his foreclaws on the sill of the room's long window and looked out at the stars. The window faced away from Ember, which was cut in half by the horizon at this latitude and further dimmed by Trimus' thick atmosphere.

Do was visible, a fourth magnitude star in the middle of an asterism the Do'utians called Gi'ab. The constellations toward one's home world looked the same, if a little smaller, Drin thought; the strangeness lay beyond. There was a splash, and a hot body attached itself to his lower right leg.

He sent his tongue down and lifted her up to his shoulder, where she was able to find a foothold.

"You must be very cold."

"I can handle it for a while. It's beautiful out there. Gonna take me a starship trip one of these years, if I don't get myself killed first."

"Earth?"

"Yeah, and Tau Ceti. My great great-grandfather came from a region of Earth called the United States, and his great-grandfather came from a town in England named York. His name was Samuel Pearce, and we're told his great great great-grandmother was raped by a Viking—a kind of human barbarian—in a war with Norway some six centuries years before that." Mary laughed. "Except, if she were like me, it might not have been rape. That's as far as I can go back. You can't see Sol from here, but I think that's Tau Ceti—near the bright star by the south galactic pole."

"Godro," Drin named the south glactic pole marker, "in Do'utian, Beta Ceti in English."

"Actually," Mary chuckled, "that's Greek and Latin, and to further confuse you, the star is also called Diphda, in Arabic."

Drin grunted. "It's Bogdo'ilda in Brogilla'a, the nation of our southern continent that started space travel." So a chance star gave reason to contemplate the vastness, both of the cosmos and of history. "We both carry the memory of our ancestors toward eternity, to give their lives meaning."

Drin felt Mary shake. "A fearsome responsibility," he added.

"I'm not afraid of that, Drin. But I think I'm about to admit I'm freezing. Help me down?"

He set her down, and she immediately sprinted for the hot pool, and knifed in cleanly.

After a few minutes she got out and looked around. "Any towels?"

As if in answer, she was bathed in deep infrared from projectors so cleverly concealed that Drin hadn't realized they were there. "Hey! Okay, I'm dry!"

Drin slipped back down to the floor and considered Mary with his right eye, and thought about the various modes of bonding in his own species. The territorial jealousy of a beachmaster was legendary, but, away from his beach, such Do'utian men went about collective affairs with a formal dignity that often verged on admiration of each other. But unmated Do'utians who avoided the beach were the backbone of his species' science and industry. In civilized times, formerly mated, or mated females who avoided calving tended to dominate arts and politics—displacing their creative and nurturing drives, the theory went. They worked well with unmated males, and often rose to the second levels of leadership. The first levels were almost always mated males, however. Where did Mary fit?

Where did she want to fit?

The room shook, seemingly with the thought, and warm water sloshed from the pool. Mary looked up to the curved ceiling far above, suddenly tense and aroused. Subtle bulges in her body reminded Drin of how much of her tiny body was bone and muscle—incorporating any Earth land life into the Trimusian ecology had been fraught with problems due to the genetic heritage of evolution in high gravity. Here, they ran with blinding speed, took incredible leaps, and, people said, could drag away burdens of many times their body weight.

Drin tried to imagine Mary dragging him away and allowed himself a low, rumbling, chuckle, glad to be distracted from less easy currents of thought.

"Don't worry about the tembler," he said, "This is quake and volcano country, and we build for it. What they told me as a child was that you could take this whole complex and drop it a charter unit, the whole length of my body, without breaking it."

Mary shook herself, some last drops of water flying from her hair, and laughed nervously, "Glad to hear it. Drin, you seem to be thinking deep thoughts. About me?" She walked up to him and placed a hand on his beak.

Exchange of affection by bumping and touching was common to both species. In Do'utians, it was between anyone, but in particular women in the same harem, or on the same project—the feelings of security and trust created by mutual touching were particularly strong. In humans, Drin was fully aware, it led, in private situations, to a performance of their mating act, which in civilized times served to create greater-than-ordinary emotional bonds between the people that did it. They apparently enjoyed it.

Did Mary expect him to pleasure her? Humans mixed affection and reproduction. But the Do'utian mating act was utterly different in feeling and purpose. It was a two-step process and not at all fun. Quickening the ovaries was something a beachmaster did instinctively to maintain his harem—it released hormones in the cows that helped make them subservient.

The beachmaster's reward for this was subservience, beak dipping, and staying. The act itself was very mechanical, not pleasurable, though for some, the feeling of power was. Later, taking and fertilizing the eggs was a compulsive, messy, and humiliating procedure that had to be done or the bearing female could die. The female was grateful, the male would typically feel the need to go on a long feeding swim. In primitive times, he would return to dominate, protect and feed his harem. Civilized Do'utians discovered in vitro fertilization a long time ago.

He needed to make some response—not doing so would be impolite. He opened his beak and laid the hand of the right branch of his tongue on her shoulder. Drin was quite happy to touch Mary and display his regard and affection for her. But he did not want to turn her into a subservient cow—that could be dangerous in a crisis. Of course, she was human and that wouldn't happen. But how would he feel when it didn't. The idea didn't work for him that way, not at all. But why was he so fascinated by the idea? Intellectual curiosity? Did he want to seem human to her, the way she seemed to try to be Do'utian with all the time she spent in the water? He found her unnaturally warm, smooth, dry flesh strange, fascinating. Would he ever be able to talk freely of these things with her? What instincts of hers were coming into play, and what curiosities?

She seemed cheerfully aware of the esthetics of her body. Mary smiled at him. "Drin, if I can feel beauty in a horse, in a swordfish, in a cat, or in you, then you feel beauty in me! I don't have to look like a Do'utian. Don't question it so much, enjoy it!"

Drin moved his hand down her arm, acknowledging. She covered her hand with his and guided it. This was between them, and harmed no one. Except that it took time.

"We need to go to work, Lieutenant," he said.

Mary took a deep breath, and exhaled. "Right." She touched her lips to his hand, dropped it and scampered to the pool side. Quickly, she got into the olive body suit she wore to work in the salt sea and on the frigid polar land.

Drin gratefully turned his mind to the problems at hand. "Mary, Gonikli'ibida apparently doesn't want to be questioned. I was warned off, very strongly."

Mary nodded. "Drin, while you were out, I did some information gathering. More gray area stuff, but I'm taking your position that the house computer is not a sentient being and the question of testifying against itself or breaking its confidences does not arise."

Drin chuckled. "The only time the currents say anything about how someone passed from here to there is when they carry a body."

"Huh?

"Ibgorni *let* you have the data."

"Oh, Well, Drin, there *are* currents of ice not far from here, and they carry a body. Could Gonikli'ibida's reluctance be personal? Something between you and her?"

Mary was a good investigator, and for once, Drin thought, a little too good. This current led over a waterfall. "Possibly. We were close, once."

"Drin..."

Drin sighed from his blow hole, almost like deflating. So she knew. But what did that have to do with anything? "We left my sister, Bodil'ib, where she died. Eons hence, she will reach the sea."

"How did she die?"

"The memory is painful. Is it relevant?"

"Would a Do'utian keep coming back? To pay respects? Or in times of great emotional stress? Have you?"

"Privately. She is gone, but she is still there—the suffering is frozen in her body. Mary, she went out alone in a snowstorm the day I left for Monitor training, and fell into a crevasse. They found her days later. Do'utians are built for the cold and it takes us a long time to die of it. We got some nourishment down to her and she seemed to rally for a while—she recognized us. But it took too long to get the equipment there."

"I'm sorry Drin. But there's more, isn't there?"

Oh, yes, there was more. How much did he dare reveal to Mary? He remembered the strange, intense, warmth of her body, and how that had said "trust me, trust me." She had saved his life more than once. Their ancestors had evolved in wildly different environments— but a common physics and logic of sentience had done its work, or they would not be here together.

"We are in conservative circles here; can you be very careful of who you tell?"

Mary nodded. "Drin, was there a bond between your sister and Gonikli'ibida that could last after death? Could Gonikli'ibida be out there, at the glacier now, looking for some way to deal with something? With you?"

"We were immature, Mary, playing games. New to our bodies, and curious. They wanted me to play beachmaster and they would play my cows. We didn't understand what would happen, inside, as we played these roles. It just isn't done with one's sister, but we didn't mean to do it. We didn't know what "it" was—our stuffy parents kept too much in their beaks. We weren't mature enough —there weren't any eggs—but Bodil, became very dependent on me. Then I left. Gonikli didn't bond as strongly with me, but she felt Bodil was her senior co-mate; that bonding can be almost as strong."

"Her first love. Drin, I can understand that. If she's as disturbed about your questions as you say, maybe she went back to where—did you say Bodil? That's a human name, too."

Drin nodded, teetering on the brink of understanding. "Bodil'ib.

My sister."

Mary continued. "Maybe Gonikli'ibida went back to where Bodil died."

Drin nodded. Gonikli might go there in a time of crisis. But . . .

"But why would this be a crisis for her. We are only trying to find Richard Moon?"

"She was close to both Bi Tan and Richard Moon. Richard Moon didn't say he saw Bi Tan die, he said someone he trusted had told him."

Now that Mary had pushed him into the sea of understanding, what lay on the bottom was obvious. "You think she was the one who told Richard Moon that Bi Tan was dead? That would be unpleasant, but less than a crisis, unless she weren't being truthful. But a lie like that would kill both the Kleth, including her friend. None the less, it looks like she was involved—but how?"

"We'll have to ask her, Drin."

"Against Borragil'ib's will?" Drin remembered images: images of challenge and images of duty.

"Very well. We should go now. He has been away from the complex and may have other duties."

Drin looked around and thought of family versus duty, and the possibility that he would not be welcome here again.

✶ ❋ ✶

Trimus' climate is similar to that of Do'utia, that is to say a little more energetic than that of Kleth, and much less energetic than that of Earth. The differences are, of course, statistical, and the immigrants from temperate Earth zones who settled in the high latitudes of Trimus claimed, ruefully, that they felt at home with the tornadoes. Do'utian immigrants noted that while the storms on Trimus are of similar intensity, they last much longer. Simulation studies point to the steady input of Ember and the complex tri axial climatic map to explain the duration of polar storms. Over the years, the main belt of Do'utian settlement has moved somewhat south of original projections.

—Go Zom's notes on the Compact and Charter of Trimus

✶ ❋ ✶

The wind made even Drin cold, and he found himself picking up his pace through the early morning gloom to generate more heat. He could smell his skin glands react to the cold; his outermost doci or so would, effectively, hibernate, but remain flexible. Mary had substituted big, wide bottomed boots for her flippers, but otherwise wore her form fitting artificial skin with an extra power pack. Her sea mask doubled as a cold mask and she'd added a transparent, wind-impervious, hooded cape with a weighted hem. Her tiny form bent against a wind that seemed to Drin to be enough to blow her away like a Kleth.

They reached the glacier after a vigorous climb of almost an hour that left Drin at an almost comfortable temperature. It lay in a valley between two mountain ranges piled high by the spread of polar rift to the north, and spilled into the sea-flooded caldera now occupied by Drin's branch of the Ib, west of the dome complex. On its way to the sea, it split into several huge crevasses. When it got there, it gave rise to many icebergs.

For Drin, the glacier aroused primordial feelings, terror of the heights, comfort in the smooth ice, horror in the knowledge that below this surface of this ice lay not food, but death.

Drin had not called Do Tor and Go Ton in on this yet, thinking that he and Marry had overreacted a bit around Yohin Bretz a Landend's tourist sailing ship—to the point of embarrassment.   And, he'd reminded himself, they were not now going toward a potentially armed and dangerous vessel, but a heartsick Do'utian woman who had seen one too many close friends die.

If they could find her and get her to tell her story, whatever it was, Drin was hopeful that he could patch things up with Borragil'ib and be on their way.

The glacier had flowed several macrounits toward the bay since his sister's death, the surface features remained very much the same—it was almost eight-squared charter units across with a hump on the west wall about two-thirds of the way toward the sea. East wall lower than the west. It was split by several large crevasses, from flowing faster in the center than at the sides. In one of these, through occasionally blinding flurries of fist sized snowflakes, Drin found his sister.

Someone had been visiting Bodil—her body was encased in clear ice that had been kept clean of all but the most recent snow. Memories. It had been in a storm like this when they found her. She had broken her back in the fall, but that would have been repairable if they could only have gotten her out in time. He shook as he thought about it.

Drin had to stop there. The visiters must have taken a different route; the sides of the crevasse came too near the walls of the valley here for Drin to find an easy way. Mary went ahead.

"Mary," Drin said at length. "There's no sign of Gonikli, so we may as well go back."

There was no answer.

"Mary?" Drin called and looked around. She had been standing at the lip of the crevasse near an avalanche site that looked like a possible way down not a minute ago. Drin looked around again. Her olive body suit should stand out fairly well against the white snow. Still no answer.

Fearing the worst, from the wind, he eased himself closer to the edge of the huge crevasse and looked down at the wall. Ominously, it seemed to overhang a little. Far below, perhaps six times his body length, he saw a splotch of olive color. How can this happen? He wondered. Had she been so surprised that she had not even cried out? Had he been so preoccupied that he hadn't heard. Had he felt a little shake? A quake? No, that had been his own feelings, hadn't it.

This couldn't be happening. Mary and Bodil in the same crevasse! Drin roared in anguish, then remembered his comset. There had to be some aircraft that could fight this storm. Best turn things over to Do Tor, he was in no emotional shape to be much help to anything.

He stuck his head over the edge again. There had to be a way down. He looked at the green splotch with both eyes—it did seem to be Mary and she wasn't moving. Now he realized how much a part of his life she had become. Familiar, expected, a certainty. Like his gun, like the Compact, like the Ib homestead, like—he remembered—his sister.

"No, no, no!" he roared at the unfeeling wind.

She had fallen about eight charter units from him, having followed a ledge that looked too narrow for a Do'utian. But he had four strong claws and the walls were snow and ice, not stone.

Drin reared up with his head pressed against the valley wall and placed a rear claw on the ledge, testing it with his weight. It held.

The snow on the wall had been densified by freeze-thaw cycles and compressed almost to ice by the wind. He slammed a foreclaw into the packed snow, claws extended, and pulled. It seemed solid enough. He risked moving his right rear leg, stretching about an eighth of a charter unit along the ledge until he found comfortable purchase. Then, he swung his tail over to the ledge; it had nothing to grip with, but could exert a little upward pressure for balance. So, hanging by his foreclaws and the one rear leg, he moved his left rear leg to where his right one had been.

So far, so good. He made another foreclaw-hold and repeated the process. He was burning energy at a tremendous rate, but felt exhilarated—he could work at near maximum efficiency with the cold polar wind taking heat away as fast as he generated it.

Thus, with his massive bulk clinging to the wall like some kind of lizard, he managed to work his way sideways toward Mary.

Halfway he set a foreclaw only to have a great swath of snow and rock pull free and go tumbling down over the edge, leaving his right foreclaw pawing nothing as he struggled with his other three limbs to stay on the wall. The snow under his left claw started to groan, shifting slightly. He began to lose his balance, tilting outward. Instinctively he shot his tongue uphill, found a rock and clung with both hands.

The wind stung his extended tongue, it would freeze in a few beats if he didn't do something.

He brought his right leg back toward his body and stabbed his claws into the snow just beside his head, and pulled.

If the snow here fell away too, he was done. But it held. He let go of the rock and pulled his tongue in. It burned the inside of his mouth with cold—but he could still feel. He tasted old ice, bitter with volcanic ash and dust. No permanent damage, he hoped. But he would have to go back.

No. Mary was down there.

Where was that polluting aircraft?

The wind blew some snow from the slide—it was loose, obviously. Experimentally, he shoved at the pile on the ledge with his tail. An eighth-squared of a cube of the stuff fell free over the ledge. Using his tail, he brushed the fallen snow from the ledge, and discovered the small avalanche had actually given him more room for his rear feet.

It took him a macrobeat to work his way through the small avalanche, but he managed it.

Ten macrobeats later, he was nearly over Mary. He tried his comset.

Nothing.

He pulled a in big lungful of freezing air, slowly so it wouldn't freeze his blow hole, then yelled her name, throwing a recklessly large amount of volume into the lower register. Anything that was going to go in this area, he figured, had already gone.

And impact caught him in mid bellow, not from above, but on his lower left leg, dislodging it from its precarious clawhold. A small shadow figure appeared momentarily then vanished into the blowing snow. What?

His attention had been on Mary and his upper claws were relaxed, and set in recently loosened snow anyway. Without the left rear leg, he started sliding down. Almost immediately, his rear legs were over the edge of the crevasse, flailing at air.

He dug at the snow with great swipes of his foreclaws snow, essentially trying to swim back up the snow slide. For a moment it seemed to work.

Then there was a terrible moaning groan and entire mass of snow under him seemed to flow, sending him into weightlessness over the edge of the giant crevasse. In one last act of sanity, he triggered his emergency beacon. Then he screamed the death scream, instinctively warning any of his kind within hearing of mortal danger. Lungs still full, he glanced off the ice wall and bounced like a rubber ball, exhale in a great, painful gasp.

He hit it again and instinctively clawed the wall. The ice tore at the webbing between his toes, but he slowed, and slowed. He'd almost stopped when his left foreleg caught a crack, far too suddenly. He felt a bone snap, and let go in immediate reaction to the pain. But he was almost down to the floor, the slope was much less steep, and he stumbled more than fell.

He bounced once more and belly-flopped on the snow that over the ages had filled in the bottom of the huge crack. Pollution! How could he hurt so much? The nerves of his leg screamed in pain as he fought for objectivity. Pulling air into his lung helped calm him. Somehow, aside from the leg, he was reasonably intact. The strained muscles in his back would feel abused for several turns, but he'd been through worse.

He gazed up at the edge of the crevasse through gaps in the blanket of blowing snow. If there was a way down, there was a way up. Walking three legged was just barely possible for a Do'utian.Better to rear up, he decided, and stagger on the two hind legs, human fashion. But first, find Mary. Every bruise and strain protested as he stiffened his tail for leverage and started to rise.

A roar like an aircraft fan buzz began echoing in crevasse, building louder and louder. Wrong somehow—but the ice walls and the howling wind distorted everything. An aircraft? In this storm? Do Tor and Go Tan finally? It seemed so. Thank providence!

Then the first chunk of ice hit him. He had time to look up and see a giant vertical column of it slowly detach itself from the wall of the crevasse and topple over right on top of him, a huge solid slab heading right for his head. He tried to move and fell, collapsing on his broken leg, his beak digging into the ice. Then an ice slab landed on his head and he lost consciousness.

★ ❈ ★

In inventing Trimus English, we gave the prefix "macro" the specific meaning of eight to the third power, and the prefix "mini" the specific meaning of eight to the minus third power. These were in addition to, and consistent with their ordinary usage implying the very big and the very little. They, with prefixes like di, tri, etc. for squaring, cubing, and higher powers, were also direct literal translations of the base eight terms from my native language, for which I make no apologies. Math was never my specialty, and I was grateful not to have to relearn it!

—Go Zom's notes on the Charter and Compact of Trimus.

★ ❈ ★

When Drin put his memories back together he was surprised to find that he was still around to remember anything. It was pitch dark. He was colder than he'd ever been in his life. He couldn't feel the end of his tail. His left foreleg was a tearing, rending, agony with each breath he tried to take.

"Mary?" he groaned, in reflex. There was no hope. There was no answer.

The situation was insulting. He was of a race that had moved worlds, that had made machines that answered their every whim, that had banished age and war. What was he doing helpless under a pile of snow? He tried to roar in anger. It came out as a kind of grunt.

Pollution, he wasn't dead yet. The first thing he had to do was to get into his ventral pouch. He had some of the tools of civilization. His comset. A gun that could possibly blast a small hole through this covering if he had enough explosive rounds.

He wasn't sealed in—he could breathe. He couldn't see it, but thought there must be an air pocket above his blow hole. He tried sucking air in, then exhaled with his valvae marinus closed. This expanded his upper chest at the expense of the abdomen, and, with an awful creaking protest that filled the sonic spectrum with white noise, the block moved slightly up, and to the side. When he exhaled again, he could wiggle a little. Some water dripped into his blow hole; his breath must have melted it. This slight evidence of affecting his environment helped his morale, greatly.

Cold at least was numbing his broken foreleg. After another macrobeat of huffing and puffing, Drin found he could roll half wiggle and half roll enough to slip his tongue out and reach his pouch. His outer skin was so numb and leathery that it didn't feel like part of him anymore. That would be something for the doctors, he feared. In the meantime, he had his gun and his comset.

Now, where was all this snow and ice most thin? He closed his eyes to concentrate on the sonic image and tried various frequencies of voice, looking for the one that made the picture deepest and clearest. His prison seemed darkest off to his right; which meant the fewest reflections, which meant, he hoped, the thinnest.

Drin squirmed and wriggled until he could open his beak a couple of doci's wide. Then he held the gun about a doci from the ice, and fired.

Ice chips stung the inside of his mouth. He probed the hole with a finger—it was deeper than he could reach. He fired twice more into the same hole, and no ice chips came back from the last shot. Struggling to reposition his beak, he repeated the procedure five more times until he had a rough hexagon of holes to the outside near the corner of his mouth.

The idea was that his hexagon of gun-drilled holes would define the weakened border of a plug that he could push out with his good right foreleg, if he could get it in position. To do that, he had to burrow forward, just a little.

His struggles had gained him a little more freedom of movement. He bit off a little ice, pressed his beak to the side, and bit some more. In about a Trimus hour, he was able to wiggle the upper part of his body sideways an eighth-sqared of a charter unit. Then he had to press himself, in excruciating pain, against his broken leg to create enough room to bring his right foreleg forward. He groaned in relief when he finally got his claw in the center of the hexagon of holes.

Drin rested. Then he pushed with every cuf of strength he could muster, holding his breath to stiffen his body as much as possible.

The ice broke and Drin found he'd punched a large hole in his prison. Not big enough for him to wiggle through, but perhaps he could enlarge it. He started tearing great hunks from its perimeter with his right claw.

"Drin?"

The faint, but clear voice froze him.

"Drin?"

"Mary?"

Drin struggled to get his right eye at the hole. Mary was standing, shaking almost violently, in the snow and wind just outside the hole. Her cape was gone, as was her mask. Her face was blotchy.

"Damn it's good to hear your voice," she said. "Is it warm in there? My power's used up."

"The freezing point of water is about the best I can do—and there's no room. I was buried thoroughly. What happened?"

"Got shot with a trank dart when I wasn't looking, and fell. Dumb. That avalanche was no accident—it was set off with some kind of weapon. Wll, we were looking for a possible murder suspect. Guess w—we found one."

"Mary, I got pushed and toppled myself. It might have been a human—maybe a primitivist working with someone here." Gonikli? An artist freind of hers? Borragil'ib? Could his cousin be yet another proud Do'utian who had found a cause greater than honor. "Time to worry about that later. I have a field med kit in my pouch, with maybe an emergency wrap in it."

"Gonna need more than that Drin. I have to—get—warm."

There was only one way to get her warm that he could think of, but it would incapacitate him further. So, he had to do some other things first. He grabbed his comset, set it on emergency relay and stuck it out the hole he'd dug.

"Set this on a rock or something, flat side facing south," he told her, "Then come in here. I'll try to open my beak wide enough so you can crawl in my mouth. Feet first if you can. Uh, Mary."

"Drin?"

"If I die, stay inside. My body will keep you warm for many hours." He said nothing of the hours of agony that it would take the cold to shut off the blood flow to his brain at the center of a shell of dead frozen flesh. He would have to endure that, for Mary's sake. The longer he could stay alive, the longer she would.

"R—right." Her hands shook terribly, but she took the comset and managed to wedge the unit in a crack of ice facing south. Then she started backing in through his hole. In the meantime, Drin found his medical kit and got it out of his pouch and into his mouth. That done, he grabbed Mary's boots, opened his beak as wide as he could, and pulled her in. With her feet freezing his throat and her backpack poking the lining of the top of his mouth, he closed her in. She just lay there and shivered.

She wasn't sealed in; he had to leave room for his tongue to hang out the left corner of his mouth—it was starting to freeze again!—and that left an air gap. He breathed for two, inhaling through his blow hole and exhaling the warmed air through his mouth over Mary, his tongue and his hands.

With Mary as secure as she could be, and to help keep his hands warm, Drin resumed work on the hole. Another four holes outlined the vertices of another hexagon, contiguous to the first. Rather than pushing it out, and letting the wind in, he outlined a third. Then a fourth.

Despite the noise of the gun drilling through the ice, Mary seemed to have gone to sleep.

At least he hoped it was sleep. He could tell she was still alive, but not much more, and unconscious. To wake her, he knew would deprive her of badly needed recuperation time.

But not knowing was a torture.

The work was going slowly; it had taken him an hour to outline a hole less than a third of the size, he estimated, needed to let him out of his icy prison. And he could feel the cold slipping into him much faster than that.

He had another worry. In all the thrashing and wiggling he'd done he hadn't managed to move his tail. Not at all. He couldn't even feel its tip any more. Chaos! He could deal with that later. He loaded another clip and resumed firing.

The hole he'd outlined was almost half wide enough for him to crawl out, if he could crawl, when Mary started moving again. She was doing something with the med kit.

There were, he remembered some surgical implements in there.

Mary patted the roof of his mouth and he opened it. She wiggled out, and sat in the hole, wrapped in the emergency blanket, blocking the occasional cold gust. Her face had some ugly yellow splotches, but her mouth was curved up at the edges and her teeth were showing.

"A little frostbite, the med comp says. And a busted rib. I'll live. Besides having had fish for dinner last night, how are you?"

How did she know what he'd had for dinner? Never mind. "My left leg is broken. And my tail is trapped. Mary, I may have to ask you to amputate it."

"Drin!"

"I can ignore the pain and the damage can be repaired, if I live." What worried him more was that, without his tail, or all of it, to counterbalance, he would have a very hard time moving, let alone climbing, on three legs.

"We're going to make it. Drin. Don't think anything else." Mary took a couple of deep breaths, exhaling clouds that would not have been out of place for him. "Okay. How far back?"

A sudden roar outside stopped their conversation, and a warm gust blew into the hole. Another avalanche, Drin thought, or a volcano?

Then it stopped and he recognized it. Some kind of flying vehicle.

Friend or foe? There were eight rounds left in this clip. If he had to defend them, there wouldn't be enough to finish his drilling. If only Mary hadn't lost her weapon in her fall. But that couldn't be helped now. He would just have to make every shot count, then hope.

A bass Kleth voice rich with overtones ripped through the wind and snow.

"Over here!"

"Do Tor!" Mary yelled.

Drin let a breath out his blow hole in a great resonant honk, part for communication, part in relief.

Do Tor did not look like any Kleth Drin had ever seen before; he hopped into view in a heavy-looking black cape over a bright orange body suit, and wore a narrow peaked cap covering his crest.

"They're alive," Do Tor yelled.

"Do Tor—" Mary's voice was down to a shout as Do Tor closed the distance "—Drin's left foreleg is broken and his tail is trapped."

"Damn right it's trapped," another voice declared, human this time. "That rock's got to weigh a hundred ton!"

Drin placed the voice quickly, making up for his lack of recognition of Do Tor. The human with the Kleth was Yohin Bretz a Landend, the erstwhile Thet City harbor pilot cum primitivist cruise ship captain. What was he doing here?

"They've got some big pneumatic jacks back at Gonikli's place," another human voice shouted. It took Drin a while to place it, and he groaned at the irony when he did. After chasing him a quarter of the way around the planet and getting hopelessly trapped, Richard Moon had come to him. Now, was the human writer back at the scene, or should he scratch another suspect?

"Their to heavy to get down here." A Do'utian. Gonikli of course.

"Get rocket crane from Pahn No City." Do Tor suggested.

Gonikli wailed and Drin knew why. It would take a day. They'd been here before. Crazily, it was less worrisome to him being the one trapped than being one of those who might try to rescue him.

"Cut me out," he said.

"Fish man, you want to come out in two pieces or one?" Yohin yelled. "I can get you out in one."

"Huh?" just about everyone else said.

"I got me ten four-line tackles back on the ship; each line'll pull three ton. We anchor them to that crag and blast some anchor bolts in the rock. Ought to do'er. Your heavy weather flyer there can lift the gear if the rest of us stay here. Just tell my crew."

Silence.

"What is a "ton" in cufs?" Richard Moon finally asked.

So they had found him.

★ ✸ ★

A cuf, one Trimus unit of force, is be one dom-charter-unit-per beat squared (567.45 Kleth go-bo; 37.06 newtons, in human base ten; or 1.85 E-5 Li'in, in Do'utian base 12). In terms of the archaic human unit "ton," which is still embedded in English literature, it would take about four eight-squared (400 octal, 256 decimal, 194 base 12) cuf to make a "ton."

—The Compact and Charter of Trimus, Technical appendix.

★ ✸ ★

"We're fighting the wind, and the cold's makin' the lines hard. Best move when you can, Commander," Yohin yelled.

Gonikli and Borragil'ib cleared away the rubble in front of Drin with beak shovels, and gave him a clear path out from under the rock. He had no idea of how his hind legs would respond after having been trapped all these hours. Incredibly, it was still light out. He felt like he'd been entombed in ice for much longer.

"All right, me hearties, pull!" Yohin yelled.

Gonikli and Borragil'ib pulled on the archaic tackles. The lines pulled taught. Something shifted.

"More! Dig in, mates, now!"

The pressure on Drin's tail suddenly lifted and feeling returned there—so painfully he wished it hadn't. He tried to push himself forward, and collapsed on his broken left foreleg with a groan.

"Come on, Commander," Yohin shouted through the gale, "Hurry, it's all we can give you."

Drin tried to raise his forequarters up on his one good forelimb and slide, or squirm forward. He began to lose it again.

Mary darted under him, and pushed up and right. It was impossible. She couldn't lift any part of him. He was far too massive. But he shifted as much of his weight to his right foreleg as he could and somehow she kept what was left off the ice. Almost without thinking, Drin pushed himself up, snapped his right foreleg forward, dug his claw into the rubble before he had time to fall, and pulled. Something broke free, his left rear claw pulled clear and he thrust it forward, scraping a foothold in the ice, and shoved his head out of his prison. Mary tumbled out of the way as he came crashing down on his throat and chest and slid the rest of the way, pushing with his hind legs.

"Loosen up there, maties, he's out! Easy now, easy," Yohin shouted.

Clear of the rubble, Drin watched Mary scramble out before the hole they'd been inside collapsed with a thud and a spray of snow and ice shards. She waved at him, then ran for cover.

Cover was a huge tent inflated in front of him, dented only slightly by the wind, set beside a low, rugged-looking ducted fan aircraft, bristling with vector nozzles. Gonikli was beside him instantly, and stuck her beak under his left shoulder. Supported that way, they were able to stagger into a warmth that normally would have been very uncomfortable, but just then was very, very welcome.

No sooner was he on a heated pad, then Go Ton hovered over him like a fury, poking this and that needle into him. All feeling left his left foreleg, except for various tugs and pulls from Mary and Gonikli under Go Ton's clucking supervision.

Richard Moon managed bring him a Do'utian field ration cube that must have weighed as much as the human male that carried it. Drin took it and stuffed it down his gullet and soon its sugars and enzymes found their way into his blood. Gradually, his head began to clear.

Everyone was standing around him, looking concerned, and waiting for him to say something. "Okay. Thank you everyone." His voice sounded weak and raspy, even to him. He coughed. "I think I'll live. I was trying to reach Mary when something or someone—a human I think—toppled me into the crevasse. You saw the rest. But what happened while we were out? In light of our investigation, this is a rather interesting rescue party!"

Everyone started to speak, but Gonikli said "Please" a little louder than everyone else.

"This is my fault. At least in part." She rubbed the tent floor with her beak. "I ended my dear friend Bi Tan's life because she was dying, and begged me to do it. She called me to her retreat—she was very private, avoiding almost everyone, when she was away from Zo Kim. She was unhappy with him and unhappy without him, and tended to pick fights, like the one with Gorman over including his contacts with Lord Thet's sailors in her manuscript and . . . I'm wandering.

"Bi Tan told me that Zo Kim was dead, and she wanted me to—help her go. She was shaking, jerking around, but she gave me a few more changes to our last chapter—about crude replicator manufacturing showing up in Thet City. She was sure that would upset people, and make them remember her. Then she begged me to bite her head off—

she placed her head in my beak, told me I was the best friend she ever had, and to do it quickly because the pain was terrible."

"It was awful. But in a way I felt honored, that she would ask me to do it instead of another Kleth. But I'll never forget the bitter taste."

"I went back to the writer's colony and asked someone, it might have been Gorman, to take care of Bi Tan's body. He and the others said they'd take care of it."

"I called Richard before the awards meeting and told him, so he could say something about her. When I found out that Zo Kim had died at the awards meeting, I didn't know what to think. Everyone knew what I thought of Zo Kim. But, but, Bi Tan was my friend. I would never have done that to her to get at Zo Kim—"

Drin felt a surge of sympathy—Gonikli was an innocent academic caught in a web of alien intrigue. Borragil'ib curved his tail around her. At last she stopped shaking and spoke.

"When Drin came to ask questions, I came out here, to talk to our . . . to Bodil. You think I'm crazy, but it gives me a kind of peace to pretend she's listening, still . . ."

Borragil'ib touched his tale to Gonikli's again. She lowered her beak.

"Commander," Borragil'ib said. "I didn't know the full story and suspected some other motive on your part. My apologies."

"That takes us to Richard," Mary said, redirecting the subject. For me? Drin wondered. Did she sense his embarrassment and beak-dragging sadness at this?

Drin saw that she had some flesh toned ointment over the spots on her face, and seemed perfectly normal otherwise. There was no way she could have done what she had done, lifting almost a quarter of his weight, . . . but he was here.

"Yes," Richard Moon said. "I was surprised that no one had notified me about Zo Kim's passing, but was prepared to make the sad announcement and present the award myself when Zo Kim came flying in, right on schedule! I was flabbergasted, and horrified. I didn't, myself, know that Bi Tan was dead, I'd just trusted what Gonikli had told me and had assumed Zo Kim was dead, too."

"Did anyone," Mary asked, very quietly and gently, "think of reporting this to the Monitors?"

"Yes, we did." Gonikli looked puzzled. "Gorman took care of it before he left for Trimus City. He'd had words with Bi Tan when some of her critiques of his work from their group showed up in Zo Kim's reviews, and he was, well, a little more cold blooded about it all. The rest of us were in a bit of a mess."

"When Zo Kim died on stage," Richard Moon added, "I knew I had to see Gonikli before you Monitors did. I found a way to go back to Hot Springs Island that didn't expose me to any records."

Wind, wood, sail and nothing else, Drin remembered. The face in the rigging.

"Aye," Yohin chortled. "So ye did. People pay my agents the usual way, which makes the usual record, but ye volunteered for crew. And did good of it, too!"

"When," Richard continued, "I didn't find Gonikli on Hot Springs Island, I talked Yohin into coming up here."

Something in the back of Drin's mind was bothering him. Quite beyond Zo Kim and Bi Tan, there were two other felonious assaults to worry about, the victims being Mary and himself! This didn't seem to be getting them any closer. What was the connection?

"Everyone?" he said, finally. "We are in the bottom of a crevasse surrounded by avalanche- prone mountains. Mary was shot by someone, who, incidentally, may have started the avalanche that buried me. Presumably that act flows from nobody in this tent, but just now that isn't such a favorable current. I suggest we get back."

"Stendt." Do Tor said, ignoring Drin's call for motion.

"Who?" Mary sounded surprised.

"Human Gorman Stendt. Quarrels with both Kleth. Present on Hot Springs Island at time. Didn't tell monitors until Zo Kim not *just* dead, but humiliated, ruined, in front of everyone. Maybe he lied to Bi Tan about Zo Kim dying."

Drin waved his beak in negation. "Stendt was with others at the colony when Bi Tan died, then he was at the awards ceremony in full view when Richard Moon got the call and Zo Kim flew in and died. Bi Tan carried no comset with her—someone who was there would have had to tell her the lie."

"He's here, too," Yohin offered. "Least he came on my ship. Ye can ask him yourself."

"But why would he try to kill Mary?" asked Gonikli, "Just because she was investigating? That would be too stupid for Gorman."

"Whoever it was didn't really try to kill me," Mary said. "The dart knocked me out where I'd fall into the crevasse, but the fall wasn't that much for a human, and it was on a snowy slope near the valley wall,—an old avalanche site I think. The only thing I could think of is that he wanted Drin to come after me; and that's what happened. Then, with both of us trapped down here, everyone else would come . . . "

Do Tor and Go Ton weren't waiting to hear the rest. They were getting in their flight suits again.

"Can we fix a crutch for Drin?" Mary asked. "We really should get out of here."

Good idea, Mary, Drin thought. If not their antagonist, there was always Trimus' unstable geology to worry about. But his inflatable splint was not going to hold any weight.

"Got an idea for that," Yohin said. "Need to get outside first. Get some wet towels—soak 'em."

Outside, Yohin wrapped the towels, one by one around the inflatable cast, where they quickly froze solid in the frigid wind, forming a rock hard composite casing around his lower leg. The inflated splint insulated the inner towels from his leg and distributed the pressures to its icy shell. Within minutes, Drin found he could put his weight on it and walk, in a sort of limping, peg leg manner.

The Kleth packed the tent into the aircraft and roared off into the teeth of the storm, hoping to spot their antagonist, or at least dissuade whoever it was from starting more avalanches.

Drin was in no shape to negotiate the mountain pass they'd taken to the glacier. To move, he swung his splinted leg forward, planted it, stepped with the other three, then swung it forward again, and stepped. They decided the quickest route back would be down the glacier to the sea. Borragil'ib arranged for another aircraft to meet the humans at the glacier foot. The Do'utians would swim home.

Borragil'ib led them toward the ramp he'd built to tend Bodil's resting place. It was, of course, on the side of the crevasse opposite the one Drin and Mary had found themselves. Their procession was single file for Do'utians, and Drin's hobbling gait slowed everyone down.

They passed Bodil's body, now just a hump in the snow on the floor of the crevasse. They didn't stop—a kindness to Drin. Drin reflected that Go Zom had observed in his commentaries that Do'utian memories are excellent, but that their manners were better.

Finally, they crawled out of the crevasse and started down the main glacier. The snow slowed them down even more than Drin's leg. As they got closer to the water, it fell and fell.

Drin was surrounded by a deep red fog—what light there was now came from Ember only—and that glowing dull red through layers of cloud. It was very, very dim. Drin's audio imaging helped a bit, but the snow absorbed that too. He followed Borragil'ib's tail with one eye, and Mary behind him with the other, all the time expecting the mountain to come crashing down on him again.

It was sheer chance that he happened to be looking in the right direction. It was training, preparation, and fright that had his gun loaded with knockout and in his mouth, rather than in his pouch. They'd just reached the rim of another open crevasse, when the snow lifted momentarily, and Drin looked back to his left.

He saw the long tube, he saw the black beard, opened his mouth and fired.

"Everyone," he shouted, "Commander Drinnil'ib. Break silence, I've just tranked a human. He was lying in ambush with some kind of weapon."

"Sheet!" Yohin exclaimed, barely audible. The heavy snow was swallowing everything. "Where are the bird men?"

"Do Tor, Go Ton? Come in," Mary shouted. There was no answer. She was on top of the assassin a minute. "Drin, It's Stendt! And I've found a launcher. It's been fired! If they've been hit, they're nearby. Stendt didn't come far so soon with this."

"I understand," Drin roared back against the wind. Pollution! Drin's Monitor comset was down in the crevasse. Mary had lost hers in her fall. "Borragil'ib," he shouted in Do'utian, using a range of frequencies evolved to cut through polar storms, "can you call and get a fix on the aircraft?"

"Commander?"

"Emergency channel, and give the operator code 572D9."

"972B9?"

Drin tried to shout as clearly as possible. "Five—Seven—Two—Delta—Niner"

"Got it." There was an interminable wait. Then Borragil'ib said. "The Kleth monitors are over the ridge, eight-squared charter units. Commander, they are down, but they managed a safe landing."

"Mary, Do Tor and Go Ton are safe." Drin shouted. He looked up and saw a star on the west horizon just south of the flat ruddy dome of Ember. Aurum III, where these makers of harpoons and rocket tubes should have gone. The storm was lifting, but clouds of question remained.

Stendt had not been aiming his weapon at Drin, but at Gonikli'ibida.

★ ❋ ★

Check the obvious. Especially the obvious.
     —Planet Monitor's Handbook, Forensic Methodology

★ ❋ ★

"We didn't," Do Tor admitted, "recognize the rocket launcher for what it was until much too late."

Drin gingerly adjusted his position on his pad so that he could see the holoscreen on the wall opposite Mary's pool in his estate room. Do Tor shuddered in the wind shadow of their damaged aircraft, already dusted with blowing snow—Kleth needed to keep active at low temperature.

The Kleth monitor panned the damage with his comset's tri-ocular video pickup. The digital holographic reconstruction was clear and sharp, probably a little bit better than the raw data, Drin reminded himself—like the untrained eye, cybernetic pattern recognition and reconstruction programs sometimes filled in detail that wasn't there. But this one seemed straight forward enough. One of the blades of the port fan of their delta-shaped aircraft had been bent straight up, rim and all. The two adjacent blades were bent away like the skin of a steelfish filet.

"It must have taken great skill to land the aircraft on its nose and starboard fans alone. So you saw the launcher?"

"Oh, yes," Go Ton said. "Looked like a telescope, or something optical. Then whoosh and bang! Do Tor bailed out and held the port wing up while I eased us down. Saved evidence."

"Well done, but you look very cold," Drin observed. "You could finish your report when you get in." A splash and a light laugh reminded him that the other half of his team was now very warm. Mary had invited Richard Moon for a swim and some gentle fact finding.

The harem-instinctive part of Drin's brain was putting out discomfort hormones at the sign of Mary being physical with someone else. Realizing this, with beak closed Drin told himself again and again that Mary was not in the "harem/mate" category, but in the "family/ sister." Getting a sister into someone else's harem before her biology forgot that she was a sister was a major theme in Do'utian literature. Do'utians were less susceptible to mutations than humans, but exogamy still offered more possibilities. And for most of their history, obligations to the bridal family had been what tied beaches together into loose the trading confederations, despite combat between their beachmasters. A sister in the harem was a traditional sign of weakness, but even in the best of families—Drin shuddered.

Bodil, with her ravenous intellect and passionate will, had attached herself to the long discredited idea that harem imprinting was really a cultural, not biological, thing which intelligent beings could choose to disregard. Curiosity had burned in her, and she had begged him for the experience. She'd seen nothing disgusting in doing what nature had evolved them for, had no fear of the minor pain involved, and no qualms about discarding any eggs.

Drin had been curious, too, but had been unwilling to shorten his tail to satisfy it. But Bodil and Gonikli had caught him alone, outdoors, in season, one day and teased him into "just acting it out." They could always stop. But the hormones they triggered had washed through him and his mind had been a semiconscious observer to the tragedy.

He exhaled as if to discharge the memories—there was work to do now. He stared at the damaged aircraft on the wall screen, picking out details—there were dark things in the white composite hull here and there—he forced it to take back his attention.

"It looks like pieces of the rocket are embedded in the hull."

"Oh, yes," Go Ton agreed. "Think the fan cut off guidance head and threw it into hull—see hole just above wing—before explosion."

"Best get data to you now," Do Tor suggested. "That rocket launcher is a puff in an updraft. It appears that Lord Thet has guided weapons now. Cybernetics and A.I. maybe."

"Good enough," Go Ton added, "to force us to kill many of them if we attempt to remove them."

Drin nodded. So it had come to that, Drin thought. When this had started, Thet had a farcical primitivist city-state dictatorship run with sharp steel sticks and the kind of nihilistic charisma ancient humans often fell for. In some respects, they were a herd animal, and untrained minds were prone to follow those who spout pretty mist. Primitivists generally came from romantic young people who, knowing little and hostile to learning fell back on their instincts. In this case; follow the alpha male. Evolution had prepared Do'utians to be more self assertive. But there were, Drin reminded himself, difficulties to indulging that mode of behavior as well.

"The Council will not be amused. But what is the connection to this case?" Drin asked.

"Drin," Mary yelled from the pool. "The connection is that Stendt had one!"

"Oh, yes." Go Ton agreed.

Drin thought, or tried to think. He was swimming in a whirlpool of data. "Very well. He needed a weapon like that, so he got it from them. And, because it was of Thet City manufacture it doesn't show up in the Trimus permit files. This makes sense for Stendt, but . . . "

"Councilor Drinnil'ib," Richard Moon spoke up. "Gonikli'ibida and Bi Tan had been working on a report about primitivist weapons manufacture—and Zo Kim's criticism was scaring off any potential editors."

I must be swimming through a swamp of pollution, Drin thought. "So Gonikli'ibida told you and Stendt that Bi Tan was dead in order to kill Zo Kim? Having the information come at him from two sources like that would probably convince him. But she knew that would kill Bi Tan, too." Drin touched his beak to the carpet. The Gonikli he knew was incapable of such callousness.

"Big puzzle," Do Tor agreed. "Who told Bi Tan that Zo Kim was dead? If no one could have done this, one terrible answer is that *no one* did. Must test at the hearing."

The sound of an aircraft approaching cut through the gusts of polar wind picked up by Do Tor's comset. "The replacement fan is finally here! We need to sign off now and help dismount it. We'll have evidence of smart weapons back to you in an hour or so."

Drin sent them off with a "smooth air" and turned an eye toward Mary. She was sitting in the shallow end of the warm pool with Richard Moon, whose yellow mane now lay wet and flat on his skull, making him seem thinner and more athletic. Now that he was firmly off the suspect list, Mary had, in effect, recruited him to help with the cybernetic tendrils of discovery that this case had grown. Their data trail now ran to Lord Thet's city state. But not continuously.

"Drin," Mary called. "Maybe if we all get our minds off the case for a while, something will happen—mmm, Richard—below the conscious level. Drin, why don't you come over here? There's something I'd like to share with you, and Richard's willing."

Drin hesitated. Mary was offering to balance books, he realized. Eight Trimus years ago, Mary had watched, and helped Drin help deliver eggs from two very gravid, very feral members of a Do'utian primitivist beach harem. This exposure of Do'utian intimacy, though accidental and involuntary, on his part, had always embarrassed him. Mary, however, had called it beautiful and natural.

She was unafraid of limits, and enjoyed testing the boundaries of experience and convention—and in Richard Moon, had found a kindred human spirit. Despite himself he, was intensely curious. He said a soft command in old Do'utian to the cybernetic servant to isolate the eyes and ears of his walls, and moved, gingerly still with his left foreleg in a Do'utian walking cast, over to the human pool.

Mary and Richard Moon were facing each other, teeth bared, and periodically biting, or pretending to bite each other, usually each other's mouths, but sometimes other parts of their bodies.

"Drin," Mary said, laughing, as happy as Drin had ever seen her, "put your hands on my shoulders and hold me, so I don't float away."

He sent his tongue out and did as she requested. Her body tasted different, somehow. Richard Moon patted one of his hands in a gesture that meant "welcome" in any body language that Drin knew.

"Drin," Mary murmured, "remember how I cradled and washed the eggs you took. I hope this feels as good and as special to you. Oh, Richard! Yes, Yes!"

Something tense and warm seemed to flow from Mary into Drin as he held her while she accepted Richard Moon's seed. However different it was for humans—Mary, for instance, would not produce eggs without a reproduction permit, and humans actually did this for pleasure rather than to survive a pain-driven biological necessity—the concept of sharing intimacy, of balancing what each had experienced with the other, appealed to Drin as did in general the idea of touching her intensely warm body and sharing good things with her.

He shut his eyes and memories of Bodil and Gonikli and that summer night before he left for his monitor training on the beach across the bay came roaring back. Terrible memories then, but now, somehow, rendered less terrible. Here on Trimus, he mused, we have chosen to remain biological beings, with all that implies. In a way, he pitied the life descended machine intelligences that roamed the galaxy like Gods. Fate is not always kind, but at least we still know what we are, he told himself.

When Mary laughed and said he could let go now, that elusive thought about machine intelligences had become a school in his mind, turning in unison this way and that. The dangers represented by the guidance system of the rocket that had downed Do Tor and Go Tan's aircraft was clear to him.

They may have seen but the air side of this ice.

"Mary, forgive my multi-track mind. I feel a, a completeness with you and Richard Moon that is philosophically beautiful—but only for advanced minds of both our species."

"Unfortunately," Richard agreed, "you are right. Councilor, we will hold this among ourselves."

"On my other track, I also realized that we are up against opponents that do not understand discretion nor value the restraints under which we live."

"Restraints?" Mary laughed and Richard coughed. Drin had to puff a bit as well.

"Technological restraints," he added.

"Do you think the people that gave Stendt the rocket launcher might have given him more such toys?"

"Smart toys," Mary added. "We've deliberately held ourselves back from having artificial intelligences run everything—which is fine as long as you don't have to outsmart one by yourself. But why would Lord Thet show off his cybernetic prowess just to aid one customer? And what is Stendt's compact-cursed motivation?"

"He could be crazy," Richard speculated. "Or maybe Bi Tan was getting too close to the truth."

"Maybe." Drin reached a decision. "It looks like a battle is going to be fought on technological grounds. So I'm going to hope they are as ignorant of Do'utian culture and history as they act. If Do Tor is right, we know who killed Zo Kim and how. But we need to know why, or at least part of it. Uncontrolled artificial intelligences are involved and in the hands of someone like Lord Thet they are not just a danger to Trimus but to the whole Galaxy! I think Stendt is the key, and if we put enough pressure on Stendt, he may tip his hand—before he understands what he is up against."

"How?"

"Excuse me for a macrobeat or so. I must talk to someone privately." If he could. If that someone could and would still listen.

But all Do'utian tradition said that the top was where to go, especially if questions hung on the next long like seaweed. Drin had to persuade the long one that Stendt was someone to be up against. But he was convinced now that Stendt was not only the key to the deaths of Bi Tan and Zo Kim, but a conspiracy to put illegal smart armaments in the hands of a charter-trampling chauvinist dictator.

Even from the depths of whatever thoughts he was thinking, the long one should respond to that.

✶ ❇ ✶

The most significant difference among the three intelligent species was size. Do'utians were from five to six times the linear dimensions of humans and massed two to four eight-cubed as much. Humans, in comparable parts of their bodies, are about twice the linear dimensions and ten times the mass of we Kleth. But our brains have each evolved by natural selection to the point where they could understand the universe well enough to end natural selection. So, despite a difference of almost a factor of a thousand in brain mass, Kleth and Do'utians have similar physical problem solving abilities.

—Go Zom's notes on the Compact and Charter of Trimus

✶ ❇ ✶

The main hall of the old dome was filled with the smells of sushi and the pleasant drinks of three species. Three raised platforms waited for the Do'utian elite; himself, Commander Drinnil'ib at the left, Beachholder Doglaska'ib in the center, and Borragil'ib at the right.

When Drin had met Doglaska'ib in person, he'd again been impressed with how huge the long one had grown since Drin's childhood. The conversation had been very short. A swiveled eye and a nod on the long-one's part. Then a turn to indicate the interview was over. But the eye had been clear and the nod had been definite.

The ancient one was in excellent shape, and climbed briskly to his pad. Drin and Borragil'ib followed and waited for the long one to speak. Two centuries ago he had opened a family fish hunt with an amusing story. But that was two centuries ago. All he said here was "Begin the review."

A mind grows heavy with the burden of things past, Drin thought.

In the inevitable irony of such things, the one without the title, Borragil'ib, took charge and explained to the human and Kleth visitors how local review worked in Do'utian territory. Essentially, it eliminated worries of unsavory interrogation techniques, because all interrogation was done in front of the Master, his recording devices and everyone else. Anyone present could ask questions, but they had better be worthwhile, for if not, the humiliation could be cold as the bottom of the Southern Rift.

Stendt was present, in dignified dress, sampling the sushi, and pretending affability—much good that it would do him. For all his apparent freedom, this suspect was in a prison of the watchful technological servants of Ibgorni, a house system that was, perhaps, more mentally alive than its master. However, things were unresolved. Stendt was in custody for what he had done to the monitors, and tried to do to Gonikli. There was still nothing to link him to the deaths of Zo

Kim and Bi Tan. Nor anything to trace the origin of the circuits of his "smart toys" as Mary described his weapon.

And if what Go Ton suspected was true, something very horrible had happened, something that powerful people wanted to hide. The rocket launcher was part of it. Lord Thet's colony had made it, and it was far from the primitive weapons he and Mary had seen eight squared turns ago.

After the preliminaries, Borragil'ib turned it over to Drin. Drin called for Gonikli'ibida.

"Mistress," Drin began, "you, and not me, were the object of the Mr. Stendt's murder attempts. I had passed him when I saw him on the trail. He was waiting for you."

Gonikli nodded. She was miserable, beak hung low, tail limp.

"There must be something you know, that he might kill you to prevent from being known. So important that he would risk killing Mary and me to draw you to us. So take us through it, again."

Gonikli did, saying what she had before.

"Please," Go Ton spoke up. "What was the taste like? And the consistency."

Gonikli shook her head. Mary's mouth opened in shock. Drin tensed. Do Tor and Go Ton had hinted said something about testing a hypothesis at the review. But they had not reviewed this line of questioning

Borragil'ib rose to his feet and Drin caught a whiff of challenge, understandable given the obscenity of the idea. Drin swiveled an eye at Go Ton, who held herself in the Kleth posture of certainty and self confidence. He willed himself not to respond and instead focused his attention on Gonikli. "Gonikli'ibida. Our apologies. The discussion must be frank. We need your answer."

She looked up, involuntarily, as one would at a mate. It cut him to the core, the strength of that imprinting after so many years. He raised his beak. She would have to admit that she tasted the flesh of an intelligent being.

"It was bitter, maybe slightly salty."

"I think her body was not prepared to die." Go Ton announced softly.

Air rushed out from from spouts and into mouths.

Gonikli'ibida moaned and waved her head from side to side. "No, she was dying."

She smelled sincere, and frightened. But Drin remembered what Go Ton had said when he applied the bite of mercy to Zo Kim. It had tasted sweet. Kleth and Do'utian taste organs were different, but the chemicals were the same and the biochemistry was similar; all races got internal rewards for ingesting high energy compounds. "Sweet" like "b-flat" meant pretty much the same to all.

"This is nonsense!" roared Borragil'ib, "Gonikli'ibida is no murderer. Kleth, you are a guest in this hall! Enough of accusations."

Drin thought furiously. If Do Tor was right, Gonikli had killed a perfectly healthy and unbereaved Bi Tan. The whiff of challenge sent from Borragil'ib had become the predominant odor in the room. He meant to defend his harem and his hall, or, Drin thought, defend his secrets under that guise. Gonikli could have killed for personal reasons, but she would not be involved in a plot involving uncontrolled artificial intelligence without her master's knowledge. Which meant, if there were Do'utian involvement, he was involved.

And that would be one of several explanations for his hostile behavior toward Drin.

Only because Borragil'ib's anger was directed at Go Ton, was Drin able to keep his head clear. The challenge scent was thick on the dais. Now Drin grasped the slippery eel of Do Tor and Go Ton's reasoning. If Gonikli wasn't lying—there was one other person who might be responsible.

"Please wait Master Borragil'ib," Drin said as softly and controlled as he could. "This may not mean what you think it means."

Mary spun to look at Drin. Drin keyed the comset he'd left in his beak and whispered. "Mary, back to the wall. Watch Borragil'ib, and watch Stendt." Then Go Ton's head bobbed ever so slightly.

"Continue, Go Ton," Drin intoned.

Borragil'ib remained on his claws.

Go Ton she produced a syringe and injected herself. "I took general anesthetic. Now squeamish people look aside." With Kleth quickness, Go Ton took a small surgical knife, deftly bared a small patch on her arm, and sliced a not so small piece of flesh from it. Just as quickly, she put a standard tension dressing on it.

Do Tor's crest fell and his wings went a little out and back. But he said nothing. Go Ton was done before Stendt dropped his sushi. Drin glanced at Mary, who stared in open mouthed shock.

As if what she had done was entirely normal, Go Ton approached Gonikli and held out the piece of herself. "Taste this."

Gonikli curled her tail looked at Drin, who wondered if anyone but Do'utians could read her horrified body language.

"You are already forgiven," Drin said. "And the truth may save your reputation."

Still she kept her beak locked shut, and rocked from side to side.

Then, to everyone's amazement, Doglaska'ib himself rose wordlessly from his center pad and walked to Gonikli and Go Ton. He opened his beak and sent his hands to take the flesh from Go Ton and offer it to Gonikli. Trembling, she opened her beak and accepted it with a trembling hand.

"Is the taste the same?" Go Ton asked.

Gonikli nodded.

Then Go Ton did something Kleth do not do, save ones that have spent much time in the company of Do'utians and people. She stroked the distraught Do'utian woman's beak with her spidery hand.

"I am sorry and humiliated for my race," Go Ton said, in the perfect English that Kleth can manage for important occasions, "for what those of my race have done to you. You, and your friendship, were used in a way that is understandable only from the view of one driven insane by inner conflict. Bi Tan killed her mate by tricking you into killing her. Please accept my apology, and my affection. Your tail is longer than any of ours in this."

Bi Tan killed Zo Kim by deliberately tricking Gonikli into ending her own life? Opportunity and means. But motive? What was the motive for such desperation?

"Stendt," Mary said, softly. But Drin recognized the human body language—she was pure fury. "What, Gorman Stendt, was your role in this? You were involved, I think, because you told Zo Kim—and you told him at the conference before any word could come from the island."

Stendt looked around, eyebrows raised. "Why ever would you think there was any such role?"

Drin surmised that he had not expected Mary's question. The room was silent, except that sharp ears might have heard Drin talking furiously on his comset, beak closed, to Monitor Central.

Drin finished his call. Mary was putting the pressure where it was needed. Now Drin would add a little more. "Stendt, you can answer Lieutenant Pearce now with dignity, or have it dragged out of you in what, I assure you, will be as humiliating an experience as the Trimus Council will permit!"

Stendt spread his arms. "All I did was show her an advanced copy of her mate's review of her book, and when she reacted I told her that's how I felt about what they'd done to mine." He snorted in disgust. "The little harpies didn't even read the final version of my work, damn them!"

"Stendt!" Drin bellowed, on his legs, the scent of challenge pouring from his pores. An act, he told himself, or a catharsis to somehow make up for what he had done to Gonikli so many years ago by dispatching her current tormenter. "Truth! Or I shall ask everyone to leave but you and me!"

Mary took her cue, and walked toward one of the curtain doors, and motioned for Richard Moon to follow. That would leave Stendt the only human in the room. It was condescendingly chauvinist psychology, and Drin berated himself for it. But it would work on Stendt, he thought.

The suspect's head snapped left and right. He waved his arms up and down, full of disappointment. He had to realize that he was alone now. Perhaps he smell the Do'utian contempt.

"Truth?" he asked, in a voice still filled with challenge. "What do you know of truth? And where is this so-called truth?"

"We have Zo Kim's effects including his copy of the manuscript on weapons trade on which Bi Tan and Gonikli were working. Gonikli, did you keep Bi Tan's copy? It can't hurt her now."

The Do'utian woman reached into her pouch and produced a standard data module.

"It is a terrible thing to remember her by, but it was the last thing she touched. I—I needed to have something. To touch."

"A certified electronic copy of the review will do for evidence," Drin said. "The copy she gave you will no doubt help us understand her feelings. It is, no doubt, filled with classic Zo Kim sarcasm. But, I gather my human colleague suspects, *not* as he wrote it."

"So I made a few changes," Stendt said, still calm, still sounding as if he were in control. "That harpy mate of hers already said it didn't work for him, I just made that a little more clear, stronger. Improved the language, took out the weasel words and qualifiers. Hell, with the review as it was their theories, and her career, would never be taken seriously. She knew that. All I did was make it a little clearer, and suggest how she could end his career too. But she was already ready to do that, anyway. They didn't get along. It would have happened anyway, don't you see? With them living apart? All I did was to make a few changes—"

"It's about the weapons, isn't it," Drin rumbled. "With Bi Tan, Zo Kim, and Gonikli'ibida all gone, that little secret would be safe until Lord Thet had himself a cybernetic war capability, wouldn't it? Just how are you involved?"

Stendt shrugged.

Drin continued. "Zo Kim said he'd suspected for days. That might have been even before Bi Tan had herself killed—the only one that could have planted that suggestion was you. The whole thing was one complex, premeditated scheme. Two birds with one stone, was it? You used them and you used Gonikli. Was your human ego worth so much?"

"There's more than my ego involved."

"Gorman Stendt," Borragil'ib asked, rising up from his pad on his limbs, claws bared. "Why have you troubled my family so?"

"I want an advocate," Stendt said, and Drin recognized a mocking tone in the human voice.

"I," the disembodied voice of Ibgorni answered, "am programmed to recognize the application of all Trimus and local Do'utian law in this and instruct you in it's application. In this case, the law requires you to answer."

"A human advocate, in private." Stendt demanded.

"Privacy is for deceit," Borragil'ib said. "Are you trying to conceal arms manufacturing by the human primitivists? And if so, why? Any refusal to answer will count against you."

"Count against me? Because I'm human? Because I can't bully people around with thirty tons of blubber?"

Stendt looked to Moon, than to Mary, for sympathy. Human help.

Drin saw only hardness in the looks Mary and Richard gave Gorman Stendt. Only a chauvinist, Drin thought, would look for sympathy from only his own kind while standing in the middle of the most conservative ethnic establishment on the planet of Trimus. If there was a defense to be made for ethnic enclaves, here was where to make it. If there were excuses of racial pride, here, if anywhere, were beings that would understand. If one wanted to plead local autonomy versus the state, here was where to make the plea.

Drin could not help but let a belch escape his blow hole in the ironic humor of it. Borragil'ib caught Drin's eye and belched as well. The smell of challenge had faded to contempt. Mary glanced at Drin and winked. Go Ton and Do Tor exchanged a glance and a flap of wings as though, they too, had better things to do than sully their talons with this idiot.

Stendt's agitation faded and his false affability returned. He shrugged and smiled. "Primitivist is a relative term. In some respects you are primitivists, too. And fools before your own biological chauvinism, posturing to each other in this archaic pile of stone."

Drin's beak opened slightly, hands on his gun. But Doglaska'ib remained impassive. Do'utian eyes rolled to him—this was a blatant challenge, but the long one seemed to utterly disregard it. Was he too far gone?

"I don't get my missile guidance chips from Lord Thet," Stendt declared.

Huh? Stay with the plan, Drin told himself. "Where do they come from, then?" he pressed.

In answer, the lights in the hall faded to black and stones in the dome above groaned. Dust fell.

Sonar chirps filled the room. Everyone was on their feet and claws. Everyone except Doglaska'ib. Well, thought Drin. He had meant to force Stendt's hand, and here it was.

But the sophistication of this writer's attack surprised Drin. Were they in time? Had they underestimated the capacity of Lord Thet's sources? Why would Thet let Stendt have this much—unless Thet had much more already.

Drin was nervous, but took his cue from the long one. Drin had warned Doglaska'ib, and the long one, presumably, had done something. If he had really understood the danger.

Stendt's voice filled the darkened room with a dim glow, sinister to those who could "see" it fill space that way. "I don't get them from Lord Thet—that idiot gets them from me."

Both of Drin's hearts surged. The school of fish had solidified into an iceberg. A mock fatfish had turned to stab his tongue with poison fangs. The hunter was suddenly the hunted. Pollution! His own chauvinism may have turned out to be as bad as anyone else's. How badly had he underestimated Stendt and overestimated Doglaska'ib ability to respond. What back-up did he have? Drin fingered his comset.

A burst of electrical fire burst from one of the wall sensors.

Stendt laughed. "I control the computer now. I suggest you do not try to use any electromagnetic devices."

"A product of your modeling computer," Mary stated, her voice a brief glow in the gloom.

Drin shuddered. He hadn't thought of artistic technology as real technology—it was, somehow, diminished, trivial. He hadn't recognized the multi-media writer for the consummate technologist he was, operating so far beyond the limits of the Charter. But, in retrospect, that's what he had to be to do what he did. So it was only a small step to have his system make smart weapons or even smart bugs—microbots to do his bidding. A saving grace was that if they could still, somehow, overcome Stendt, they would put Thet back in his place as well. But Stendt didn't act like the loser in this, and Drin began to wonder if some of his worst fears might be realized.

In the silence, Drin could hear the wind outside. But it was not quite loud enough to illuminate the room. Then a brief whoosh and a momentary flash of sound suddenly filled the room. A broken ceiling panel lying on the floor in front of the dais, where no one had been standing.

"I suggest that nobody try to move. I can drop a hundred tons on anyone here."

The sound flash had shown Gonikli moving slowly toward Stendt. He would kill her without a thought, Drin realized. Then they would both be dead, Gonikli and Bodil.

"Everyone, hold still," Drin bellowed. "He doesn't intend to kill us or he would have. Don't provoke him." Noise subsided. His voice revealed the Gonikli had halted. Thank providence.

Drin rolled an eye toward Stendt. "What do you want?"

"Good thought, Councilor. Now, I suggest you turn over to me all recording modules of the research that Gonikli and Bit Tan did right now. I have your main computer, you see. I also have the structure of your dome, and this whole complex in my hands."

Drin glanced at the ceiling. It moaned, as if its vast panels were adjusting themselves to Gorman Stendt's will. Drin's faith in his heritage readjusted itself as well. Perhaps Doglaska'ib had decided to ignore Drin's warning. The long one's mind was not what it used to be. Or, despite his efforts, had the human's bootleg microcircuits and software actually succeeded in taking over?

Drin raised himself. "You can't destroy all the evidence by killing us," he said, not sure if he believed his own words. "Copies of our files, and those of Bi Tan and Gonikli are in Trimus City."

"Then get on your comset and have them deleted, Councilor-Commander of Monitors." He laughed. "I'll be able to verify it from here—and your systems are too stupid to lie to me. Evidence? We're beyond that concern. I just don't want anyone else doing what I've done. As for killing, why kill what I can control?"

There was a collective gasp. "That kind of threat will get your mind reeducated," Richard Moon said. "Give it up, Gorman. Save yourself while you can still take it back."

He'd gone too far that, Drin thought. The human had gone much to far to avoid reeducation. Drin smelled gage and swiveled an eye to Borragil'ib. "Hold it in, cousin," he whispered. "A charge here could cause dozens to die." Then Doglaska'ib's mouth opened slightly, just enough for Drin to see an everything-is-all-right sign made by one of the long one's hands. What? The long one still didn't comprehend what was happening?

"There's no going back now." Stendt's voice had lost the tense overtones, the edge Drin had come to recognize as the equivalent of the challenge scent. It was as if he were already contemplated the burdens of his ill assumed leadership.

"I'll give it up when I'm tired of it," the human continued. "If any of you have learned anything from my human histories, you've learned that we progress through the acts of great individuals. People with an integrated, holistic, vision of the way things ought to be and the ability to seize the day.

"In the meantime, the thirty-century stagnation of Trimus is over. Its population, or at least its human population, will be allowed to evolve toward their natural destiny, without the constraints of the Charter. Why providence selected me, I do not know. But I am a consummate artist in nurturing simulated worlds—now I shall nurture a real one. What you have to understand it that I am in charge now. Here for now, and eventually everywhere on Trimus."

The lights came back on and dust curtains leapt into operation. Stendt looked around in confusion.

"Not exactly." The voice of Ibgorni echoed from the dome. Cleaning robots whirred to remove the pieces of fallen ceiling.

"I've played along with you," the Do'utian cybersystem continued. "Your toys are now, and have been, under my control, but was useful to see what you would try to do with them. That last offense of yours will be sufficient to force appropriate measures by Trimus authorities.

We will not have to concern ourselves with disciplining a human here, which would be best for all."

Drin settled back down, spouting relief. The voice was Ibgorni, but the words, in their understated humor and confidence were Doblaska'ib's. The long one had simply found a traditional Do'utian way of handling the situation—a tradition of living with cybernetic servants that was as long as Stendt's race had existed. One which their ancestors had not entirely given up when settling Trimus. A human might have called it fighting fire with fire. With no conviction and no punishment, there would be little public exposure of the Ib family, nor what Ibgorni had apparently become. Drin was relieved at that as well.

The scent of relief flooded the hall. Mary bounded up to the stage to nobody's objection and flattened herself against Drin behind his left eye with her mouth near the tight hide that covered his left high frequency ear

"Drin, who's really in charge here? Doglaska'ib? Or Ibgorni?"

He shook his head slightly. It was not a question he could ask. How deep was their connection—over the centuries, had Doglaska'ib's ancient body and the cybernetic system become merely different vehicles for the same mind? With the body trotted out when ceremony demanded? How long would that continue?

Drin looked at Borragil'ib. Perhaps until that one had grown long enough. Or was challenged. Drinnil'ib, himself, was a possible challenger—though far down the line. He had a vision of a future in which he tired of being Councilor-Commander of the Monitors, and came home—to something like this. Would Mary fit into—*this*—if he did?

Could Doglaska'ib see that too?

And what connection, Drin asked himself did the long one have with the others, out there? Perhaps they were being watched allowed to be themselves—but within limits? Who monitors the monitors, and who monitors *them*. Drin had a vision of himself as part of a philosophical food chain of paternalism. What was on top? Was there indeed a point to it all? And what if he someday decided that, at least for him, there no longer was any point?

Mary shoved him to get his attention.

"Excuse me, Mary. Lost in thought. Who's in charge? . . ."

As if in answer to Mary's question, Doglaska'ib's biological voice echoed in the hall for the second time. "Human Gorman Stendt is remanded to the custody of the Trimusian authorities. His cybernetic devices here and elsewhere are being deactivated. The review is over."

Made in the USA
Las Vegas, NV
08 December 2023

82389545R00114